Enticed

Enticed

A DEMON WATCHER NOVEL: BOOK 2

by

GINNA MORAN

This is a work of fiction. All of the characters, organizations, and events portrayed in this novel are either products of the author's imagination or are used fictitiously.

Cover design by Silver Starlight Designs
Cover images copyright 123RF

For Inquiries Contact:
Sunny Palms Press
9663 Santa Monica Blvd Suite 1158
Beverly Hills, CA 90210, USA
www.sunnypalmspress.com
www.GinnaMoran.com

For Eddie

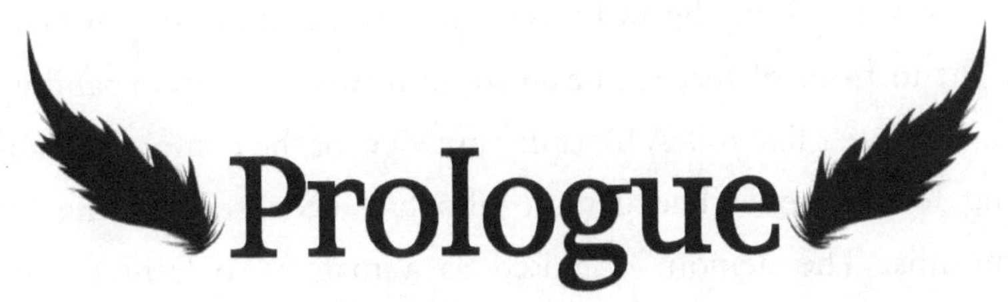

Prologue

EIGHTEEN YEARS AGO

"**P**LEASE, KRISTIN. I'M begging you. There has to be something you can do. I'm losing him, and I can't bear it. Not after everything," I say, rubbing the tears from my face.

It was never supposed to be like this. Raphael was never supposed to love me, nor I him, but he saved my life years ago, when my training as a hunter for the alliance failed me. I looked that horrifying demon in the eyes—eyes so black and empty, yet so full of fire, it felt like my soul was descending into Hell—and I froze. I knew I was looking death in the face and was about to die.

And so I prayed.

My angel, my beautiful Raphael, appeared out of nowhere, right in front of me, his beautiful pure white wings expanding for what felt like miles, blocking my view of the demon beckoning for my soul. The demon who had been stalking me for months. The demon, disguised as a man, who fathered my partner before he fell into the hands of Hell like his demon dad.

My hair whipped behind me, streaks of gold highlighting the bronze color in a halo of Heaven's light. Raphael's radiant power cut through the black night like the sun had risen, forcing the darkness away. I held my breath, my dagger drawn, my heart racing so fast I was sure it'd give out at any moment.

And then the beautiful angel turned to face me, my Raphael, the being I fell in love with the second his blue eyes searched mine. I dropped to my knees, a sob wracking my chest, and I released a cry to the angel who answered my prayer. The angel who sent that demon back to Hell and saved my life, my soul. Saved me.

But then I destroyed him.

Our love was his undoing.

He fell for me, because of me, and then I lost him to Hell.

"There is one way, but I can't guarantee anything, Grace," Kristin says. "It requires a sacrifice, and I'm not sure you're willing to pay that kind of price."

I clutch my hands to my chest. "I don't care. I'll do it. I'll pay anything. I just—I can't lose him again."

"Your soul," she says. "I can't accept anything less."

A door slams, and I tense. Kristin rushes around the table, drawing her dagger, holding her rainbow amulet spelled to protect her against demons like my beloved. Footsteps sound through the quiet house, growing louder on the wood floor. I never in my wildest dreams thought I'd ever fear the man I loved, but here I am, clutching my own blessed dagger, prepared to fight, though I never do.

"You have a friend over, Grace," Raphael says. "I can hear her breathing. Her heart sounds lovely. And her soul—oh..." Raphael stands in the doorway, Hell's fury erupting between his palms like liquid lava ready to burn the place down. "A witch."

My hands shake, and I move around the table, still clutching my blessed dagger. "This is Kristin, Raphael. Mom introduced me to her years ago."

"Lenora is always full of surprises—a witch? What a treat. And where's the old hunter now? Hiding in the shadows in wait to cut out my heart, I'm sure," he says, pressing his palms together to snuff out his liquid orb of demonic power.

I force myself to smile, sniffling. "Of course not. She's just getting used to the idea of..."

"You can say that I'm a demon, Grace. I've come to enjoy such a life with you. If only you'd stop carrying around that sacred weapon. I'm not going to hurt you. Have I ever tried to ask for your soul?" he asks. "This is—we'll adjust, my beautiful huntress."

In moments like these, it's hard to remember what he has

become. But his blue eyes flash green in the overhead light, reminding me my angel has fallen.

Raphael opens his arms, and I slide into them, feeling his muscular chest through his tailored suit. He never wore anything formal until recently, and I can't help but miss the way his jeans used to hang on his hips—how his T-shirt pulled across his taut chest.

Raphael leans down, brushing his lips to mine, and I taste the sweet vanilla flavor that always clings to him. He inhales a small breath, nipping my bottom lip, and then he pulls back and smiles at me.

"Just like I remember but better. You don't know how much I want to corrupt everything good about you," he whispers. "If only you'd let me."

I swallow the lump in my throat, straightening my shoulders. Tilting my head up, I meet his blue eyes, my vision blurry with tears.

He reaches out and touches my face. "Oh, don't do that. I'm thankful to finally be away from those who will never change. Who'll spend eternity all high and mighty like they're better than everyone. They're just missing out on—" He bites his bottom lip between his teeth. "Oh, I'll never let them have you."

I release a small sob, covering my mouth with my hand.

He frowns. "Oh, Grace. I'm sorry. I—I can't help myself sometimes."

I've never in my life heard a demon apologize, yet here

Raphael is, kneeling on the ground, wrapping his arms around my legs. I swear I can feel the cool breeze from wings no longer on his back, but the haunting memory will stay with me forever.

"I'd do anything for you. I want to give you the world and everything you love about it," he says. "But there's a need in the pit of me, burning away the memories I'm trying to hold onto."

"It's only going to get worse," Kristin says, interrupting our private moment.

Raphael snarls, horns jutting through his once beautiful forehead as he loses control, revealing his true body. I fear for my life some nights, but he always manages to compose himself.

I reach down, poking the palm of my hand on one of his black horns, trying to cradle his head to me so he'll stop focusing on Kristin. My blood drips on his cheek and then more splashes on his white dress shirt, staining it red.

He's to his feet before I have a chance to move, his strong fingers locking around my wrist. His ice blue eyes stare at the blood pooling in my palm, now dripping to the wood floor. He stares at it like it's the most mesmerizing thing in the entire world.

Shaking his head, blinking his eyes, he breaks his attention. He reaches for his breast pocket and pulls out his black handkerchief, pressing the square of fabric to my palm. "Your life is so fragile. I worry, Grace."

Kristin steps closer, yanking my hand from Raphael's. "Demons don't worry. They don't care."

Raphael ignites power in his hands. "You're right, witch. I don't care. This is an old habit I'm working to break."

I stand between Kristin and Raphael. "Stop, Kristin. What are you doing? You said you'd help."

"Is he really worth it, Grace? This is your soul we're talking about," she says.

"My soul is lost regardless!" I fling my hands out, sending blood splattering across the wall. "I did this to him. I stole everything. I *knew* better, but I couldn't help myself. I loved him too much. I still love him. If you don't do this, I'll give my soul to—"

Kristin squeezes her eyes shut. "Don't even say it. Don't even think it."

I release a breath. "I mean it."

Raphael places his hands on my shoulders. "What's going on? Grace, you're bartering your soul? I—"

I suck in a breath. "It's *my* soul, Raphael."

"I'd like it to be mine, not some—" He snarls again.

I spin around, placing my hands on his chest. His true demonic body breaks through again, stealing his beautiful façade. His eyes flash red, like firelight glows within them. His chest heaves, his heart punching against my hands, and I straighten my shoulders.

"Control yourself, Raphael. This isn't you," I say.

"But it is! You did this!" he yells.

A shudder rushes through my whole body, tears burning my eyes. A small wail sounds from my mouth. It takes everything in me not to drop to the floor to curl in on myself. Raphael's strong. He's always been strong for me. But now? He's lost. And he's right.

I'm responsible for this.

His destruction will haunt me for all eternity.

"Kristin, let's do this," I say. "He's more important to me than life, Heaven, Hell. I need this. I need him to be okay in the end no matter what happens to me. You have my soul to use to save my beautiful angel."

"He'll still be a demon," she says. "But I can create a link to humanity. A vessel of sorts."

I bring my hand to my heart. "No, you don't mean a..."

She presses her lips together. "A child."

A million thoughts race through my mind. How could I possibly bring another life into this world? It's not fair. A child can never stand a chance with Hell in its veins. I did this to Raphael, but how could I do this for him?

I shake my head. "I—"

"Grace," Raphael whispers behind me. "My beautiful Grace. I cannot ask for such a sacrifice."

I steel myself. His words cement my decision. In this moment, I know I must. If I could get even half of what Raphael was back to him, it'd be worth my soul. Worth my life and existence. Because, in this very second, I know he's worth it. He'd never let our child down. He'd be the angel I love despite everything. Despite not having wings.

"This isn't for you, Raphael. This is for me." I turn to Kristin. "Do what you must."

Kristin's eyes sheen over with tears. "Are you sure?"

I nod.

"Grace, no," Raphael says, the angel I love shining through his fire.

I turn my back on him and face Kristin. She moves to the table and grabs her bag, pulling out an ivory dagger made of some sort of bone. The rubies on the hilt glitter in the overhead lighting.

"Witch, why are you doing this? I know the consequences," Raphael says.

Kristin jerks her head up to glare at Raphael behind me. "You may have forgotten, but love makes people do stupid things, and I love Grace, too. Utter a word and you won't live to see our creation."

I frown. "What? What consequences?"

She ignores me, walking around the table. Without warning, she grabs my wrist, slicing the ivory blade across my already bleeding palm.

Raphael sucks in a breath. "We have time. Let's discuss this."

I'm afraid we don't. "I've made my decision."

Kristin moves past me and stands in front of Raphael. "Open your shirt."

He unbuttons his dress shirt without arguing, just gazing at me with his intense blue eyes. They peer through my flesh and bone and right to my soul I'm bartering to save him. My whole life has been full of regret. From the Hunter's Alliance to failing my own demi-demon partner. Not being more careful with Raphael, for forcing myself into his heart. His fall.

But Raphael as a whole? I don't regret him or my love for him, even now as a demon.

"You're my saving grace," he whispers, his eyebrows lowering on his forehead. "My beautiful Grace."

"Blood is blood from light to dark. Take this soul, take this heart. Summon life from the pit of Hell, hear my words, hear my spell. A child we ask for made from night, a child with a soul of light. Bound in blood, a soul now torn, take this body for a new life born." Kristin places the ivory dagger over Raphael's bare chest and shoves it into his heart.

I scream.

"A piece of soul, a piece of heart, creates a child made from dark. Black to red, blood now spill, hear her screams, feel her will. Blood so pure with demon life, feel the pain, feel the strife. Blood is blood now demon bound, Heaven and Hell hear the sound. A child's cry, the sound of life, a child's cry cuts like a knife. Give this demon a new life now, make him feel, make him bow."

Black blood spills across the floor, burning up in a blaze of fire, singeing the wood. Raphael drops to his knees, bowing forward at my feet.

"Blood is blood from dark to light, protect this child, give her sight. Demon bound but a soul so true, protect this child, she's a part of you. With Hell's fury and Heaven's might, you will stand up and always fight. Born from grace and love's pure light, this child is yours, born from night."

Kristin's hair flies around her head in a breeze I can't feel, and she wipes the blood from the dagger onto her hand before ripping the hem up on my shirt. She presses her open palm on my stomach, my skin searing under her touch. A handprint brands my smooth skin, and I cover my stomach, nausea rolling through me.

Raphael scrambles forward, pulling me into his lap. He brushes the hair from my face before gently touching his hand to the burned skin on my stomach. His brows pinch together, and a tear drips from his eye and onto my cheek.

"Demon bound, blood so true, a human soul will give to you. Flesh and spirit split apart, now sewn together by a beating heart. Black to red and red to black, may Hell and Heaven never take this back. If descended down, Hell breaks through, but Heaven can save and take her from you. A union of blood, soul, and bone, this child given will be your own."

Pain erupts in my stomach, stealing my breath away. I cry out, the light not unlike what used to radiate from Raphael battling the fire now in his eyes in my vision before me. I clutch my stomach protectively and heave, black blood spewing from me and across the floor.

Raphael holds me close, kissing my temple. "Grace, my beautiful Grace. What have you done?"

"You saved me, Raphael. It's my turn to save you."

"But I'm afraid."

I reach up and touch his cheek. "Have faith, my fallen angel."

Kristin clears her throat, drawing our attention away from each other. "It's done. I hope he's worth it, Grace."

I nod. "He is, but what of the consequences?"

She smiles weakly. "Those are mine to bear." Turning her gaze to Raphael, she says, "And you, Traitor of Heaven, it's time you and I made a deal."

HELL BEASTS RISING

A BLACK FEATHER tickles my nose, and I sneeze. "You're blocking my view."

Cool fingers dig into my hips, distracting me from the small group of people crowded together a few feet away. Ezekiel hugs me even closer from behind, his whole body pressing into me so I can feel the ripple of his muscles flexing with his subtle movements.

His wings wrap forward, brushing against my arm and hiding the lower half of my face. It's not like he needs to literally shield me with his downy black feathers, but he does it anyway.

Maybe to stop me from running forward on a whim, or maybe because he likes the feeling of our closeness, but either way, it's driving me crazy. My demon blood battles it out with my humanity inside me. I can't decide if I should risk breaking my elbow by jerking my arm into his bone-hard stomach or risk his purity by spinning around to tempt him with a kiss.

I do neither.

Reaching up, I shove the wing in front of my nose down an inch. It caresses my lips as I speak. "What do you think they're doing here?"

Ezekiel releases a small breath in my ear and ruffles the feathers on his wings, sending a few into the air in front of us. "I don't know."

I sneeze again. "Let's find out."

Ezekiel groans against my neck. The small vibration from the hum in his throat ignites fire through my blood, my desire getting the best of me. Damn beautiful angel. It'll be his fault if I accidentally—okay, purposefully—corrupt him. He knows how much he messes with both my human and demonic side. "And then do what? We're supposed to lay low, remember?"

I squirm in his hold until he loosens his hands enough for me to turn around to face him. My forehead touches his chin, and he tilts his head back an inch to see me clearly. Ezekiel meets my gaze with intense mocha eyes and a firm jaw, preparing for the string of complaints he knows are about to fall from my mouth.

But I can't help it. It's been weeks since we arrived in Los

Angeles, the perfect city to hide in, considering the angelic army tries to stay away from heavily demon-tainted areas. And demons love people, which this beautiful yet sometimes terrifying city, has plenty of.

Ezekiel moves his jaw, puffing his lips out. His kissable mouth, nearly in reach, distracts me so much so that I can't remember my brilliant argument to persuade him. I need him to let me move close enough to listen in on the pack of werewolves, who showed up in our human populated neighborhood this afternoon. But I also need his mouth against mine.

"Please," is all I can muster.

"Please?" he repeats, smiling. "You know it's going to take more than asking nicely to convince me. Why break our good streak of staying hidden now?"

Hiding in plain sight, yet away from demonic and angelic affairs, has been the only other thing besides Ezekiel to keep me safe and undetected since being forced to fake my death by the magic of my dad's witch soul keeper. After temporarily breaking the magical veil, which imprisons the demonic population from sunrise to sundown, the angelic army realized what a danger to the universe my existence poses. If it weren't for a pack of hellhounds starting a war with Heaven, I'd already be dead. It's a good thing Ezekiel prefers me alive and breathing.

As for demons, I could very well tip the balance in their favor, considering I could destroy the one thing Heaven has to maintain the balance between good and evil. If I fell into the wrong hands, my life as a mortal would be over—but that also goes for if I fell into the supposed right hands, too. A half demon like me, the daughter of Heaven's Traitor, with enough power to destroy the universe, has no place in existence except for by the side of the one being created solely for me—Ezekiel, my own full-blooded angel Demon Watcher.

Dad said Ezekiel never stood a chance with me because I'm like my mother, the woman whose existence made the mightiest angel fall in love with her—if only it weren't their undoing and her end. But I can't think about it. I refuse to let Ezekiel's love for me make him fall from grace. If he does, I'm doomed. So is the world.

If I didn't like existing so much, I could turn myself over and hope for a merciful end because Heaven loves self-sacrifice. But unfortunately for the angelic army, they tried to send my dad to Hell. So, I'll continue to hide in plain sight for the rest of my life on Earth with my soul permanently in the hands of my beautiful angel. Might as well make the best of it.

"Um—"

Ezekiel brushes his lips to mine in a surprise kiss, drawing me from my thoughts. "You need a better argument."

I shake my head, glancing from the sky to not get lost in his eyes again. "Oh, I have one. I just—knock it off. You keep distracting me. Don't you think we should spy to make sure they're not here to make a den or something?"

Releasing a sigh, Ezekiel drops his arms from me and steps back. My skin warms without his cool touch, and I swivel on my boots to turn back to the pack. The empty street greets me.

Nothing but the shadows of the Jacaranda trees remain in the spot the werewolf pack was conversing.

A blip of panic squeezes my heart. Losing sight of the werewolves shouldn't make my body have such an intense reaction, but I can't help it. Werewolves ruined my life. They set my dad up, making him look like he was committing crimes against humanity to the angelic army, and it nearly cost him his eternity on Earth and also my mortality. Sure, Dad might've broken werewolves into hellhounds for years when I was a kid, but he's a reformed demon. He now helps monitor and punish demons if they try to rise to power.

But his past will never be forgotten by the angelic army or werewolves. And I'm a daughter now paying for her father's sins.

"Crap, where'd they go?" I ask, tugging my hand to stroll to the shadow of the tree where the werewolves were standing.

"Maybe to a local safe house." Ezekiel steps beside me and points at the sun lowering in the sky. "Night is coming and there's no way they'd be caught outside the safety of a blessed barrier come sunset."

"Unless they're hellhounds," I mutter.

"It was one pack. You can't hold it against them all, Faith," Ezekiel says, sliding his fingers through mine.

I frown. I don't hold it against them...much. But Dad warned me the werewolves were rising, which means they're working with a witch, possibly the same witch who tried to send me to Hell to return as a full-blooded, soulless demon. Werewolves need a witch to use Hell magic to bind their souls to Hell, allowing them to transform into hellhounds on Earth, still mortal and unbroken, which makes it possible to remain werewolves during the day and some of the fiercest predators at night. Demon hunters of the Hunter's Alliance and the angelic army, even the most ruthless demons of the night, might not survive an encounter with an unleashed Hell beast, especially a pack.

"As crazy as it sounds, I don't even blame them, but it doesn't make me feel any better. We just moved, and I don't want them drawing the attention of Heaven or Hell here. I don't want to have to leave again, either. I just—"

"Maybe the city was a bad idea. We could go anywhere." Ezekiel frowns while peering past me. "A remote island? Possibly somewhere cold and snowy where it's only me and you."

I shift in my boots and smile. "Are you sure you'd want that? I'd have a lot of free time to corrupt you."

Chuckling, Ezekiel brushes strands of my blond hair behind my ear. "You'd love that, wouldn't you?"

"Not as much as—"

A low growl sounds through the air, sending the hairs on my arms rising. Ezekiel steps closer and hooks his arm around my waist, spinning me closer to him. He unfurls his enormous black wings, stretching them toward the sky, causing the purple Jacaranda flowers to rain down around us from the tree.

Stiffening, I ignite demonic power into my hands and peer around the quiet neighborhood from Ezekiel's muscular arms.

Our mundane day out to run errands wasn't supposed to turn into a werewolf misadventure. I'd much prefer to lie low with Ezekiel, teasing him about his purity and jokingly threatening demonic corruption, but I can't pretend this isn't happening.

I can't let the rest of the world take care of the rise of the werewolves. They don't have the gift of sight like I do. When I was dying, I gave Ezekiel my soul. I should've died and gone to Heaven in that moment, but Ezekiel loved me too much to mercifully kill me. He took my soul before my time, leaving me a soulless shell with an ugly white eye to prove it. And because I didn't die, and a thread of my soul still connects me to life, I can see the world beyond the veil with my demon blood—Dad's fallen angel blood, too.

"Over there." Ezekiel points at a chocolate wolf slinking between the cars parked along the street.

"Where are the rest of—"

A cacophonous melody of howls rings through the air, piercing my sensitive ears. Closing my eyes, I push the noise away and concentrate on Ezekiel's heartbeat to mute the world. The small pack of werewolves, now in their wolf forms, jut from in between two houses and toward the street. The chocolate wolf growls and jumps back toward the cars to race away.

With Ezekiel's angelic shield, we remain hidden from the view of the werewolf pack, now seemingly out for the chocolate wolf's blood in a hunt. Humans and demons can't find me as long as Ezekiel keeps his angelic shield in place, but unfortunately, it doesn't protect me from the angelic army, who I fear the most.

Pulling away from Ezekiel, I strut forward a few feet after the wolves pass us. This is the most excitement I've seen in weeks that hasn't involved the destruction of my life, witches out for my blood, or the world imploding around me. I can't help myself from wanting to see how this plays out.

Ezekiel's cool hand laces around my elbow, stopping me in place. "No, Faith. If they're leaving, we should let them."

I shrug away and continue to follow the snarls and growls fading to blend with the sound of street traffic from the busy highway not far from here. Picking up my pace, I jog for a block before dashing at a full-blown sprint. Ezekiel launches into the air behind me. Wind whips through my hair, sending it across my vision. His shadow casts over me, blocking the sun.

Swerving, I charge toward the sidewalk and the line of trees. If Ezekiel swore, he'd be cursing to high Heaven, because there's no way for him to dart down to grab me and sweep me off my feet—and not in a good way. He knows how much I hate flying, even if I enjoy how it feels like his arms were made for me.

"Just keep your eyes open for angels, will you?" I call, glancing up at him flying above the trees.

"Seriously, Faith? They're the least of my worries," he responds, running his hands along the tree tops to send leaves and blossoms pouring around me like a fragrant storm of nature.

I shield my eyes with one hand, keeping my gaze trained on the ground. A loud crack sounds from above, and I yelp as a tree branch clatters to the sidewalk in front of me.

"Ezekiel, knock that crap off," I say. "I'm following the damn wolves."

Another tree limb hits the sidewalk too fast for me to clear, and I trip, somersaulting to land on my back. More leaves and blossoms rain on me, pelting my face, sticking to my long hair. I spit a petal out and scramble to my feet.

I summon Hell power in my palms, swiveling toward the soft thud sounding in the street a few feet away. "You're not supposed to intervene, you know. You can't make me stop chasing them if I don't want to."

Ezekiel narrows his eyes at me. "There's a little leeway with divine intervention when it comes to protecting you, Faith. Raphael would hunt me down and rip my wings off if something happens to you under my watch."

I groan, fisting my hands, snuffing out my power. "Empty threats. My dad wouldn't dare touch you. Now, come on. You can either stay with me or just stay out of it."

Ezekiel frowns, strutting forward to close the space between us. "What's wrong? This doesn't feel like your normal trouble-making self."

I sigh, darting my gaze to the street. I concentrate on listening to everything around me, sorting through the sound that comes from everyday life in a human suburban neighborhood outside of downtown.

Low growls slither around me, making me shiver. A wolf yips. Another barks.

A human screams.

"Faith," Ezekiel says.

I blink, hugging myself. "They're still close enough to catch."

Before I have a chance to run forward, Ezekiel grabs my hand and brings it up to his cheek, feeling my warm knuckles against his cool skin. The gesture helps me relax enough that I don't rip my arm away to make another run for it.

"If you can tell me what the point in following them is, then I'll consider not tossing you over my shoulder and flying out of here," Ezekiel says, pursing his lips. "Though I really want to."

I clear my throat, a dozen lame excuses tumbling through my mind. How can I tell him the truth? That I want so desperately to find the werewolves because I need to make sure they're not running back to Mary—the witch responsible for creating the hellhounds who went after my dad. The same witch who turned Aria, my werewolf best friend and her pack against me. Not a day goes by that I don't think about Aria and watching her beautiful wolf body transform into a hellhound or how much killing her burns my already fiery heart. How much anger I carry for not trying harder, for not being strong enough. For not saving the traitor pack of wolves who helped me save Dad. But Aria and her pack made their choices, and free will is all we really have in the end.

I'm afraid to tell Ezekiel that I want to hunt the wolves to make sure Mary isn't lurking in the shadows. Because even though I saw my power consume her, I feel deep down she's alive and as powerful as ever. Her melodic voice haunts my dreams, making it hard to sleep most nights, even in Ezekiel's arms. Her spells entice me, trying to hypnotize my inner demon, tempting it to break free to destroy what's left of my humanity.

"You wouldn't understand," I say instead of coming up with a lie. It feels wrong to even try, knowing that Ezekiel is incapable of lying to me.

He sighs, tilting his head to the side. "This isn't about the wolves."

I rub my lips together, sucking my bottom lip between my teeth. His gaze shifts to my mouth, his heartbeat thrumming faster.

"It's about Mary." I cringe, hearing my voice say her name out loud. It's my heart's turn to thump, crashing around my chest in a bad way, probably as worried as I am that speaking her name out loud might possibly summon her from the depths of Hell on the arm of Uncle Lucifer himself.

Ezekiel's forehead wrinkles, his whole face pouting more than I am, making him look more boyish than hardened angel—like his mortal age when he ascended—barely nineteen. But age doesn't exist with him now. He's immortal. Above humanity.

Even after all these weeks alone together, I'm still trying to learn everything about his life before me, though he's adamant that his life started when I became his purpose. Grossly romantic. I love it.

"Mary is gone," he says. "She can't hurt you."

I should believe him. "I'm not so sure. I hear her."

"I can't lie to you, Faith. And her voice?" He touches his fingers to my temple. "That'll stay with you. She forced you to touch Hell. That's not something you can hope or pray away no matter how much I wish we both could. I'd do anything to see to it. Trust me. I'll protect you, always."

I lean forward, resting my head on his shoulder. "Okay. Maybe we should go hom—"

A scream rips through the air, cutting off my words. The sound slices through me, stealing all other sounds from my hearing. I cover my ears to muffle the wail, but it's already seared into my brain, resonating around my head.

I can't ignore it or turn my back on someone in such agony I'm sure the universe can hear. Instead of fleeing from Ezekiel, I take his hand and pull him with me in the direction the were-wolf pack had chased the chocolate wolf. Ezekiel runs beside me, his wings flapping to push us faster along.

"God, help me," a masculine voice cries, the pure torture in his voice gripping my heart. "Please, stop. I told you I can't."

Ezekiel skids his boots across the pavement, forcing me to slow down. A few dozen feet ahead, a naked man lies on his side in the middle of the street. Five wolves surround him, growling and snarling. A tan wolf with a bloody muzzle launches at the man, sinking its teeth into the flesh of his side, making him scream again.

Watching the wolf pack attack, slowly and purposely biting the werewolf in human form, sends a wave of anger through me. It's not uncommon for packs to turn on each other or to break a member to fall in line. And something about watching it unfold in front of me, reminding me of Christopher, the traitor wolf who lost his life to help me save my dad, automatically summons my demonic power into my hands.

Ezekiel tugs my arm, pulling me toward the sidewalk and into the cover of the trees. "You can't attack them. It risks exposing us."

I clench my jaw. "I can't stand here and do nothing either."

"Faith."

I release a guttural noise from deep in my throat and snuff out my power. Covering my eyes with my hands, I take a deep breath. The world shifts around me, transforming from the suburban neighborhood and into a dry, dead world with brown, hazy air, a sandy desert landscape with an onyx path leading nowhere and everywhere, and twisted, gnarled trees with screaming faces within them, stretching toward the sky.

My heart falters at the sight of bursts of flames drawing my attention toward the wolf pack. Circling the street in front of me, the pack of hellhounds glows brightly under the white-hot sun of the demonic sunlight prison realm. I count only five, which means the man the werewolves attack in front of me has not willingly given his soul to a witch to bind to Hell with magic in exchange for power.

Seeing the Hell beast through the veil, using the magic

branding on the back of my hand Kristin, my dad's witch, created to help me control my sight, sets off raging alarm bells within me. If the werewolves are hellhounds, I was right. This far exceeds the Moonlight Shores pack. Even if Mary isn't here, it's possible she had a coven to supersede her.

I drop my hand, my chest heaving. Ezekiel pulls me close to him, wrapping me in his arms. I blink, confusion lining my forehead. He didn't hug me to hug me—my legs gave out on me, fear gripping so tightly that I can't breathe.

Covering my face again, I peer at the hellhounds once more, hoping my eyes deceived me and maybe Ezekiel was right about the trauma of touching Hell still lingering with me. But the hellhounds remain.

I drop one hand from my face, igniting power into my palm. The world hazes around me, and I stare in horror at my blackened, burning hand, glowing under my power.

I gasp, snuffing my power out while dropping my spelled hand from my face. "Ezeki—"

The sounds of boots touching down on the asphalt, two— no three—thuds, drifts to my ears, forcing my mouth to shut. Wind blows through my hair, stirring up the fallen Jacaranda blossoms. A golden feather drifts to the ground next to us, sending a tsunami of panic raging through me.

I don't have a chance to move before Ezekiel yanks me toward the nearest house, staying under the cover of the trees. The soft whisper of ruffling feathers, like two pieces of silk rubbing together, locks my attention to the three angels who dropped from the sky.

Divine intervention at it's finest.

"Stay calm, Faith," Ezekiel whispers. "The wolves will keep their focus."

I nod my head without a word.

"On the count of three, we're going to run."

I nod again.

"One." His breath tickles my ear. "Two." Blood pounds through my head to the same racing rhythm of my heart. "Thr—"

Blinding light steals my vision.

Howls rip through the air.

I freeze.

"Run, Faith," Ezekiel says, nearly dragging me away.

But I can't run.

I can't breathe.

Fear paralyzes me.

Tossing me over his shoulder, Ezekiel dashes in the opposite direction of the angels. As soon as the tree line disappears, he bends his knees and launches us into the air despite the threat of exposure to the angels of the angelic army.

But they're the least of my worries now despite the fear I had for them the last few weeks.

I cling onto Ezekiel, watching the world shrink the higher we ascend. Three radiant angels, glowing with Heaven's light, blast power at the werewolf pack. They scatter, running away from the bleeding, broken man they tried to tear apart. The angels never even bother to look toward the sky. Why would they? The threat they face is forever grounded. They're not hunting me and Ezekiel. As far as they're concerned, we're gone. I'm lost to Hell, and as for Ezekiel? Angels disappear on their own journeys all the time, following their divine instincts.

A truck screeches to a halt, plowing into one of the running wolves, and I watch as a demon hunter from the Hunter's Alliance hops from the vehicle, ready to back Heaven up.

"That was close, Faith," Ezekiel says, shifting me in his arms.

I nod without taking my eyes from the battle below. "Uh-huh."

"Please, try not to test us so much. I couldn't bear it if I..." Ezekiel's voice disappears with the sound of my heart pounding in my ears.

A figure strolls through the trees, cloaked in moving shadows, sending ice through my fiery veins.

"No," I whisper, stiffening.

The figure steps from the trees, peering around. And then I see them—glowing red eyes.

"No!" I yell again. "Ezekiel, it's her!"

Ezekiel flaps his wings, spinning us through the air like the threat will come from the clouds. "What? Who?"

Tears burn my eyes, my throat aching. "Mary."

BRAVE ANGEL

EZEKIEL SPINS MIDAIR, propelling backward while taking in the suburban neighborhood far below. I shield my eyes from the icy air, squinting to get a better view of the hunters chasing off the wolves while the angels care for the fallen man.

"I don't see her," Ezekiel says, dropping lower.

I raise my hand and point. "She's right over..."

She's gone.

Her glowing red eyes and moving shadows no longer haunt the tree line. Fear trickles through me, and I rub my eyes, trying to clear my burning vision. I know I saw her. I'd never forget her black hair and fiery eyes, the evil that clings to her very essence not unlike that of a demon.

"Where?"

I groan. "I know I saw her, Ezekiel. But she's gone."

"Faith," he says.

I shake my head, burying my face into his shoulder. "You don't believe me."

He shifts me in his arms so I'm perched on his hip with my legs wrapping around him. "Of course I believe that you saw her, but it doesn't mean she was there."

"Then who helped the werewolves?"

He doesn't answer because he doesn't know.

Descending so quickly that my stomach rises into my throat, Ezekiel drops from the sky to land with a muted thud in the middle of a park. He doesn't let go of me until I unwrap myself from him and wiggle to get back to my feet. I bend over, clutching my knees. Breath is hard to come by, my body struggling to adjust from going from the clouds back to Earth in the quick motion I'll never get used to.

Ezekiel rubs his hand on my back, trailing his fingers across my shoulders to gather my hair behind me. "Just keep breathing."

I groan. "You fly like a maniac."

He chuckles. "You know why I had to."

How could I forget?

He reaches out and twines his fingers with mine, guiding

me out of the park and toward a shopping area buzzing with life. "Let me make it up to you. I know you've been antsy lately and only ever leaving the apartment for groceries will soon drive us both crazy. There's that little restaurant we've passed a few times—"

"This sounds like a date," I quip, the fear clinging to me now gone with the idea of going out.

He shrugs. "I guess it is."

"You'll have to let down your shield to order. You sure you want to risk it for a meal with me and my trouble-making?" I smile, nearly giggling, because I never thought I'd ever be this excited to eat out with my angel on an official date.

He smiles right back at me. "Maybe you're wearing me down."

"Corruption is right around the corner."

"Or maybe it's because we've eaten spaghetti every day for two weeks."

"Aw, and I thought this was for me and not the food."

As it turned out, neither Ezekiel nor I are great cooks. We're worse at following directions. I hadn't realized how spoiled Dad made me until it came down to having to do things for myself. And Ezekiel, he's used to the bare minimum. Angels survive on handouts from the Hunter's Alliance, since like demons, they're still somewhat tied to mortal bounds though they're immortal. Eating is one of those constraints. So is pain.

"It is pretty bad, isn't it?" I add, thinking how I never thought self reliance would feel so strange. Good yet disappointing. Sometimes overrated. My demon half definitely misses being spoiled.

He shrugs. "We make it work."

Sliding his hand around my waist, he tugs me along toward a small restaurant with seating on an enclosed patio. It's not exactly the fine dining I'm accustomed to eating with Dad, gown and all, but it's the type of place Cadence, Dad's hunter girlfriend, used to take me to for lunch.

Ezekiel stops short of the door and turns to me. "Careful not to touch anyone. I'm only lowering my shield for me."

I frown. "Really? The place is empty."

"Kristin was adamant. It's more dangerous to expose you to anyone who might want to use your lack of a soul or the fact that you're Raphael's daughter to their advantage. Tainted humans can cause as much damage as demons, and you're mortal."

Sighing, I nod and wait for him to open the door. I enter first, and Ezekiel stays right behind me like a comforting shadow on the way to the ordering counter. Something about this strangely normal moment, listening to Ezekiel order for me, choosing everything I like without having to ask me, and then surprising me by motioning me to sit down outside, brings both joy and sadness to my being. Joy, because I've missed feeling like the world wasn't out to get me, and sadness, because this isn't how my life is all the time anymore.

Ezekiel sits next to me instead of across from me, brushing his knee against mine. It'll appear as if he's eating way too much alone, but it's not like people pay that much attention to others to notice how quickly the food disappears.

I take a couple bites of my dinner, stabbing at my taco salad with my fork. Silence falls between us, and I listen to all the little sounds coming from people shopping, cars driving by, a dog barking. I usually concentrate on keeping the world quiet, but something about all the noise eases my nerves. It mutes everything threatening to leave me weak—something Dad would frown upon. *Damn, I miss him.*

"You know, you can talk to me about anything," Ezekiel says, swirling the ice around in his cup of water.

"I know."

"This whole situation isn't exactly ideal, and I'm sure being around me every second—"

I reach out and cover his hand with mine. "I like your company, Ezekiel. I hated being alone during the day when my dad was gone. Why do you think I snuck out all the time? Why do you think it was so easy for the Moonlight Shores pack to fool me?"

He stares at his plate instead of me without answering.

"I'm just—can we talk about something else?"

"Anything."

I twist my lips to the side in consideration. "You."

"Me? Why me?"

"It's only fair, considering how much you know about me. Maybe it'll help me corrupt you." I deflect from having to expose my fears to Ezekiel by resorting to teasing. I can't help it.

When things get serious, my first instinct is to lighten the mood. It's always helped me cope when facing demons—because with demons, things tend to always be dark.

He leans back in his chair. "Well, there really isn't that much to tell. When someone ascends to join Heaven's ranks, you cut all mortal bonds and ties. It's more like a past life, and the memories fade pretty quickly."

"Dylan seems to be the same as he was before," I say, bringing up one of the few full-blooded Demon Watchers I know apart from Ezekiel. And Dylan? He's like my big brother. He knew me before he died and ascended to serve in the angelic army.

"There are always exceptions depending on your purpose, but I'm not one of them, Faith. My eternity really did start with you."

I scrunch my face and crane my neck to peek at him. "That never stops being cheesy or sad."

He laughs. "You like it."

I grin, touching his knee. "Don't even know how you could recognize that through all your purity."

He only smiles as a response.

"Oh, wait. I know why. You weren't always so pure, were you?"

A deep blush sweeps across Ezekiel's face at my question. He sips his glass of water like he needs something to do to decide how and if he should respond to me, considering angels can't lie.

I giggle. Full on giggle. Getting such reactions from him makes my demon blood pump. He's been so serious and brooding, pouty even, lately that I'll take whatever I can get.

He clears his throat but doesn't say anything.

I snort. "What? You can discuss *my* mortal desires but answering a simple question about your own when you were a nephilim is too hard? Is it against angelic law or something?"

"Your mortal desires are much more fun to talk about," he says, shifting his gaze to look at me.

I raise an eyebrow, moving my hand up an inch on his leg. "Just talk?"

I'm pretty sure he's never going to recover from where this conversation is heading. His heart picks up pace, the light in his eyes darkening into something incomprehensible—human even.

"You're testing me," he whispers, his voice low and husky, nearly vibrating across his lips.

My own heart rams against my ribcage. "I wouldn't dare."

"Because, you know, the sun is setting soon..."

And we'll have an entire world to ourselves. How could I forget? To cast the spell to fake my death, Kristin tied me to the Veiled Realm, which is the night world version of the prison realm that locks demons away in the day. Luckily, time speeds by there at a faster rate than on the Earth plane. If it didn't, Ezekiel would be in serious trouble due to my boredom. Mostly, I sleep. It took some adjustment to transition from a night to day schedule, but it's nice. Almost normal. The angelic army is less active during the day, too...not sure for how much longer.

I tilt my head toward the sky. "In five minutes."

"I promise a better date next time."

Next time. I never knew such a little plan could weigh so heavy on me. Thinking about tomorrow, let alone some unforeseen time in the future hasn't been easy. I treat every day like my last now. I can't help it.

I smirk, nodding. "You would dare give me something to look forward to? You know how I feel about hope."

He leans in, brushing his lips to my cheek. "It's all for me. The hope, the plans. You."

I laugh. "Uh-oh. You sound a little devilish. You sure those wings of yours aren't going to get struck by lightning?"

He frowns. I've gone too far. "That's not how it—"

Reaching out, I press my fingers to his lips, cutting off his words. The air hums around us, mist swirling over my skin, now steaming as the Veiled Realm steals us away. Ezekiel kisses my palm, making me smile. Instead of watching the world around us transform, I study every feature of his face.

His stubbly jaw twitches as he swallows, making his Adam's apple bob in his throat. The sudden bright moon rising in the sky bounces silver light off his mocha eyes. He cradles my hand to his cheek, a million thoughts flashing across his face, every one of them begging for me to figure them out because he only ever speaks his mind in unsuspecting moments when I crack through his angelic guard.

Stepping back, I raise my hand over my eye to peer

through the veil and into the Earth realm. Our half-eaten plates remain on the table where we left them, and I kind of wish I would've finished mine, because who knows when I'll get another few minutes to pretend my life is normal.

Ezekiel tugs on my elbow, trying to get me to stay with him in the present rather than lose myself in a world I can no longer be a part of for who knows how long—possibly forever. Dad swore to me he'd figure something out, but I'm not so sure he can. This is far beyond the scope of his power. He can protect me from Hell, but Heaven is another story, not if he wishes to stay on Earth. I would never ask him to give up his eternity for me, either. Not when my life on Earth is like a minute in comparison to his, though I wish I could have one precious minute more with my family.

"Faith," Ezekiel whispers, touching his hand over my hand still covering my eye. "The world will be there come dawn."

A flash of light catches my attention, and I shift away from Ezekiel pleading for my attention. Any other night I would gladly give it to him, but I can't shake the awful familiarity the intruder werewolves elicited within me the second they appeared in my neighborhood.

"Are you so sure about that?" I ask, taking a few steps toward the street.

A hellhound, in all its burning glory, charges down the block to turn the corner. Now might be the perfect time to investigate. I have an advantage no one on Earth does. I can see through the veil without being seen.

"Yes," Ezekiel says, sliding his hand through my free one.

Bright headlights shine through the Earth realm, startling me, and I drop my hand as a car zooms toward me. I shake my head to orient myself to the Veiled Realm. Ezekiel unfurls his massive wings, stretching them toward the sky.

Now, that's one way to get my attention.

"Well, I'm not."

He groans, flapping his wings, stirring the mist around us. "How do I persuade you otherwise?"

I offer a smile. "Let me follow the hellhounds."

He twists his lips to the side in consideration. "And then what?"

I shrug. "Nothing. I just want to see. It'll help me sleep better."

Straightening his shoulders, he gives me a steeling look, lowering his eyebrows on his forehead. "I can help you with that."

I hold out my hand to him. "And you can help me with this, too."

"I guess it's better doing this from the safety of this side of the veil."

A muffled howl cuts through the air between worlds, sending my arm hairs rising. Only the loudest noises usually come through. Pushing the whisper of fear away, I summon all the courage I can muster.

Ezekiel swears the Veiled Realm is safe, and I know I should believe him.

But tonight, something feels different.

Nowhere feels safe. Not even in the arms of my brave angel.

BOW TO A WITCH

"DOWN THERE," I say, pointing at the street below that transforms into the onyx road leading into a dense forest of gnarled trees. Ezekiel can't see what I see, so I have to narrate everything to him. "It's going inside a house."

Dropping down, Ezekiel sends my heart into my throat with the motion. I release a small, unwanted squeal and cover my mouth as he touches his boots to the path. Cool mist steams over my skin, much warmer than the world around us. Ezekiel sets me on my feet, flapping his wings a few times to push the fog away.

I swallow, staring at the ghost of a house in front of us. Mostly, the Veiled Realm is made up of dead things of nature. It's pretty barren. But occasionally, we stumble upon houses made up from the materials around us. Upper level demons have loads of time on their hands, and I can see them creating somewhere to hang out during the day.

"I don't want to go inside," Ezekiel says, standing beside me. "It's like walking into a demon's lair when it's not home."

"Well, it's the perfect time to do so. Not like anyone will come home anytime soon," I argue, stepping forward anyway. Just because he doesn't want to go inside doesn't mean he won't follow me anyway.

"You sure the Hell beast went in?" he asks, rubbing his hand through his dark hair.

I nod. "It's a normal house on the Earth plane."

Ezekiel flaps his wings, stirring wind through my hair. "Obviously not. Demons choose locations wisely. Something drew them here."

Moving forward, I head to peek into the cutout that creates a window. A shiver trails down my back, and I clutch my hands to the windowsill. I'm not sure what I was expecting—a demon hanging out with a pack of broken werewolves—but I definitely wasn't expecting to find a pack of werewolves, some in human form and others in hellhound form, standing around a demon bound in blessed chains.

Smoke drifts from the demonic man's wrists as he struggles

in the chair. "You're making a grave mistake. What did the witch offer you? I'll double it and make your time on Earth worth your while. If you don't take my deal, I'll assure you that you will—"

One of the human werewolves splashes a cup of water into the demon's face, making him holler and thrash in his burning bindings. My stomach reels at the sight of his smoldering, melting skin.

"Shut up. We don't make deals with demons. Why pay a price when we can take whatever we want for free?"

I hate to admit that the hellhounds make a point. If only their power didn't mess with my world and life. Demons and angels have a purpose to fulfill. It keeps the balance of the universe in order. Some evils are necessary. But the hellhounds? They have no place. They shouldn't even exist. I'll never understand how they could trade their entire eternities for such a short amount of time to hold power. *Because they think immortality is within their reach...*

But I doubt the angels will open a portal powerful enough anytime soon. It might've been my dad's only saving grace considering he was never really a threat. But just because the angels might not open a portal now doesn't mean they never will.

"What's happening, Faith?" Ezekiel asks, drawing my attention away from the imprisoned demon.

"Hellhounds have captured a demon."

"But why?"

The demon screams, yanking my attention back to him. I

hold up my index finger to my mouth so Ezekiel doesn't ask me questions I can't answer yet. I'm sure it's frustrating not being able to see what I see, but it can't be any more frustrating than how I feel half the time when no one ever wants to answer my own questions.

"Everything has a price," the demon mutters.

The hellhound in human form laces his fingers on the back of his head. He laughs turning to glance over his shoulder at his pack mates. My stomach twists in knots at the sight of the familiar man. I can't recall his name, because he stayed far away from me anytime I was at Aria's house, but I definitely know he's a part of the Moonlight Shores pack.

Those hellhounds, working beside Mary to gain power, scattered after I stopped her from taking advantage of the portal she planned to use to bring a new Hell to Earth to tip the balance away from Heaven and Hell and into the hands of witches and werewolves—two species said to be born from the Veiled Realm and both who have fallen before demons with no help from the angelic army, Heaven's crusaders.

That night not only changed my life, but it changed the world, too. Rifts happened in the Hunter's Alliance, and when people don't stand together, they fall apart.

"Yeah, and it's you who'll cover the costs," the hellhound says. He turns to another pack mate in human form. "Give me the dagger."

A woman with long blond hair hands over a curved dagger made of black metal and red rubies, not unlike the one that

Mary burrowed into my stomach. Fear steals my breath, and I pant, trying to pull myself together as the edges of my vision shadow.

"Faith, what's wrong?" Ezekiel says, latching his fingers to my wrist. "Drop your hand and talk to me."

I hold firm. I can't turn my gaze away from the dagger. Not yet.

"Faith," Ezekiel pleads. If he wanted to pry my hand from my eye, he could, but he doesn't. He's trying to get me to see reason instead of forcing divine intervention upon me.

The hellhound twirls the dagger between his palms, waving it in front of the demon's face to taunt him. The werewolf is definitely more Hell beast than human, playing dangerous games and relishing in someone else's torment just like demons do.

"One demon heart, coming up," the hellhound says, pulling his arm back.

The demon growls, releasing its true body for the world to see. Blood red spikes cut through his forehead and down his temples, so long that bars of shadows cross his face. Black liquid trickles from his eyes, now onyx without signs of pupils or irises like before, and he opens his mouth to reveal several rows of shark-like teeth in a now widening mouth.

"Tell me what you want!" The demon roars, thrashing against the chains. He struggles so hard that one of his hands falls off, now severed from the pressure he put on the blessed metal as it burned his flaking skin.

The hellhound stops short, piercing the demon with the dagger only a few centimeters into where his heart hides within a cage of demonic power in his chest. The demon gnashes his teeth, spitting black liquid at the hellhounds, smoldering the fabric of his T-shirt.

I dig my nails into the window frame. "They're going to use a demon for something. Do you think…?"

"Demons access Hell all the time, but it's not the same as opening a portal powerful enough to send someone like your dad back. It really does take an angel—a powerful angel—to do something like that," Ezekiel says.

"Are you sure?" I ask.

"Well, I can't be a hundred percent certain." His answer ignites panic within me. "But I wouldn't worry, Faith. Heaven knows what's happening now. They'll get it under control. They always do. Trust them."

I groan. "You did not just ask me to trust the angelic army."

He clears his throat, touching his hand to my back. "I'm sorry. I know you have it in your mind that they're the bad—"

"They'll kill me, Ezekiel," I snap, cutting him off from even trying to make me see reason in an unfair, unreasonable world.

"I have faith that things will turn out as they—"

Another scream rips through the air. The hellhound presses the dagger deeper into the demon's chest, but it doesn't make him explode in a waterfall of goo. It does nothing but make the

50

demon wail.

"They're cutting out his heart," I say, directing the conversation back to what's going on. "Why isn't he exploding?"

"Must not be blessed. Demons are resilient and can withstand quite a lot. They'll regenerate in the sunlight realm, too," Ezekiel says.

"But why take his heart?" I ask.

Ezekiel shifts next to me, and I wish his presence was enough to yank my attention away from the grotesque acts unfolding through the veil.

"Stop," the demon says. "I'll do anything."

The hellhound barks a laugh, sliding the dagger free without removing the demon's heart. "Get Heaven to open a portal to Hell."

The demon stops fighting, relaxing against the chains, now loosened with his handless arm free. "That it?"

The hellhound nods.

"You have a deal."

Panic rushes through me, freezing my fiery blood. I gasp, dropping my hand from my eye and spin to meet Ezekiel's dark gaze. He rests his hands on my shoulders, searching my face for answers I struggle to say out loud.

"The-the demon. They—" I groan, squeezing my eyes shut. "The demon made a deal with the hellhounds to get the angelic army to open a portal to Hell."

I bring my spelled hand back to my eye, my stomach twisting at the sight of the hellhounds releasing the demon like they didn't just have him held captive with blessed chains while torturing him with holy water. But Ezekiel was right. Demons are resilient. They're adaptable, too. More so than angels.

"Oh, no," I whisper.

Ezekiel holds me tighter, keeping my whole body from trembling. "Tell me exactly what they said."

I repeat the exchange between the hellhounds and the demon. My brows furrow as I think about them over and over again. Something isn't right. I've heard Dad negotiate thousands of deals, and the hellhounds missed their stipulation. Without saying it at the moment of exchange, it leaves them open to shifts and having it misconstrued.

Smart demon. He has nothing to lose if he doesn't follow through with the deal, and the hellhounds already let him—

"One more thing," the hellhound says, holding the dagger up to the demon. He takes a step back, but one of the hellhounds, in all its flaming glory, snaps its frothy jowls at the back of the demon's legs.

"We already made a deal," the demon says.

The hellhound shakes his head, holding up the knife. "That's not how this works, Hell's minion. You aren't negotiating the deal. We are. And there's one more thing."

I tense.

The demon ignites an orb of black liquid in the palms of his hands. "You can't change the terms."

A hellhound howls from behind him. "I can, and I am. Your deals aren't binding with me. I work for power far greater than you. And because of that, you must bow to a witch."

Snarling, the demon thrusts his hands toward the werewolf. The power doesn't even get within reach of the hellhound because another one of its pack mates locks its flaming mouth to the back of the demon's legs and yanks his feet out from under him.

"Ezekiel, what can we do?" I ask, not taking my eyes off the demon. "They're going to make the demon bow to a witch. Do you think it's Mary?"

Hearing me say her name out loud sends my teeth chattering. I can't shake the ever-present despair gripping my heart, threatening to send me to the ground.

"I don't know, Faith."

I release a small cry of frustration at his response. Because he didn't say no, it means he really doesn't know now. Not like before. Something has shifted. I don't know if it's because he can feel what I feel, but I was praying he'd flat out say he truly believed Mary wasn't behind this, that she didn't escape Hell.

"What am I going to do?" I ask.

"What do you mean?" Ezekiel asks.

"She's going to come for me. She'll drag me to Hell again. I know it."

Ezekiel wraps me in his arms from behind, trying to get me to look at him. I can't though. I can't help but watch the demon and hellhounds yell at each other in muted voices I can only understand through reading their lips. And because Ezekiel distracted me, I missed portions of their conversation.

"You're safe with me, Faith. Only Kristin and your dad know you're alive. Even if Mary or another witch does try to shift things, you won't get caught up in the disaster again. And Raphael and everyone else are on high alert."

A flash of light erupts in my vision. I snap my mouth closed instead of arguing. A cloaked figure steps from the hallway, but I can't see the witch's face with her back to me. My heart nearly explodes at just the sight, knowing that it could possibly be Mary only feet away from me on the other side of the veil.

I summon demonic power in my hands, holding it in front of me like the veil isn't enough protection.

The demon thrashes on the floor beneath one of the flaming hellhounds, and I swear a breeze stirs from the room to me, lifting my hair from my shoulders. My heart works in overdrive, and I gasp, preparing to send my power at the witch, hoping it'll break through the veil to destroy her before she can ever hurt me again.

"Faith, what are you doing?" Ezekiel asks.

"She's going to get me, Ezekiel. I have to stop her," I say.

"She can't hurt you," he says.

"You're lying," I say. "You're not supposed to lie."

Bright red flames erupt in the house in front of me through the veil. The demon fights and thrusts his power at the hellhound, knocking it into a wall. I guess the deal is off. He'd rather go to Hell than bow to a witch.

The black cloaked figure glides across the room toward the

demon. Shadows obscure everything about the witch, making it impossible to confirm or deny whether or not Mary is back on Earth in the flesh. If I could just—

"Faith!" Ezekiel yells.

The figure disappears into thin air at the same time the demon explodes, sending guts and blood cascading through the room.

I heave, my stomach threatening to release the small portion of dinner I ate. Ezekiel yanks my hand from my eye, not giving me a choice into whether or not I'll get to watch the hellhounds on the Earth plane any longer.

Tears blur my eyes, turning my vision fuzzy, and I sob. Ezekiel wraps me in his wings, rubbing his hands on my back. A thousand painful emotions whirl through me, making it hard for me to even stand on my feet.

"Ezekiel," I say, sniffling, barely managing to get the words out. "I—I—"

"Shhh," he whispers, embracing me while kissing the tears from my cheeks. "Just take a breath."

"I can't. I can't do this."

He pets my hair. "Then let me help you."

I sniffle again. "Okay. Please. Just make it stop."

With a flash of blinding light, Ezekiel and I disappear.

SURPRISE VISIT

"**B**LOOD TO BLOOD, red to black, a fall from Heaven will send you back. Hell's fury, so hot and true, will cut your soul, releasing you. With your death, comes new life. A demon born, Hell's warrior of night."

A scream rips through the air, startling me awake, and I scramble to my feet. One second I was crying on Ezekiel's shoulder and now I'm back in our apartment. Bending down, I yank a dagger from under my bed. Something about the chant in my ears stops me from summoning demonic power. I aim the dagger at the door glowing with brilliant light seeping in through the cracks around the frame.

Blood pounds in my ears, and my hands shake. The familiar spell repeats over and over again, and I can't help but wonder if it's a warning. No, Mary wouldn't warn me. It's a threat. Somehow the hellhound pack managed to lure the angelic army right to my door.

Hands touch my shoulders. "You're okay, Faith. We're home and safe. You were having a nightmare."

"I heard a scream," I say, blinking my eyes.

Ezekiel hugs me, snuggling his chin into the crook of my neck. "It was you."

I exhale a shuddering breath. "And the light?"

"A new day."

A new day. *It's the sun. It's just the sun. Pull yourself together.*

Groaning, I turn and sit on the edge of my bed. Memories of last night consume my thoughts, making it hard to gather any sort of bearing. I hadn't expected Ezekiel to use his angelic light on me to knock me out in the Veiled Realm.

"Ezekiel, you have to wake me up before we cross the veil. I can't stand crossing between worlds without being aware. I thought—damn it." My heart slams into my ribcage, trying to pulverize itself. "I can't live like this. This is—G—" I bite my tongue to silence my thoughts. Not only am I now afraid to summon my demonic power, I'm afraid of whispering any sort of prayer. Stupid hellhounds and witches and angels.

"What happened last night? Are you sure the world is still okay?" I ask, resting my elbows on my knees. The world presses against me, like Heaven and Hell will stop at nothing to pluck me right from existence for reasons out of my control.

The bed shifts as Ezekiel sits next to me, leaning back on his arm behind me. "Everything is fine, but you freaked out. I think your lack of sleep is getting to you."

"Or Mary."

"Faith, I don't know what else I can do to help you realize—"

"Believe me. Let me go out again. Let's find the werewolf intruders. We can—"

"We can't do anything. For one, you need more sleep. You're exhausted. And two, we're two people and not an army. Let someone else handle it."

He makes it sound so simple.

I shift, swinging my legs onto the bed. Ezekiel pulls me onto his lap, sliding his arm under my legs to curl me against him. His beating heart thrums in my ears, and I hold my breath to listen to only it, pushing every other noise from my head.

"You can't keep this up," he continues.

"Oh, yes I can. The Veiled Realm rejuvenates me," I argue.

He laughs. "Believing that doesn't make it true. You're only half demon. Even if you weren't, demons heal during the daylight realm, not the night world we visit."

I groan.

"Why don't you just snuggle with me for a bit and relax? If you can't sleep, I can help you again," he says.

I shake my head, almost tempted by his offer to cuddle—

not by the angelic nap time, though. "Don't you dare. You didn't hear her like I did. You don't feel her in your bones like I do now, either."

He releases a small breath. "You know, I believe you hear her, but I also think it has more to do with you and everything around us. Seeing those hellhounds got to you. Mary can't get to you ever, even if she managed to escape from going to Hell. I never let my shield over you down. Never," he says, his voice confident, though confidence does nothing to comfort me. "And I won't ever do it for me again, either. I'll do whatever it takes to assure you."

I sigh, covering my face with my hands. The world shifts around me, the stained carpet of our tiny apartment turning into dead grass under my boots. Brown haze fills the air under a sun that should burn my skin, yet I don't feel anything through the veil locking the light prison realm from me.

A shadow falls on the ground next to me, stretching out to blend with the tangled shadows of the twisted branches above my head. A hand reaches out, and a tiny shock buzzes against my knee.

Jerking my head up, I meet Dad's vivid blue eyes smiling from his spot sitting next to me on a boulder in the same place I still see and feel the lumpiness of my well worn mattress. Haze surrounds us, veiling between us. I'll never get used to the strangeness that comes along with covering my eye that sees the realm while letting myself still see Ezekiel sitting next to me on the plane my body is in.

"My beautiful Faith," Dad says. The last person I had expected to show up in our apartment—well, sort of in the apartment—was Dad. His presence pulls so many good emotions from me—love, happiness, relief—that it's easy to forget he shouldn't be contacting me. I had no idea how much I needed to see him until now.

I wish so much to hear the smoothness of his voice. Stupid veil, muting the world. It's not like I can ask him to yell either. A screaming demon in the daylight realm attracts the worst attention.

"You have no idea how happy I am to see you," Dad says, grinning at me with a smile that soothes the panic battling in my chest.

I smile, reaching out, shocking myself again to rest my hand on his. "As happy as I am for this surprise."

"More," he says.

We smile at each other. I'm afraid to take my soulless eye off him in fear that he'll say something I'll miss if I'm not reading his lips. He looks as handsome as ever, never changing apart from his luxurious suits. Today the blue of his tie matches his ice eyes, and a small opal pin glitters on his lapel.

"The angel's treating you well but not too well, right?" he asks, peering past me at Ezekiel, but neither can see each other. I could get lost in this conversation, pushing away all the stuff I need to tell Dad about the hellhounds. About the possibility of Mary.

"You can use his name, Dad," I say with a laugh, pushing

my negative thoughts away.

"Raphael," Ezekiel says from next to me. "He should know to never visit our home, especially with the sudden werewolf activity yesterday. Tell him, Faith."

I ignore Ezekiel, keeping my focus on Dad.

"But it burns my poor demonic tongue to do so," Dad says, fake grimacing. "I bet one soul that he just complained about my surprise visit."

I laugh again. "Sorry, I don't have a soul."

My words make Dad's smile falter, tilting his lips into a frown. He blinks fire from his eyes, heaving a sigh, probably wishing I didn't remind him that Ezekiel possesses my soul. My eyes probably do a pretty good job at that, forever mismatched, one as blue as Dad's and the other as colorless as a soulless body abandoned on Earth when a demon is sent to Hell with all the souls contracted to them.

Dad leans his head on his curled hand, his elbow resting on his knee. There's something about seeing Dad through the veil, in a world where he's invincible and strong, that makes me yearn to be able to join him. If only it didn't mean I'd have to be a full-blooded demon. "I'm going to break one of his wings for that when you get to come home."

He says it like he's certain it'll be possible. But I don't see how it is. Not after last night. Mary's spell still hums in my ears, reminding me that if she had succeeded, I'd have returned from Hell because of Ezekiel—except I'd have changed. A demon without a soul, a minion for Lucifer, controlled by Mary. It's a fate worse than dying by the angelic army's hands. I'm starting to realize that the more I think about it. If Mary is truly back, if she still has her wicked heart on me, the angelic army might be my only saving grace. Because death is better than turning into a demon despite what Dad would say or think. I just—I could never be like him without a soul.

I roll my eyes. "You're all talk."

He glares. "I'll break both."

"You'll have to get through me." Grinning, I hold my fisted hand up like I could ever get in a punch if I tried.

He groans, bowing his head, but still looking at me sideways. "I never believed in karma until this second. The universe thinks it's being hilarious. You truly are your mother's daughter. Be careful, Faith."

"We are careful."

"I swear, Faith, you better not be insinuating—"

"Ezekiel said that human desires—"

Dad snarls.

I tip my head back and release a loud laugh. This conversation is way better than anything else I could think of to say.

"I'm kidding!" I say, though I sort of wish I wasn't. Even after him questioning me about Mary, or helping me sleep, even if I'm slightly annoyed with him, I can't help thinking about the date he promised. A better date. A real date. If only Ezekiel's love didn't run so pure, and he wasn't always on guard to my antics, I wouldn't have such a hard time even considering doing anything on Dad's list of things he'll break Ezekiel's wings for if either of us tries to explore "my human desires" as my sweet, sometimes infuriatingly pure angel calls them.

"And I'd say being your spawn might make me worse off than being Mom's daughter," I say.

Dad flares his nostrils. "You're right. Doomed. The both of us." He smiles while he says it, but his eyes glass over for a split second before he blinks to clear them. The daylight prison world might make him strong, but I can see how my humanity must sneak to him, especially with only a veil between us.

"Well, I don't know about you, but I'm not going down without a fight."

"It'll rain fire and brimstone," he adds.

I bare my teeth and raise my hand up, the one not covering my eye, in a fist, and Dad puts his arm around me, holding up his free fist, too. A shock crawls across my shoulder blades, but I don't turn away. I lean into him, knowing that if he says anything, I might miss it.

"Faith, I don't mean to interrupt your moment with Raphael," Ezekiel says, "but someone's here."

Fear tightens my muscles, and I sit up straighter. I look at Dad. "Dad, someone's here. Can you hang out for a while? I have some things I need to tell you, but I have to go in case it's—"

"Kristin can wait a moment longer," he says, cutting me off.

I heave a breath. "What? Why is Kristin here?" Maybe she knows. Maybe she's here to tell me I'm screwed and to enjoy my last day alive. Maybe that's why Dad's here, to say goodbye.

Dad presses his lips together. "We have business to take care of."

Oh, no. This might be it. Dad says everything he doesn't like is business.

Cool fingers lace around my wrist and gently pull my enchanted hand from my colorless eye. Dad disappears, leaving Ezekiel in the space in front of me, staring at me like if he tried hard enough, he could see Dad, too.

"You didn't tell him about the hellhounds," he says.

"I was getting around to it." I drop my hand to my lap, staring at the puckered branding of an eye across the back of my hand. "But I think he might know. Go ahead and open the door."

Ezekiel crosses the room, his feet soundless on the carpet. He peers through the peephole of our studio apartment's door just to be sure before he opens it. Demons might not be able to see through his shield, but other celestial beings can. My Demon Watcher is in a dangerous position, walking a line between serving his purpose and protecting me when both Heaven and Hell saw my body turn to ash. If he turns his back on his purpose...I can't even think about it. I'm lucky that I *am* his purpose.

"How did you find us?" Ezekiel asks, blocking the door, drawing me from my thoughts. "Is my shield—?"

"Your shield is fine, featherhead. I used Raphael's blood. Normally, tracking someone shielded is impossible, but Raphael isn't an ordinary demon. Right, Heaven's Traitor?" She says it like she can hear and see dad. Maybe she can.

I put my hand over my eye, viewing both worlds at once. Dad stands in front of Kristin, his arms crossed over his chest, but he looks past her and at me instead. Kristin turns her back to face me and motions me to come closer. Dad can see me through the veil because of our blood. If Ezekiel was on the other side, he could see me because he holds my soul. No one else can see through, though.

Kristin tugs my hand from my face and puts it over her own eye. "Blood to blood, a demon's kin, give me sight, let me in. Thin the veil so I can see, Heaven's Traitor watching me."

A strange sensation crawls over my skin, freaking me out. Spells—even Kristin's—knot my insides. Without warning, she pulls my hand from her face and uses a spiked thimble over her thumb to cut my palm. Ezekiel unfurls his wings, but she holds my hand up, making him stay back.

"Demon bound and demon born, blood meets blood, the veil now torn. Use this vessel split in two, show her demon peeking through." Kristin waves my hand through the air, my blood smearing before us like it coats a glass I couldn't see before.

Peering at me instead of my own reflection is a demon with blackened skin, glowing red eyes, and a ridge of horns poking in a perfect line across its forehead. Blond hair sticks to its bloody cheeks, and I gasp, reaching out to touch the bleeding veil.

The demon—my inner demon—suddenly vanishes, leaving Dad smiling at me even though my enchanted hand isn't held up to my eye.

I step back right into Ezekiel's taut chest. I was so focused on the bloody veil separating Dad from me that I didn't hear or see him move. Kristin squeezes my hand, trying to summon more blood in my palm. Like water on scorching asphalt, the blood sizzles and dissipates with every passing second.

She smears my blood over the veil again. "We don't have much time."

"What's this about?" Ezekiel asks.

Dad touches his fingers to the veil, gazing at me. "Such a gift to see both your beautiful eyes, Faith. How I miss you so much." I can hear him clearly, like he's standing in front of me.

Only a demon could appreciate the freakiness of my color-less iris. Maybe just a dad, even.

"Raphael, this is not the time," Kristin says. Only one other person in the universe can speak to my dad like that, and it's because he's in love with her. Kristin on the other hand? I haven't quite figured it out. She works for dad, yet he lets her get away with things he'd power blast other people for.

He curls his lips up in a snarl. "It's always the time to remind my daughter how precious she is to me regardless of what that angel—"

"I saved her," Ezekiel says, cutting Dad off. Dad and Ezekiel haven't really had the opportunity to work things out, and while I'm looking forward to the day I can reunite with Dad, the idea of bringing Ezekiel along in his physical form scares me. It wouldn't be the first angel versus demon battle. I can only hope with me standing in the middle, they might actually hold themselves back.

I stand between them, the veil struggling not to burn away, stealing Dad from Ezekiel and Kristin's sight. "Enough. Someone tell me what's going on. Is this about the hellhounds?"

Dad releases a breath. "You know? How?" He turns to Ezekiel. "You're supposed to protect her."

I purse my lips. "Stop it, Dad. Hellhounds arrived in our neighborhood yesterday. A whole pack. I think some from Moonlight Shores."

He nods. "You're right. It's causing quite the problem. The Hunter's Alliance has been given no choice but to re-evaluate their ties to non-humans, ruffling the angelic army's feathers. It threatens the truce in place with demons...not to mention the sudden hold the angels put in place against opening a portal to Hell for any unruly demon—both from angelic and demonic creation."

Ezekiel presses his fingers deeper into my shoulders, tensing. "So, there are no consequences for—"

"Oh, I've come up with plenty of punishment—"

"I thought demons couldn't create portals powerful enough," I say, craning my neck to meet Ezekiel's grimace.

"Seems they're not taking chances."

I close my eyes, both worlds disappearing. "I told you, Ezekiel. It's Mary. This is what she wanted, a fight for power." There's no other explanation for hellhounds to continue to rise.

Mary didn't perish by my hands. I knew my instincts were right. Her voice haunts me.

"What?" Dad and Kristin exclaim at the same time.

"I hear her sometimes in my dreams, when I listen to the silence long enough," I whisper.

Ezekiel's eyes widen. "You think it means something? I assumed the broken spell left some residual effect on Faith's mind, stirring these fears from her subconscious. Had I known—"

Kristin tugs a dagger from her bag. "I was afraid of this happening. Witch's use spells to protect themselves, including creating doppelgangers."

"A doppelganger?"

Slapping her blade against her palm, she says, "A lookalike. Most witches use one to protect themselves. I don't, because I'm contracted to your dad."

"Are you sure?" Ezekiel asks.

Her gaze flicks from him to me. "There's only one way to find out."

I extend out my hand. "I guess since I'm already bleeding."

She smirks. "Featherhead, I need your palm, too."

"You can't be serious," Ezekiel says, surprising me.

"It's your hand that holds Faith's soul," Kristin says.

"Maybe you should have thought about that before putting it on my daughter," Dad says, pressing against the veil. His voice lowers, the blood hovering between us nearly disappearing.

"I—"

I press my hand to Ezekiel's chest, standing on my tiptoes and whisper, "If you don't want to do this, then I respect your decision. Just get ready to run come nightfall. I can't stay here after last night."

Ezekiel's shoulders relax, and he tugs my hand from his chest, bringing it up to his cheek to hold there for a second. He kisses my palm, the corners of his eyes crinkling as he gazes into my eyes. It takes everything in me not to look away. Before, when he'd look so intently into my eyes, I knew he was searching my soul for things I couldn't see. Now? There's nothing. Yet he still manages to make my heart race.

Dad groans. "I expected eternal punishment for my mistakes, but this is beyond torture. Cruel and unusual punishment is Luci's specialty not Heaven's."

I crinkle my nose, grinning at Ezekiel, and he beams me a bright enough smile to push away any darkness clinging to me.

"I need a decision now, Zeke," Kristin says.

Hearing her use the nickname he despises reminds me of Aria, who had given it to him in the first place. It's been sixty veil crossings between worlds, and it still feels like one of these days, Aria will be waiting for me when I arrive with the sun.

Ezekiel notices the pout on my bottom lip and reaches up to touch it. "Okay," he says. "But not for either of you. This is for Faith."

"Finally, something I can approve of," Dad says.

Kristin turns to Dad. "Sorry, Raphael. I need Faith's

blood."

He frowns. "Until next time, Faith. I love you."

With a wave of her hand, Kristin smears the blood from the air, destroying the looking glass into the sunlight prison realm. My heart aches, Dad fading away. I cover my eye with my hand once more, and he waves before heading to the gnarled trees to disappear into the eerie forest.

"All right, featherhead. This is going to hurt like Hell," Kristin says, waving an ivory dagger in front of us.

Ezekiel sighs, giving Kristin his hand. "Faith, brace yourself."

I frown. "Huh?"

Kristin straightens her shoulders, flicking her gaze from Ezekiel's hand to my face. Sucking in a breath, she positions the ivory blade over Ezekiel's palm. "He's right, Faith. You should probably sit down."

Panic laces my heart, and I drop to the floor, crossing my legs.

Without another word, Kristin swipes the blade over Ezekiel's palm. I expect him to yell out in pain, to thrash, to unfurl his beautiful wings. To do something to react to the pain she swore he'd feel not unlike Hell.

All he does is capture me in his dark stare.

I release a tiny, breathless laugh. "You guys are not funn—"

Pain, worse than anything I have ever felt, rips through me to my core. I yell out, agony coursing through me, sliding up my hand. It's worse than how I imagine the pain to be from the fiery bites of a million hellhounds. It hurts the same way sacred items feel against my demonic power or how it felt to wake up without my soul—but worse. Much, much worse.

I scream again.

A WITCH'S KISS

"**S**OUL TO BLOOD and blood to soul, tie the two, make them whole. Unholy body but spirit divine, give her the answer, give her the sign. Angel's blood so pure and light, show the truth, give her sight. Bound to Heaven, anchored to Hell. A soul reveals, to my spell. For a demon's kin, who's angel tied. In the shadows, no witch can hide."

The pain dissipates in an explosion of fire, and I open my eyes, scrambling back. Standing before me, Mary smiles with her arms outstretched, beckoning me closer. Her green eyes shift to red and sparkle against the flames surrounding her. A veil of mist blurs her in and out of view.

"My dear child, how lovely it is you've summoned me," Mary says, gliding forward without using her legs. "I knew you'd hear my whispers and couldn't resist the allure of power I have to offer you."

I ignite an orb of Hell power between my hands. "Stay back."

She doesn't stop. Moving forward, she reaches out and grabs my face in her hands. Her now red eyes turn black, blacker than night, blacker than the void left inside me where my soul used to be, the complete opposite of my one white eye.

She inhales a deep breath. "I can take that from you. You'll be more powerful than ever if you let me."

I try to pull back, but her nails pierce the skin on my neck below my ears. "Take what?"

"The fear."

"Kristin! Make it stop," I yell. This can't be happening. Mary can't be standing before me. As much as I try to remember this is a vision, I can't deny the pain burning where she holds me. I can feel the fire around us, heating the room.

"A witch under a demon's contract shall never taste the power as sweet as what hides in you. But a witch free to serve all of Hell shall devour every last bit of power you have to offer."

Bringing her sharp nail to my mouth, Mary runs it over my bottom lip. Blood drips onto my chin. She leans forward and presses her lips to mine. My blood turns into lava, licking my skin in fire as it lands on my chest, searing through my shirt.

I scream, summoning more demonic power.

"Blood is blood, red to black. A demon born, I'll take you back. A witch's kiss brands the skin, there's no hiding now, I'll get in. An angelic shield can always break. And when it does, you're mine to take."

"Ezekiel!"

My voice rips through the foggy air, and I unleash my power at Mary. She explodes in a storm of fire and red light, a dangerous beauty that imprints on my vision. Cool hands slide around me, and I convulse, pain blinking me in and out of consciousness as Mary disappears completely.

"Angel wings, blessed and black, carry your soul, bring you back. Angel blood, pure as light. Lock you in, protect your sight. Angel love, fierce and true, fight the fear by protecting you. Soul to blood and blood to heart, sever the bind, break them apart."

Kristin's voice cuts through my ear-piercing screams. I snap my eyes open, flailing my arms, shooting my power around me. The witch ducks. She clutches her rainbow amulet, and the power splits around her and hits the wall, melting the framed picture of an ocean Ezekiel hung up last weekend when I told him I missed Moonlight Shores. The wall smolders, and Ezekiel shoots his own heavenly power at it to suffocate it before I set the whole place ablaze.

I heave a ragged breath, hiding my face against Ezekiel's shirt. Droplets of black liquid scatter across the soft gray fabric.

I touch my lips.

"You're bleeding," he says, pulling up the hem of his shirt to press it to my mouth.

Licking my lips, I taste the sweetness of my blood, almost like it has been infused with sugar. "This wasn't how I wanted answers," I snap, turning my glower to Kristin.

Kristin closes her eyes for a second in thought, and then she shifts to look at the destruction I caused to the wall. "I'm sorry it was so unpleasant, but there was no other way. Did you—"

"Mary said she knew I'd hear her whispers and that I *summoned* her. What does that even mean?" I ask.

Kristin curses so softly under her breath that if I wasn't listening so intently, I'd have missed the words. "What else happened?"

"She kissed me," I say.

Kristin's eyes widen. "This is worse than I thought. She shouldn't have been able to touch you, but—"

"But what?"

"We must leave. Now."

My brows knit together in confusion. "I don't understand."

"You've been officially marked for Hell." Kristin peers around the room, combing her fingers through her black hair. Her face scrunches, her sudden fear strong enough that I can smell the incense pouring from her with the scent.

"But my soul—"

She gathers her bag and yanks a bottle of water from it. Shaking it, she pours it across the bloody floor. "I don't know! Okay? It's not like I have experience in soulless demi-demons whose guardian angels mess up. I was only trying to find out if she was alive, but she must've intercepted my spell."

"Are you kidding me?" Panic cuts through me, stealing every good thing seeing Dad again stirred within me.

Kristin points to my angel. "Ezekiel, make yourself useful. Help me cleanse the place. Faith, pack your bag. Five minutes."

The urgency in her voice commands me to get to my feet instead of arguing with her or quipping about her lack of skills. Ezekiel steadies me when I wobble, motioning me to shield my eyes. Bright light floods through the room as he unleashes his heavenly power to burn through my blood to leave nothing behind. Even when my blood vanishes, I can't stop feeling like there should be something more I can do to protect myself.

I race to my bed, unhook my backpack, and stuff everything from the nightstand into it. Being without everything I'm used to was hard to handle at first. It's been years since I've worn the same thing twice in the same month, sometimes never—but now? I've worn the same jeans for two weeks straight. Pack light, run fast. Leave what you can't carry. Keep only what's important, which includes a handful of photos, a weapon, and the locket with a picture of Mom and Grandma on one side and Dad on the other with a tiny barb I cut off a stray feather from Ezekiel's wings.

I automatically touch the locket dangling between my

breasts. Pain erupts over my heart, burning under the platinum chain. I pull my bloody shirt askew for a better look, and shadows crowd my vision. A heart-shaped branding glows across my chest. My red, puckering skin screams under my touch.

"Ezekiel," I whisper so quietly, I'm not sure he heard me. I turn toward my makeshift vanity with a mirror propped against the wall on a folded table and take a closer look. It's not a heart on my skin but a kiss print. *A witch's kiss.*

My breath quickens, and I brace myself on the rickety table. Dizziness spins through my mind, overwhelming me. My trembling hands shake so much that my mirror topples over and shatters on the floor. I whirl around, searching the room for anything I can use to fix it. Spotting my knife on the kitchen table, I rush forward and swipe it off.

"Faith? What are you doing?" Ezekiel expands his wings, using them to push himself forward faster than his legs can take him. "Faith, stop."

"I need to get it off." The thought consumes me, clawing at me like if I don't follow through, I'll die.

I press the knife to my skin, the cool metal making my skin smoke. I can't stop my fingers from trembling, my body resisting my mind. The sharp blade catches the fabric of my shirt and rips it instead of slicing into my skin. All I can think about is cutting this damn kiss off me. If it's off, then Mary can't get to me. I survive another day. I'll be okay.

Ezekiel reaches for the dagger. He doesn't understand why I need to do what I'm about to do, and I can't let him stop me.

I don't have time. It must be done.

I jerk back, attempting to cut the skin from my chest again. The sacred blade meets the brand, and my skin sizzles and burns with agony. I yell out, dropping the knife. Hopelessness rushes over me. It's not going to work. The brand resists the dagger. Tears burn my eyes, my vision turning red and then black. I fall back to the floor, scratching at the branding, trying to use my nails to dig it off my skin instead.

"Blood is blood, red to black—" Mary's voice rips through my mind, poking at my skull to bury into my brain.

"No!" Thrashing, I whip my head back and forth, hitting it on the floor in the process. Everything is turning against me. My mind, my body, they want to see my demise. They're tired of everything I put them through.

"Faith!" Ezekiel yells.

Even my angel is against me.

"Get it off me," I beg, hoping he'll listen to my pleas. "Get it off. Get it off!" I'll pray to him if I have to if that's what it takes.

Ezekiel lunges forward, grabbing my hands, squeezing them so tightly. "Tell me what. What do I need to get off you?"

I jerk, igniting demonic power in my fingers. He's taking too long. My skin burns, smoldering. The rancid smell of my burning flesh assaults my nose. I gag, my stomach heaving, and black bile—blood—spills from my mouth and all over the floor.

I release a cry. "Ezekiel, please. Get it off. I'm begging you. Don't let me suffer. Please, you have to get it off me. Get it off." I can't stop repeating the words.

Wind whips from Ezekiel's wings, the soft breeze making the brand mark on my chest sting worse. "Kristin, help me. I don't know what to do."

I scream louder, breaking free from his grip. My hands jerk up to my chest, and I rip my shirt from the frayed fabric where I caught the knife. I pinch, squeezing at the burned kiss brand like if I can get my nails just right, I can rip it off.

"Hold her down," Kristin says, kneeling next to us.

I swing my arm out. I want nothing to do with her. It was her spell that put me in this position. This is her fault. "No, stay away from me. You don't know what you're doing."

Ezekiel grabs my hand. "Faith, listen to me. Kristin can help."

Shaking my head, I release a cry. I try to yank my hand free, but Ezekiel doesn't let me go. "I don't need her help. I just need to get it off. Give me my dagger."

"Tell me what it is," Ezekiel begs, his voice low and full of something I haven't heard in his words before. Fear? Panic?

"Please!" I scream, tucking my chin toward my chest. "It's right here. Can't you see it?"

Ezekiel scoops me into his arms, locking my hands at my sides. I buck my legs, fear cascading over me in hot waves. Kristin stands over me, staring at me with her head tilted to the side. She's going to make it worse. I know it.

"I think she's still hallucinating. I should've never let you cast that spell. I knew better." Ezekiel's usually smooth baritone voice sounds raspy, now laced with anger I've never seen him direct toward anyone apart from those who sought to harm me.

Kristin brushes my hair from my face, making me wince. "Faith, I need you to take a breath and tell me exactly what's wrong. I can't help you if I don't know what's happening."

"The kiss! She kissed me. Get it off my chest!" I yell, finally managing to spit out more words. But my body still fights like my hands decided to take over to do what needs to be done because my mind is too scared of the pain to come.

Reaching out her hand, she opens my shirt more, peering at the smoldering spot of the kiss branding. "Faith, there's nothing there. Calm down."

I wail, thrashing. "You're lying! You're just like her. You want me to suffer."

Kristin frowns without saying anything.

I thrash. "Get it off, Ezekiel!"

Kristin runs her fingers gently across my chest, ignoring how much I fight. The sudden coolness of her fingers clears my mind enough to realize she can't see what I see. Neither can Ezekiel. My skin burns and smolders, yet she doesn't react to the heat. She stares at me with her hard, almost black eyes. Puffing a breath, she blows strands of her nearly black hair from her face.

She pulls her hand away, the pain intensifying without her touch. I fight to free myself from Ezekiel. If they're not going to cut it off, I need to. "Please," I beg.

Kristin takes my hand, the one with the eye she branded

herself on my skin, and re-opens the wound with her nail. A small drop of blood pools, and just seeing it calms the tightening nerves in my stomach, making me focus on the new pain, on the drop of blood. It's red. Beautifully red and human, not the black blood of my inner demon. Kristin pokes her finger into the drop and then rubs it across her closed eyelid before pulling my hand up to cover it.

My chest starts smoldering again, and I cry out. "No. No more spells."

"Demon bound and demon born, blood meets blood, the veil now torn. Use this vessel split in two, show her demon peeking through." Kristin sucks in a sharp breath, dropping my hand. For a second, I swear I see the shadow of horns across the wall.

"What is it?" Ezekiel asks.

"A brand mark. I thought the kiss was a warning, but the witch is trying to stake her claim on Faith. She can't get through you, so she's trying to use Faith against herself. The kiss will continue to burn her as long as your shield remains in place. She's trying to get you to let it down," Kristin says.

"What?" Ezekiel asks.

Another wave of pain washes over me, and I scream again. "It hurts. Please, someone do something."

"It'll take me an hour to prepare, Faith," Kristin says.

Her admission sets me off, my brain and body fighting. One hour is a blip in time compared to all of eternity if Mary were to find me, but my body screams that an hour is way too damn long. I'll surely die before that and end up in the same eternity.

Swinging out my arm, I clock Ezekiel right in the jaw. He loses his grip on me, and I scramble to my feet, reaching for the dagger only feet away discarded on the floor. Wind whips through my hair as my watcher flaps his wings, and I spin and throw a burst of demon power in his direction.

I can't wait an hour. I need the burning to stop now. If it takes a witch and an angel a freaking hour to fix this, I'm doomed. I can't wait that long unless...

I reach for the dagger. Ezekiel knocks me off my feet, and we fall through the air. He spins me on top of him, taking the force of the fall onto his wings that scatter black feathers into the air. One drifts and lands on his chest.

"Faith," he whispers. "What are you doing?"

I blink at the dagger I aim at that pretty black feather over his heart. "Drop the shield, Ezekiel."

His brows pinch together. He reaches to take the dagger from me, but I press it more firmly to his chest. Freezing beneath me, he extends his arm up, hovering it inches away. A red sheen burns my eyes, and I blink the haze from my vision. Small drops of blood splash on his shirt and absorb into the gray material now covered with other dark stains, probably all sorts of my body fluid.

"I'm not dropping the shield, Faith," he says.

I press the knife tighter. "Please, I don't want to do this. But the pain—" I gasp, my breath shuddering. More red tears drip from my eyes, splashing on his shirt. "Please."

He moves his hand away from the blade and runs his fingers under my eyes, smearing my bloody tears. His serious face, shadowed in the veil created by my blond hair, tries to lock me in his intense mocha gaze.

"You're strong," he whispers.

"Drop the shield!" I scream.

I reach out to hit him, to show him exactly how much pain I'm in because he won't let his shield down for one measly hour. One hour of leaving me open for attack in exchange for this unbearable pain to stop. It's only one hour. I'm willing to risk it.

Blocking his face with one hand, he grabs my hand with his other. He pulls me down on him, my chest searing from the pressure. I jerk and thrash, kick and punch—I even snap my teeth at him, trying to take a bite of his neck. My inner demon grips me, attempting to possess me to save me from the agony.

"Ezekiel, please. Why are you doing this? Why are you making me suffer? I thought you cared about me." My screams turn into sobs, and he still holds me against him. "Please, if you love me, don't make me suffer. I'm not strong. You're strong. You can protect me. Show me what an awesome Demon Watcher you are. It's one hour. You can do this."

"Ezekiel," Kristin says.

Rage rushes up me from my stomach to my heart, igniting the branded kiss once more. I snarl at her, summoning every bit of scariness my dad encompasses, and throw it in the witch's direction.

"You suck," I say. "You're a terrible witch. Dad should just end your contract. You're worthless—"

Ezekiel flips me off him, pressing my back into the floor, cutting off the fiery words burning off my tongue as hot as the brand stinging my chest. He presses all his body weight into me, bringing my hands over my head. His leg rests between mine, and he restrains me without squishing me.

"Faith, look at me," he whispers.

The moment I do, fire erupts in my heart. "I can't! It hurts! Your shield hurts. You're hurting me. Why do you want to hurt me?"

His eyes glass over, and he blinks. A tear hangs from his bottom lashes, sparkling in the light now radiating from his wings. It escapes his eye and splashes my cheek.

I stretch up and touch my forehead to his chin. "Please."

Leaning down, he brushes his lips to mine. "I'm sorry but no, Faith."

"What? But—"

He presses his forehead to mine. "Forgive me."

"Ezekiel!"

The world turns white.

6

ɮBRANDED

RAINBOW LIGHT DANCES through the mist like crystal prisms hang in the air to create this mesmerizing dreamscape. My chest aches, but the burning isn't so bad with the cool air coating my skin.

"You're wicked when you're desperate, Demon Spawn." Ezekiel's soft voice trickles through the air from behind me, and I spin to face him. "You know how to test me in ways I could never imagine."

I suck my bottom lip between my teeth, bringing my hand up to my heart to feel the warmth against my fingers. "I hurt."

It's all I can manage to say.

He closes the distance, pulling me into his arms. Ever so softly, he brushes his cool fingers over my chest above my heart, my ripped shirt displaying enough skin to redden my cheeks with how his dark gaze inspects every inch of me.

"I know, Faith. And it hurts me to see you like this," he says. "I wish I could do something more."

"Except drop your shield," I say.

"Never that."

"Even if it meant life and death."

He sighs. "It doesn't."

"Feels like it."

"I know."

Ezekiel unfurls his wings, expanding them out before curling them around us. He tilts his head against mine, his lips hovering just out of my reach. Every exhale of cherry blossom-scent breath he breathes, I suck into my lungs. He stares into my eyes, capturing me in his gaze, forcing me to focus on him and only him.

I pout my bottom lip out, and it grazes his. "I hate this, you know. I feel like I'm living on borrowed time. I'm a lost cause."

His breath quivers, cooling the heat burning from the cut on my lip caused by Mary. "Your life isn't a lost cause, and even if you're living on borrowed time, it doesn't mean we can't find more. Have hope."

Hope. Funny. Hope is for those who have nothing else to

cling onto. Hope is for those who need an excuse to keep going because all is lost, and there is nothing left. Hope is a waste of time. I don't need hope. I need a plan. I need my guardian angel to stop treating me like I'm a dying breath away from turning into his enemy.

"You know what I want to have? A moment where I don't think the sunlight is the angelic army, or to look in the mirror and see this stupid colorless eye, or to have to restrain myself because I want to—"

Damn angel kisses.

They always come when I least expect them and are worse than a rude interruption. Because they steal my breath away, fill up my empty shell of a body with a glimmer of light to replace my lack of soul. They ignite a fire in my heart while reminding me how human I am when warmth blushes my cheeks. And he's kissing me more and more lately.

Ezekiel cups my face, caressing his feathery light lips against mine, yearning yet cautious. Just testing and teasing, leaving me craving more. Always begging me to respond and to push the limits. It's only fair that I'm not the only one breathless.

Wrapping my arms around his back, I brush the base of his wings. They disappear, leaving behind tight muscles to explore. I run my fingers in the spot his wings would be if he didn't hide them, tracing circles, mapping out every inch of him while he lets me.

I shift, wrapping my legs around him, my thighs pressing

on the sides of his torso, my hands moving up to comb my fingers through his dark hair to deepen our kiss. Ezekiel always starts, kissing me first on his terms, and I let him because I know it drives him crazy. Seducing an angel has always been on my list of fun things to do, but it's indescribable having him yearn for me without trying.

He pants, pulling back slightly, but I lean in again, sliding my tongue between his cool lips to run over his tongue.

The world spins, and I find myself staring up at a strange heavenly light glowing above me. It's not the sun, but an absence of darkness.

Ezekiel peers down at me, haloed in the light, his wings casting shadows across my face. I'm on the ground—but not really the ground, more like what a cloud in solid form might feel like—now stretching out, grinning up at my Demon Watcher because I did something he liked, something he was afraid to have too much of.

"You're not a good distraction from all this unbearable pain with so much space between us," I say, reaching out my hand.

He twines his fingers through mine and pulls me to my feet, hugging me against him, breathing into my hair like he can't get enough oxygen in his lungs. "You evil, evil Demon Spawn," he says, his voice light and playful, making me grin wider. "You realize this is a dream, right?"

"Oh, I thought it was a fantasy," I say, pulling away to meet his gaze.

The blush crossing his cheeks makes me smile so wide that my face hurts. I wish I could bottle his blush up to paint the world in, the color being the perfect shade of rose to represent how every look and surprise kiss makes me feel.

"Faith," he whispers, his heart thrumming in my ears, a melody I don't know how I ever lived without. It's become the constant reminder of all the love he shares with me despite everything.

I nip his lip. "I'd say not to start what you're too afraid to finish…"

His lips twist, frowning at my joke. "This isn't a good time."

"You say that every time."

"Faith."

I snuggle against him. "I'm kidding, my pure, sweet, beautifully innocent angel. Despite what you think, my sole mission in life isn't to corrupt you."

He laughs, tipping his head back, his voice sending my heart crashing into my ribcage to beat against his. "And here I am, thinking about how much I wish you would."

My mouth falls open and surprise widens my eyes. "Careful, watcher."

"You're all talk, Demon Spawn," he says, poking the bottom of my chin to close my mouth. Then he kisses me again.

I smirk. "I can change that."

He chuckles. "I want to…"

"I didn't think you did. With those wings I sometimes confuse you with a—" I laugh before I can finish my lame joke.

He narrows his eyes, fake glaring at me. "Don't even finish that sentence."

"Chicken." I snort and cover my face.

Ezekiel tugs my hand from my face and smirks. "I'm not afraid of you," he says, his voice deepening with a desire I'd love to explore.

I raise an eyebrow, pursing my lips to meet his eyes with a glower I hope makes him laugh. "You should be. I'm one death away from being a demon."

"Faith..."

Uh-oh. I ruined the playful moment with words neither of us likes to think about, but it's a reality I ponder every other minute, especially with the aching, burning skin now above my heart, threatening to dig into me.

I shrug. "What? It is what it is. I can't pretend this isn't happening. You can create all the dream worlds for me you want, but it doesn't change that Mary's alive and breaking through to my mind." I wave at my chest. "And now this? I'm doomed."

"I'd never let anything happen to you," Ezekiel says. "I'd rather fall."

My chest tightens at his admission, the words always hanging in the back of my mind, but it's the first time he's said them out loud. The thought alone scares me. Because an angel who falls is a traitor of Heaven like my dad. And then what? He holds and protects my soul. I can't lose him. I can't spend my life watching him through a veil like I do my dad—if I'd even exist at all.

He can't fall. Never.

Tears sparkle in my eyes, and I blink, causing them to pelt my cheeks. "Ezekiel—"

He frowns. "Hey, no. That's supposed to make you feel better, not make you cry."

"I'm sorry, it's—"

"Demon born but Heaven bound, hear my spell, hear the sound. A cry for help, a whispered plea, show the kiss, let me see. Blood to blood, light to dark. Burn the kiss, destroy the mark. An angel's feather pure and light, protect Faith, protect her sight. Cool the burns on her skin. Seal the pain, trap it in."

The world shakes, and Ezekiel flickers in and out of my vision. The bright light and rainbow mist dissipate at the sound of Kristin's spell, yanking me from a bearable existence into something I remember Hell feeling like.

I snap my eyes open and thrash, the pain seeming to burn right through me. Ezekiel hugs me tighter, and Kristin aims a red feather—a blood coated feather—over my chest. The edges of my vision blur, my voice ripping through the air, threatening to erupt my own eardrums.

Kristin's mouth moves, but I can't hear the rest of her spell over my screams. She presses the bloody feather onto the branding, smoldering my skin like lava flows through the kiss print. I suck in a gulp of air, ice flooding over me, snuffing out the fire I'd trade my soul for to extinguish if it were still my own.

Tears pour down my cheeks, the hair framing my face now sticky and wet. I heave, still gasping, still remembering the pain of the brand, though the pain is no longer there. Ezekiel shifts me, kissing my cheeks, gently touching my chest afraid he'll do more damage.

Ever so softly, he brushes his cool lips over my heart, like his kiss can take everything bad from me and put it onto himself. I shudder, hiding my face in his neck, adding my tears to the array of body fluids I've left on him. If I wasn't so weak, wasn't so relieved by the coolness of his lips, I might be mortified.

"Okay, that's enough. We have to go," Kristin says.

Ezekiel helps me to my feet, and I stare around what has been our home for the last few weeks. I was getting used to it, to the size, the blank walls, and I'm sadder than I realized I'd be that we have to leave so soon. I take a step forward, my bare feet splashing the pink-tinted wet floor, and my head spins.

Kristin stops in front of me, taking my face into her hands. "I need you to pull yourself together. I know you've lost a lot of blood, but I can't have you passing out. We might need your power."

I swallow, blinking through the weird stars in my vision. "I'm good."

Ezekiel finishes gathering our belongings—everything that can fit in our one backpack—and he makes his way to the door first. He steps outside and looks around the courtyard of our apartment complex and motions that it's all clear. I still can't get over how I'm nervous about the sun, especially after yesterday. I don't have the veil to protect me from angels, and Mary's trying to destroy the shield that protects me from everyone else. I shouldn't feel so helpless. I'm Raphael Blackwell's daughter. This is a disgrace.

Ezekiel expands his wings, offering his hands to me and Kristin. Flying with two people isn't a problem, though I prefer to be solo if I'm forced to fly at all. The ground is safer. I can't trust the skies to be clear of the angelic army even above the city, and they could easily swarm us midair to knock me from Ezekiel's arms. I'll fall to my death and they could just be done with the girl who threatens everyone's safety.

And Ezekiel would have to let me go. I can't let him turn his back on his existence for me, because it still wouldn't end well for the both of us.

"I'm parked on the street," Kristin says, looping her arm with mine to pull me faster and past Ezekiel. "I don't fly, featherhead."

I smirk at Ezekiel's frown. "Finally, someone I can relate to."

Ezekiel doesn't say anything, not wanting to argue with a demi-demon and a witch. Who would? He hides his wings instead and falls into step beside me, sandwiching me between himself and Kristin. His arm brushes mine, and I slide my fingers into his. There's something about chaining myself to a witch and an angel that helps ease the panic coursing through me. It also helps me to remember how to move my legs. My eyes blur in the sun, the spots in my vision getting worse and worse by the second.

"Twenty more feet, Faith," Kristin says. "I'm parked up ahead."

I've never been more relieved in my life to slide into the front seat of what Dad would call a junkyard-worthy vehicle. The white SUV is well past its prime with its torn leather seats, filthy floor mats, and cracked windshield. But when I get in, feeling the cool leather—at least cool to me—I close my eyes, my body relaxing.

Kristin slams her door, jarring me back to reality, and I flip down the visor to peer into the mirror. I gasp, touching my chest. A new branded mark mars my skin, slightly askew under where my locket hangs. It's the imprint of a feather identical to the ones on Ezekiel's wings. It's so lifelike that I try to pluck it from my skin, yet nothing is there.

I don't know why, but my first thought is how Dad's going to freak the heck out when he sees it. It's basically the same as me tattooing Ezekiel's name right over my heart. He'd probably prefer Mary's kiss print to this, decorating my skin.

Kristin pulls from the curb, glancing at me in her peripheral vision. "Sorry about that. It was either giving you a permanent mark or telling you to toughen up. It won't protect you if Ezekiel drops his shield, but it'll stop Mary's spell from encouraging you to torture, seduce, or murder featherhead if he doesn't relent to your wishes. And in all honesty, I think you could break the poor angel. You have it in you."

"I'm used to being tested," Ezekiel says, speaking up from the backseat. "I would never let Faith down."

Kristin peers at him in the rearview mirror. "Until she makes you feel like you are."

"Okay, let's not go there. Dad's bad enough to Ezekiel already—"

"Because he seriously messed up—"

"Could be worse. Like I told Dad, I could be dead."

Ezekiel's lips hide in a tight line when our gazes meet in the visor mirror. Neither of us needs the reminder of what happened that day with Mary. Taking my soul was my last request. I was bleeding out. It was supposed to be the end. I even touched Heaven. But Hell was more determined.

I adjust my seatbelt to swivel in my seat. "Don't listen to her. I wouldn't want anyone else but you holding onto my s—"

The SUV jerks, and I bang my back into the door. Ezekiel automatically reaches out, locking his arms around me to keep me in place as Kristin rams into something that thuds on the hood, smacks the window, and rolls across the roof. She swears and slams her brakes, sending a cloud of burning rubber into the air.

"What was that?" I ask, unbuckling my seatbelt, preparing to lunge from the SUV to make a run for it.

"I took too long with the spell. One of Mary's pets found me," Kristin says.

"But the shield—"

"Featherhead can't shield me. My pendant neutralizes me.

No light or dark power," she says.

"And you couldn't tell us that sooner?" Ezekiel thrusts his door open. "Come on, Faith. We need to leave."

I open my door to step out. A growl sounds through the air, sending dread down my back in the form of a shudder. I'd recognize the sound of a werewolf from anywhere—and this one was among the group of hellhounds last night. Her bones crack and shift, almost sounding like sand being shaken in a metal can. Her heart speeds up along with her breathing. A growl reverberates through the air again, making me cringe.

The werewolf slinks right past Ezekiel, not even showing him any attention, but it—she—pauses in front of my open door, snarling, froth dripping from her jowls. But it's not looking at me, either. She trains her gaze on Kristin, who reaches into her bag to retrieve the ivory dagger still stained with blood.

"Shut the door," she whispers.

Ezekiel reaches out to shut the door, but he's not fast enough, and I'm frozen.

The werewolf launches forward.

It's about to break Ezekiel's shield, the only thing left protecting me.

RISE UP

THE WEREWOLF'S BACK legs land right on my lap. It barks and growls, snapping at Kristin, who reclined her seat and now lies under the heavy-pawed wolf, way too big to be in the front of the SUV. Its head hits the roof, and Kristin runs the knife along the werewolf's side instead of stabbing it in the kill spot in its chest.

Blood drips from the knife, and the werewolf scrambles around the small space. I ignite power in my hands, ready to blast the beast.

"Don't kill it!" Kristin yells.

"But—"

I don't have a chance to argue with her. Ezekiel locks his strong fingers around the werewolf's tail and jerks hard, pulling the beast off us and back out of the SUV. He ignites angelic light in his hand, blinding the wolf before flipping it onto its back, straddling it to keep it in place.

I scramble from the enclosed space and to my feet. Ezekiel extends his wings out, blocking me from the werewolf's view. It thrashes, snapping its teeth, refusing to give up, even with the unbreakable hold Ezekiel has on it.

"A beast of night and firelight, bound to Hell, hear my spell. Shift your bones, split your heart, hide your fur, rip apart. A hunter's desire, I will break, seal your eyes, your vision I take." Kristin rushes around the car chanting, cutting her own palm to drip her witch's blood into the werewolf's eyes. "Sever the bond, to the witch. You're mine now, make the switch. A demon's wolf, bow down to me. A creature of Hell, broken you'll be."

The werewolf howls, arching its back. Ezekiel squeezes it tighter as the wolf's bones crack and move, Kristin's spell forcing it into its human form. The sandy fur expels from the wolf's skin, shedding in a way unlike anything I've ever seen. A woman groans, curling in on herself under Ezekiel. If I were him, I'd have flown into the air at the sight of the naked, hairless woman, but he doesn't move.

She releases a loud, howling wail, clawing at her eyes to scratch at the smooth skin of her cheeks. "What have you done?"

"Get her in the car, Zeke," Kristin says. "We have to keep moving before Mary locks in on her. She won't be able to access her vision, but it'll only slow Mary down."

Ezekiel scoops the crying woman into his arms more gently than she deserves for trying to attack us. He even takes off his own shirt to cover her, reminding me of how pure of heart my guardian watcher is despite who this wolf is or that she's Hell-bound. His compassion cuts me deeply, reminding me of what I lack.

The woman sobs, feeling around the seats like there's a way for her to escape in the state she's in. Kristin grabs some bungee cords from her cargo space and fits them on the werewolf's wrists, stopping her from trying to fight.

"Come on, Faith," Ezekiel says, holding his hand out to me. "It's not safe for us here."

"Wait," Kristin says.

"No." Ezekiel laces his fingers around my arm, but I pull away. "I have one job, and it doesn't involve whatever you think it is you're doing, witch. Haven't you done enough damage to Faith already?"

Kristin glowers. "Haven't you?"

I step in between them, raising my palms out to each of them before Ezekiel starts shooting heavenly light all over the place and Kristin starts bloodletting and casting spells. They both look ready to fight over me, and the last thing I need is to be pulled apart even more than my body and soul already are.

"Why do you want us to wait?" I ask the witch, turning ever so slightly toward Ezekiel. I wouldn't put it past him to sweep me off my feet and into the air without my permission. He's gone from the occasional divine intervention to full on Heaven's Warrior since Kristin bound me to the Veiled Realm.

"I need you so I can track Mary. I can reverse the link of the mark and maybe put an end to the rise of hellhounds. If I could get a handle on things, Raphael could—"

"Ezekiel, we're staying with Kristin," I say, cutting her off. If Dad could somehow use this to his advantage, put a stop to the rising threat of unbound hellhounds while also sending the powerful witch that threatens my very existence back to Hell, maybe I can breathe for once. Maybe he won't be seen as Heaven's Traitor anymore, and he can somehow make a deal with the angelic army and I could go home. If I prove myself, they'll have to let me. It's getting the chance to even try that leaves us on the run. They don't need me. Need makes a huge difference.

"I'll adjust my protection spell," she says to me. "She won't be able to track me soon enough."

"Faith," he says, expanding his black wings. "It's dangerous."

"My existence is dangerous, but especially because of what that witch did."

"There's always another way, one that doesn't risk—"

"Risk me dying? Risk me turning into a demon? Risk the entire world, because I have the sight and power to crack the veil of the daylight prison realm?"

Ezekiel shakes his head, stepping closer. I inch back toward Kristin. She takes my hand like she could tether me to the ground when we both know Ezekiel could launch the three of us into the air.

He sighs and crosses his arms. "Yes to all of that. But also risk everything Raphael has done to see to it that you remain untainted and pure—so beautifully moral and human. I know what Kristin needs to do, and I'm afraid—"

"The daughter of Raphael Blackwell's destiny does not include being locked away in a fortress apart from the world, Ezekiel. I did not sacrifice my best friend's soul to save Heaven's Traitor to use his offspring to only siphon humanity into his demonic existence. Faith is a vessel born of power—both light and dark—and she—"

"Hold on," I say, interrupting her. "Before you go putting some prophecy into motion or whatever, which thanks but no thanks, you were friends with my mom?"

Kristin offers a stiff nod but glances at the moaning werewolf instead of elaborating.

"Get in the back," I tell Ezekiel. "We're staying with Kristin."

"Faith," he says, frowning. "You can't be serious. We need more time to prepare. Hellhounds and the witch are actively hunting Kristin because of her mistake."

I motion him back into the car at the same time I slide into the front seat. If I let him convince me to see any sort of reason, I might back out. Something inside me gnaws at me, begging me to not let fear consume me. It goes against how Dad raised me. I'm not to cower from evil. I'm to rise up and make evil fear me. "I'll make a deal with you."

"You sound like Raphael."

I smile, taking his intended jab as a compliment. "If you feel I'm in immediate danger, you can fly me away without my permission. We'll hide in the mountains, desert, wherever you want, and live out the rest of my human life with no more complaining from me."

Ezekiel climbs in the backseat. "No more complaining from you? Sure."

"As long as I can corrupt you."

He laughs, the seriousness disappearing from him along with his wings. "Maybe a little."

Kristin gets behind the wheel and puts the SUV into gear. "Damn charming angel," she mutters. "Making everyone forget he was the one at fault for the bad that happened. Using his high and mightiness as an excuse and then judging you for trying to fix things."

I smirk at Ezekiel in the rearview mirror. "Ezekiel's not high and mighty."

"His light blinds you." Kristin glares at Ezekiel in the rearview mirror, acting like he's not sitting two feet away.

I turn toward the window to peer out. "I'm not blinded, Kristin. We all have our faults. He was trying to do the right thing by me."

"That's what I'm afraid of. He has one job."

I sigh, pushing my hair from my face. Ezekiel doesn't comment on Kristin's assessment of him, but he stares at me in the visor mirror. "And he's doing it."

"As long as he's worth it, right?" This is starting to sound less like concern over me and like a personal vendetta she carries toward angels. "At least that's what Grace used to say."

I blink. I was right. "She did?" I ask, pushing away her judgment toward Ezekiel because she refers to my mom, and Dad never talks about my mom apart from the occasional quip that gives me nothing much about her. My grandma never spoke of her either. But Kristin? I can feel the love and sadness lining her voice, and unlike Dad, she doesn't pretend it isn't there.

"She always blamed herself for Raphael's fall." Kristin stomps the gas pedal, speeding faster than necessary.

"Because they were in love?" It's what I had assumed since discovering Dad was Heaven's Traitor.

"Angels aren't punished for loving people. They thrive and flourish under love. But your dad chose a different purpose than the one given to him, which had irreparable consequences."

"I didn't know angels could do that." My voice barely sounds over a whisper as I say the words.

Kristin turns her focus to the rearview mirror. "Hasn't Raphael told you that anything's possible? This is stuff he should have told you about, especially now."

I shrug. "We haven't exactly had time."

Her eyes glass over, and she focuses on the road. "Well,

since everyone seems to think you're some fragile doll and won't tell you how the world works or even your damn family history, I guess I should."

"Careful, Kristin," Ezekiel warns.

I swivel and glare at him.

Kristin rolls her eyes and tilts her head to me. "Some angels don't fall, Gra—Faith. Some jump."

Something really has gotten into Kristin. She nearly called me by my mom's name. "Ezekiel won't."

She shifts lanes, her eyes glassy with her own thoughts. "Just be careful, Faith. That's the same thing your mom said, but at least Raphael didn't possess her soul."

"He won't," I repeat, glancing at Ezekiel. His wings blink in and out of existence.

"For both your sakes, I hope you're right."

The sun hovers low in the sky, threatening to sink into the horizon in less than an hour. I used to love watching the sunset, counting down the minutes until Dad was released back into my world, but now? My chest tightens, my heart pressing against my ribcage, and my hands tremble. I dread it. I dread crossing into the Veiled Realm no matter how much teasing Ezekiel and I do about having the world to ourselves. But now it's half my life, my punishment for being a demon's daughter.

A scream rips through the air, and I press my hands over my ears to muffle the sound of the unbound hellhound. Her eyes, cloudy and empty due to Kristin's spell, still manage to gaze in my direction like she can see me even blind. She gnashes her teeth, fighting against the chain restraints Kristin wove around her wrists and ankles.

"A beast unbound, but never free, show me the path, let me see. As darkness falls and the veil thins, give me access, let me in. A demon's blood and angel's light, break the link, release from night. A sacred object from me to you. Will stop Hell from breaking through."

Kristin dips her fingers into the giant bowl of holy water stationed on the table to her left. Rubbing her finger across the wolf's skin, she smears the water. Her skin smolders with the spell, sending a tendril of smoke through the air. The woman hollers, froth foaming her mouth as she fights the chains.

Rainbow light streaks in from the stained-glass window, and I turn to gaze at the intricate picture of an angel with pure white wings captured in the glass. It stares right at me, sending a blip of fear to my core. If the picture could smite me, I'd probably already be lost.

"Faith, I need your power," Kristin says, waving me over. She drops a metal medallion into the palm of my hand. "Melt this and then release it into the bowl, will you?"

"Hell power from angel's light, ignite the curse and lock it tight." Kristin nods her head to me.

Taking a deep breath, I summon a small orb of ruby red power. It swirls over the strange black metal, turning it molten red.

"Wait!" the woman screams. "Please, don't do this. I'll tell you where she is. I'll do anything."

I hesitate before dripping the liquid metal into the holy water. "Where is she?" I ask.

Kristin steps between me and the woman. "Don't talk to her. She's made her choice. She must live with the consequences like everyone else."

"But if she'll tell us—"

"Faith," Kristin says.

I swallow, closing my eyes, feeling the molten metal coating my hand, but it doesn't burn me. "I just—why can't there be another way?"

"This is the only way to guarantee anything. She must be broken," Kristin says.

I puff out a shuddering breath and close my eyes. The woman screams again, piercing my ears with the noise. I turn my hand over and drop the liquid metal into the holy water like Kristin instructed. Hell courses through me like an evil rope, tying up everything good inside me. Being here in this church, helping Kristin perform a demonic incantation, hurts my very being.

Ezekiel meets my eyes with his sad stare. He feels it, too. Our world together, which was tolerable, now burns with something dark. This type of spell comes at a cost. To save myself, the woman's soul will be sacrificed. I shouldn't feel bad. Kristin is right, she made her choice. But allowing her to use me to break the hellhound like Mary forced my hand to break Christopher doesn't hurt any less.

Ezekiel turns away from me, shifting his gaze to the smiting angel in the stained-glass. Something like this could ruin us. He didn't want to come here. He wanted to run again, hide, just remain by my side for the rest of my existence until my life—his purpose—ended.

And now look at us.

I can't help wondering if this is worth it.

Flicking her gaze to me, Kristin frowns. "Almost done. Just think about this as fighting evil with evil because good falls short. I know it feels wrong, but—"

I shake my head. "Just finish it." I honestly don't care about the right reasons. All I care about is putting all this behind me so I no longer have to live in the position where I have to make these kinds of choices.

Kristin reaches into the bowl and pulls out the metal chain, formed from the melted medallion. But instead of black, it glows red not unlike my power. "A collar from Hell, from a traitor's spawn. Leash you to night, take you at dawn."

The woman's screams increase in volume, clawing into my head, turning my vision blurry. My chest heaves. I need to get out of here. I need the world to stop so my whirling mind can catch up. So my insides settle. Hands lock around my waist, pulling me back. The soft sound of ruffling feathers breaks through the anguish and guttural sobs consuming the woman, stealing her voice. I was too focused on the screams to realize Ezekiel moved.

He spins me in his arms, enveloping me in strong arms that

promise to keep me together. He cradles my head to his chest so I can't turn back around, protecting me the only way he knows how to by trying to get me to focus on him and his melodic heartbeat now too soft to hear over the soul screaming wails.

But I must see. I need to see. I can't just listen as the humanity of this werewolf morphs into the form she willingly gave her soul for, which Kristin's turned against her. As much as it kills me, I have to bear witness to the evil born from my blood and magic. Because if I am caught, if the world fails me, at least I can find peace knowing that maybe Heaven is right about me, and even though I want nothing more than a long life, the harm I can cause, the evil I can inflict, is far too great. I will not be my father.

"Ezekiel, please," I whisper. "Don't protect me from this."

He loosens his hold. "But you shouldn't watch."

"Yeah, I should. I'm afraid if I don't, it'll become too easy for me to make excuses. I should feel this horror in my soul. It should haunt me. I never want to live my life where this doesn't faze me."

Ezekiel slowly turns me around, keeping his arms around my chest. "Heaven should never doubt you, Faith, no matter what you are capable of."

Kristin wraps the collar on the woman's neck, and fire bursts from the spot it touches her skin. She thrashes so fiercely the chair topples over. She smashes into the ground, howling, but still, she fights. Ezekiel expands his wings out, wrapping them forward, subconsciously trying to block my view. I step away from him, shaking away from his arms and wings and freeze in place.

Fire crawls from the woman's neck, devouring her skin, leaving behind the familiar grease of a hellhound's form before it bursts with firelight. I cringe, my stomach rolling. Her screams cut off when the fire reaches her mouth and her bones crack and shift. She yelps, a weird cross between a sob and a scream with a mouth that can no longer form coherent words.

I cover my eyes with my hands, the world transforming before me, the hazy air smoldering with the flames unleashed by the witch's broken wolf—the wolf leashed and tamed by my actions and power. And in doing so, leashing the woman to Dad, forcing a master upon her like those who seek to control a wild animal.

A shadow falls into my vision, and I stare at pristine dress shoes. I jerk my head up to meet Dad's gaze as he stares at me through the thinning veil. Beside him, feet away, lies the broken werewolf in all her hellish glory, bowing at his feet, ready to serve him. And serve him she will. She will be the example the rising packs will take notice to and maybe the wolves will realize the true cost of their supposed power. Mary might be powerful, but she's still mortal. She'll never be a match for Dad. And when Mary takes notice of the demon-bound hellhound, she'll come. She won't be able to hide. And then we can fight.

This one wolf is a small sacrifice to save many and to show them that this eternal feud isn't the way. At least, that's what I keep telling myself.

"My beautiful Faith," Dad says, his voice muted by the veil. "My devoted daughter."

I step forward and hit the wall of the church, one not there on his side of the veil. I bang my fists on it, trying to bash it down so I can close the distance between us. I have a minute until sundown, and a minute to see him face-to-face as the veil thins for both of us. I can't miss the chance. Something about touching Dad, hugging him, even for a split second will fill me with the courage to face another night. Another day.

Peering around, I consider running to the door to exit the church, but there's no time. I turn my attention to the stained-glass window with the glorious, judgmental angel and his pure white wings. Before I can raise my hand, it shatters, exploding in front of me. Rainbow glass cascades across the floor.

Ezekiel smashed it with a flap of his wings, the gesture more unsettling than it should be. It was a window. Nothing more.

Ezekiel helps Kristin drag the Hell beast, now covered in black oil, out of the church and past the blessed barrier. I try to slide around them, but Ezekiel blocks my exit. "You don't want to see this," he says, trying to pull me into his arms to protect me again.

But he can't protect me from my sight. The flaming beast remains bowed by Dad's side, though her body on Earth slumps in the grass feet away.

"Move," I say, pushing my hands against Ezekiel.

He only hesitates for a second and then allows me to leave

the church. The sun sinks into the horizon, igniting the valley below in oranges and golds. The world shimmers, the cool mist of night pressing against the brown haze.

"Faith," Dad says. I hear his voice loud and clear. "Hurry."

Dad meets me halfway, and for the first time in weeks, I can feel the weight of his arms around me. I release a small cry, tears blurring my eyes. Twilight takes hold in between blinks to clear my vision, and the veil rises once more, cutting me off from Dad.

I only got a second.

And it wasn't enough.

"No!" I scream, swiping my hands out through the empty air. Raising my hand to my eye, I peer around. Dad's no longer in front of me. He's with Kristin, running his fingers along the flaming head of the werewolf I helped break with dark magic and demonic power, an act no demi-demon is capable of alone.

And with the thought, everything rushes back to me in hot waves. The sound of the woman's pleas. The crack of her bones. Her screams.

I sob, my chest heaving, and I pull my hand away from my eye. I can't look at the hellhound anymore. It's too painful. Too much of a reminder of why I'm in this dark realm, desolate and barren, with only the moon to light my way. It's supposedly to protect me, but maybe it's protecting the world from me.

I sit down, my legs shaking, and close my eyes. The images remain, now branded forever in my mind.

Wind tousles my hair, and the scent of cherry blossoms

drifts over me. I expect Ezekiel to say something, anything to make me feel better, but all he does is plop down next to me without a word. His wings, glowing with heavenly light, stretch out and fold back. A black feather drifts through the air, landing on the dead ground before me. I scoop it into my fingers and cup it like holding one of his feathers will somehow make this better. But not even the weight of his arms can do that.

"I'm a monster," I say. "If you didn't hold my soul, I'm sure I'd be Hell-bound."

Ezekiel doesn't say anything.

"I just—I want things to go back to how they were. I miss my dad. I miss my home. I miss Cadence." I swallow the burning in my throat. "And you know what? Despite everything, I miss Aria. That woman—she made her choice, but what led her to do such a thing? What was worth it to her?"

Ezekiel takes my hand and slides his fingers between mine. "I wish I could tell you, Faith. This is why I didn't want to get you involved."

"But I am involved."

"And it's hurting you so much."

"I shouldn't expect anything less. I'm a demon's daughter after all. I was born from Hell. My mom sacrificed her own soul for my dad. She put me in this position, you know. Her and Kristin. My dad. I was born from my mom's desire to bring some semblance of humanity back to Dad. Born from their selfishness."

"You were born from their love, Faith."

"You say that like you know for certain."

"I do. I know you were born from hope, too. And faith—like your name."

I roll my eyes. "Silly angel. Keep telling yourself that to make you feel better about my existence."

He touches my chin, making me look up at him. "That's not true. I feel your soul every second of every day, and there is nothing dark or evil about you. You were born from light. Heaven's highest in rank."

"Who fell."

"Doesn't change anything. You aren't Raphael."

"But I could be, and then what? Ask Kristin to make me my own vessel so the world can try to live with me? With whose soul? I'd rather die. I'm sure Heaven would finally answer my prayer then."

"I love you, you know. I love how pure and honest you are. Not many would feel badly for the damned, and not many can see through the flames, care for those lost, want to help them anyway," Ezekiel says, tugging me onto his lap. "I love you even with all that fire inside you, because fire and light aren't much different. They both push away the dark."

I frown and he laughs.

"Are you sure you love me?" I can't help asking. "You don't think it's my humanity getting into your essence?"

"It's not, and I'm certain. I thought my love was obvious."

It was. It was as clear as the veil I see before me. But like the world on the other side, it feels out of my reach. Better off to stay far from my hands so I don't destroy it. Ruin it. Ruin everything about Ezekiel. Like Kristin said, I have it in me to break him.

"I—" I press my lips together and kiss him instead of responding. I can't say those dangerous words out loud. I won't risk it no matter what Kristin said about angels not falling because of the sole act of loving.

"You don't have to say anything," he whispers into my lips.

So I don't.

And then the world disappears.

A DEMON SHE'LL BE

"**B**LOOD TO BLOOD, red to black. Break the shield, get her back. Demon born and Heaven bound, hear my spell, hear the sound. An angel's cry, a witch's plea, I'll take her body, a demon she'll be."

Jerking up, I gasp, igniting demonic power in my hand before immediately snuffing it out. Sunshine pours through the broken window of the church, and I shield my eyes from the bright streaks cutting across my vision.

Ezekiel brushes his lips across my temple. "Morning."

I groan. "What the Hell?"

"You needed sleep."

"For the whole night?" I ask, annoyed.

"How else am I supposed to help you heal?"

I hold up my hands, seeing the cut Kristin dug across my palm nearly invisible. I would've healed pretty quickly because of my demon blood, but I am kind of glad he helped me. Something he probably couldn't do as well on Earth. Angels specialize in souls, not bodies, but Ezekiel knows mine well enough now.

"Like a normal person. With time." I don't know why I argue. There's just something about traveling across the veil that ignites the fury within me, like if I stay too long, I forget what and who I am. It's unsettling and disorienting having time pass without my knowledge. The longest I've usually slept, even under Dad's care, was maybe six hours tops, and always in the day.

"I'm not wasting any more than I have to."

My grimace slides up into a smile. "How do you deal with me? Normal humans usually say thanks."

"You're not a normal human," he says. "Which I love about you."

I rest my head on him. "You're crazy. And I'm sorry. I don't mean to be a pain. I know I don't tell you I appreciate you enough. How did I end up so lucky? Any other angel would've—"

"I'm not any other angel."

"And I lo—" That word—*love*—refuses to leave my lips like my mouth is incapable of saying it.

It's his turn to smile. "You can say it, Faith. I promise the sky won't open up and steal my wings away."

"How are you so sure?" I ask, pouting my lip.

Shrugging, he says, "Because love can't ruin the world."

I raise an eyebrow. "Just the universe."

He smirks as he leans in to kiss me so softly that it's like an exhale against my lips. He helps me to my feet and straightens his rumpled shirt. I stare around the empty church and at the scorch marks across the wood platform of the altar.

I gaze at the worn pews, the litter of candles—some broken, others melted down to nothing—and then to the broken window where the stained-glass angel glared down at me. Strolling to it, I peek into an empty lot the church backs up to. I lift my branded hand to my eye, peering through the veil, half expecting to see the broken werewolf woman and Dad, waiting for me to peek in.

The black onyx path greets me from in front of a strange building made of material not from this plane—bones or ethereal stone of some sort. A lower level demon circles a tree a few dozen feet away, stuck in the same spot until nightfall. Unlike upper level demons, they remain trapped where Dad can travel as he pleases.

Ezekiel tugs my hand from my face. "You've spent enough time there. We have things to do."

"Like what?"

"Breakfast."

"And?"

He rubs his lips together. "Maybe a little angel corrupting."

I press my hands to his chest, desire burning through me, though I know he's partially joking. "How so?" I ask, drawing my finger up to his shoulder only to trail it back toward his stomach.

He inhales a breath, the light in his eyes turning dark for a second, stealing my breath. "Well, I thought you could—"

"Don't even finish that thought, featherhead." Kristin steps in the room. "We have a witch to hunt."

"What?" Ezekiel and I ask at the same time.

The last thing I want to do is go on a witch hunt, not with my angel opening up enough to drive me crazy in a good way. After yesterday—and the day before for that matter—I could use a time out to test our boundaries, especially with him adjusting the line.

"Why did I go through all that trouble to help you bre—" I swallow, forcing the words to sound out loud. "Break a werewolf if we still have to look for Mary? I thought Dad could handle it, and I could help him fight."

"Yes and no."

Ezekiel groans. "Hasn't Faith been through enough?"

Kristin places her hands on her hips. "More than I ever wanted her to have to go through. You might not realize this, or be able to see it past her humanity reflecting back onto you, but Faith means more to me than even my own soul."

"Obviously, since you contracted it out to Raphael."

I cringe.

"With good reason." She crosses her arms across her chest, steeling herself against Ezekiel's quips.

"There's never a good reason to deal with demons."

She sighs. "It was for Faith. For her mom."

I hold my breath, silently listening to them, hoping they don't stop talking. Because they seem to pull out information from each other without even trying, something I can't do without them putting their guards up.

Ezekiel turns his narrowed eyes to the floor. "I'm sorry. I didn't know that it was you who assured her upbringing."

"Which I had no idea was actually fulfilled. You don't have a clue to the torture I've been through the last seventeen years, thinking my own sacrifice was for nothing."

I scrunch my nose. "Wait, what? Did I miss something?" It's like they've started speaking telepathically to leave me out.

Kristin reaches out and touches my shoulder. "It's nothing, Faith."

I shake my head. "No, it's definitely something if Ezekiel apologized to you. Tell me."

"Really—"

Placing my hands on my hips, I narrow my eyes. "I'm not a child. You don't have to protect me."

Ezekiel takes my hand. "It's not you she's protecting, Faith."

I blink. "Dad?"

"The fall changed him, Faith. The man you know has come a long way. He tried his best, but some things were out of his control. No matter how pure his blood was, Hell got to him. He couldn't resist it. It was how he managed to get through everything."

"That's why my mom asked for your help?"

She nods. "I couldn't deny her or Lenora. Your grandma helped me when no one else would. She saved my life from a demon." Heaving a breath, she turns her gaze to the floor. "And so I negotiated with Raphael to guarantee you'd remain with your mom and grandma. I wanted you to have a life uninvolved with demons for as long as possible. But I never in a million years thought that the alliance—"

"Would intervene?"

"Heaven doesn't take kindly to traitors. A demon is a demon all the same."

"Things are changing," Ezekiel says, speaking up.

He's right. There's a new order in place.

But even that's at risk. "Mary's taking advantage of that," I say. "She's taking advantage of me."

Ezekiel reaches for my hand, flashing his wings for a second. "We won't let her anymore. I can see it more clearly now that I understand where you're coming from."

"So then you agree?" Kristin asks.

He straightens his shoulders. "Let's hunt a witch."

"Without my blood, right?" I'm not so sure I can handle losing any more blood or deal with any more spells.

Kristin frowns. "Sorry, Faith. I need your palm."

Oh, unholy Hell.

Ezekiel kisses my palm for the hundredth time like his lips will magically ease my throbbing skin. I've been told most of my life that my injuries looked worse than they actually were or to walk it off. Grandma, while being my most favorite person in the world, wasn't really in tune to suffering. Pain was a part of life—at least part of hers as a hunter. I know that now. No one has ever kissed my boo-boos away, and it's especially silly an angel's doing it to me now.

"You know where else hurts?" I ask, trying my best to keep my bottom lip puffed out in a pout though I shake with my looming laughter.

Ezekiel tilts his head slightly, his gaze traveling over me in a quick sweep to assess some injury he might have missed.

Holding my finger up, I touch it to my jaw, fighting with myself not to smile. "Right here."

He raises an eyebrow, studying me. His dark eyes are enough to steal my laughter away to turn it into something more seductive.

I move my finger to my neck. "And here."

Both his eyebrows shoot up on his forehead.

I run my finger up to my lips and stop. "Also here."

He chuckles, pulling me closer to brush his lips to my forehead. "Nice try, Demon Spawn. Now isn't the time for distractions."

"It's always a good time for distractions. Kristin's been gone for—"

Speaking of the witch... Kristin pokes her head from behind the door to a yellow Victorian mansion nestled in the middle of the appropriately named Desertville. Surrounded by miles of barren landscape and protected by a blessed chain-link fence, the house seems pretty well protected but also secluded enough to not draw attention to us. I had expected a pack of snarling wolves or a coven of Hell-bound witches to rush from the door, but only an old woman with gray hair, glasses, and a house dress answered to welcome Kristin in.

Kristin waves her hand, motioning us to exit her SUV.

Ezekiel hops from the vehicle before me and searches around the vast landscape. He offers his hand out to me and doesn't let go of my fingers as he tugs me along. The Victorian's fresh yellow paint gives the place a friendly feel, and peach colored roses bloom under the front window.

"What are we doing here, Kristin?" Ezekiel asks. "Being here jeopardizes all we've worked for."

"The seer works for neither Heaven nor Hell. She won't say a word. I promise."

An old woman peers out of the house from behind Kristin. Something familiar lies in her wrinkled, almond-shaped, honey brown eyes. I can't put my finger on it, but she's the first stranger I've met in a long time that hasn't ignited imaginary alarm bells within me.

"No need to drop your shield for me, Ezekiel. I don't need to see you, and you shouldn't have to wait in the car," the old woman says. "Welcome to my home. Don't mind all the furniture covers. I've recently returned to stay here for a while. My son is being quite the nuisance and my granddaughter has taken a leave of absence to do some soul searching, I'm afraid."

Kristin and the old woman move out of the doorway, and Ezekiel steps in first like some monster will jump out from behind the red antique chair in the corner. I follow behind him and past the old lady who doesn't look in my direction at all. Her eyes remain trained outside until Kristin closes the door.

"Faith, Ezekiel, I want you to meet one of my allies. Vivian Dubois has also been gifted with sight, though naturally," Kristin says.

"Dubois?" I ask. I peer around the room and spot a cluster of photos hung on the wall covered in floral wall paper. "You're Cadence's grandma?"

The old woman, Vivian, doesn't respond. Ezekiel keeps his shield in place. Instead of fighting with my guardian angel, I cross the room and touch the old woman on the shoulder. I expect her to jump, yelp, possibly faint, but she greets me with a warm smile so familiar it makes my heart hurt.

"Oh, Faith. You're as lovely as your picture," Vivian says. She reaches up and touches her weathered hand to my cheek. "My granddaughter has always spoken so highly of you and your father."

"She told you about my dad?" I ask.

"Didn't have to. Nothing gets by me," she says. "Well, almost nothing. I was quite surprised to have your dad's soul keeper knocking on my door, asking to use my sanctuary for you all for a few days."

I frown. "We're staying here?"

Kristin nods. "The blood leads to this area."

"The local wolf pack has had quite a rocky history with demons and their children, I'm afraid," Vivian says, speaking up. "They never bother me much. Learned to stay away a long time ago."

My hands tremble, and Vivian squeezes them tighter, pulling me into an unexpected hug. Ezekiel remains out of view, yet I know he's extending his shield to block my presence, and the only reason Vivian can see me is because she's touching me.

"Oh." I don't know what else to say. I knew we were on a witch hunt, but it feels more real coming here to face a potentially dangerous pack of Hell beasts.

"Don't be scared, dear," Vivian says. "My house is better protected than even the Hunter's Academy. No one bothers an old woman like me, anyway. Plus, if they did, I'd see them coming." She turns to look behind me with a smile. "Oh, Faith. Your watcher is quite the sight. I feel even more blessed to have such a being in my home. Welcome, Ezekiel."

I turn and catch sight of my watcher standing a few feet away. I hadn't expected for him to show himself, but he never fails to surprise me.

"Thank you for allowing us refuge, Storyteller," he says.

Storyteller?

Vivian chuckles, her voice raspy with age. "I haven't heard that nickname in years." Vivian flicks her eyes to me. "You can take Cadence's room. It's upstairs with a balcony. Cadence keeps a ladder around back, but of course you won't need it. Help yourself to her wardrobe, Faith. I can run into town if you need anything, Ezekiel."

"That is very kind of you, but I'm fine," my angel responds.

I'm pretty sure he's wearing his last shirt, since he lost the other one to the woman we broke into a hellhound, but I don't mention it. Ezekiel's needs vastly differ from mine. It makes me wonder about how Dad used to be before Mom. I can't even recall a time he wasn't wearing a suit or tuxedo. Demons tie their power to status and wealth not unlike humans—but angels? They don't think about what they are without and appreciate what they do have. I'd say I'd like to think that way, but after wearing dirty jeans for longer than I care to admit, screw that. I can't wait to try on something from Cadence's wardrobe.

"How about I make us some lunch?" Vivian asks.

My stomach growls right on cue, and I swear it shakes the whole place. "That would be great."

Kristin turns to Vivian. "Your hospitality will not go unrewarded. Raphael—"

"Will need not do anything apart from seeing to it my granddaughter remains safe," Vivian says.

"Always." Kristin touches the old woman's shoulder and swivels to face me. "Be ready in an hour. I'll be outside if you need me."

I press my lips together. "Okay." I want to beg her to give

me more time, to let me at least sit down and relax for a moment, but we've already spent a portion of the day traveling. If Mary is around, we can't wait. We must get to her when she thinks she has the upper hand.

Kristin leaves through the front door, and Vivian pats me on the shoulder and motions to the stairs before telling me to make myself at home. I peer around the living room once, taking in the eclectic arrangement of antique furniture. Following Vivian's directions, I head up the stairs and find Cadence's room. There's no denying it's hers. The clothes in the closet remind me of Cadence from when we first met—mostly black and leather, lots of dresses and heels—and fishnets. Lots and lots of fishnets.

A collection of daggers lies on a satin cloth on her old dresser, and I run my fingers over the shiny metal. Ezekiel comes up behind me. I bring my hand up to touch his as it rests on my shoulder.

"What are you thinking?" Ezekiel asks, staring at my reflection in the mirror above the dresser.

I shrug. "I miss Cadence. I hope she's okay. I just—"

"Wish someone would tell her?" he asks.

I nod. "I know what it's like to think someone's dead. It hurts."

"We went through a lot to guarantee your safety, Faith. It's important those who witnessed your body burn remain witnesses. It's what keeps the witch's spell together. Heaven and Hell— and someone who bridges between like Cadence—assures no one apart from Mary will look for you."

"Until Mary tells the world."

"And create competition?"

"My life isn't a game."

He rests his chin on my shoulder. "I know that."

"I wish everyone else did."

"I know," he repeats. He knows anything he says will never truly help or change my feelings. "We'll make them see."

I meander away from the dresser and head toward the closet. There's nothing I want more than to feel somewhat human again, and changing from my dirty clothes might help with that. Ezekiel feels my desires because he struts to the attached bathroom and turns the faucet for the water on and begins filling the tub.

"I haven't taken a bath since I was a kid, and I'm not starting now," I say, placing a hand on my hip, my brows raised.

He reads the labels of a few bottles on the shelf near the tub and pours in a mixture of them. I grin, shaking my head, as he continues to ignore me. Having an angel draw me a bath was something I never knew I'd want on my list of things to do before I die or descend, but it definitely is now.

Ezekiel smirks at me from the bathroom, waiting to see what I'll do. Something shifts in his eyes, the light he usually carries dimming slightly, and I suck in a breath. Because he's not gazing at me like he usually does. He's drinking in my appearance in a way I've been begging for him to look at me since our first kiss.

I hook my fingers on the hem of my shirt and slide it over my head and then shimmy out of my jeans. I don't know what comes over me, but there's something about catching him in a moment like this that sends me wanting to test him for a reaction.

He gapes at me, his eyes wavering from mine to my bra for a quick second, and his Adam's apple bobs in his throat. It's not the first time he's seen me in a bra, but it's the first time I've revealed myself to him on purpose.

Weeks ago, he'd have been unfazed. He'd have looked at me with innocent eyes, treating me like standing before him as I am now wasn't a big deal. But now? It feels like a world-changing moment—his dark eyes trailing over my body, mapping every last bit of me to save in his mind instead of searching for the soul I no longer possess. I glimpse my own humanity reflected back to me in his unwavering eyes.

I reach back to unhook my bra, really wanting to test our boundary.

He releases a soft whisper of a moan from his throat, his veins flexing in his neck and arms. His racing heart breaks the heavy silence between us. Ezekiel must flap his invisible wings because tresses of my hair blow behind my shoulders.

Slowly, I take a step forward.

My movement snaps him out of his intense gaze, and he manages to look away, the light returning to his eyes. His serious mouth turns up into a smile. My emotions run wild while his cool and his angelic pureness snuffs out the desire he hides inside. Crossing the distance, closing what feels like a canyon of space between us, Ezekiel gently takes me by the arm and motions me to the bath.

He kisses my forehead, and I know the moment between us is officially over. "I'm going to do a quick fly around to scope out the area. I'll get you when lunch is ready."

I slowly nod my head, my whole body still burning with blush. The last thing I want is for him to go. The last thing I need is for him to stare at me like a guardian rather than the boy who yearns to know me on a human level—but Ezekiel isn't human. And to my annoyance, I can test his self control all I want, but he's prepared to deal with my humanity. Standing on my tiptoes, I brush my lips against his and press my warm body into him. He smirks against my mouth, touches my cheek once, and exits the bathroom, leaving me standing alone.

Damn. I didn't realize how bummed I'd be over Ezekiel's denial. Sure, this isn't the first time. But this time felt different. He let his steely guard down for me.

Sighing, I glance at my reflection in the mirror above the sink, catching sight of the feather imprinted on my skin. I run my fingers across it, tracing it, imagining the softness one of Ezekiel's real feathers holds, before finally pulling myself away.

I finish undressing and get into the hot water mixed with fragrances that should relax me, but all I can think about is how Ezekiel stood there, watching me with eyes filled with—not darkness—even if something dimmed in his shining eyes, it wasn't shadows. It was...almost human. Like with demons, humanity affects every being in the universe differently. With Ezekiel, I'm not so sure how. But it gets to me in a good way, more so than the good grace constantly clinging to him.

I lie back in the tub, suppressing my thoughts about Ezekiel. Hot water rushes over me, feeling way better than I could've imagined. Cutting my hand across the bubbles, I gather some up to blow just like I did when I was little. I can't help it. Everything has been so bloody and murderous, evil and full of Hell fire, carrying bubbles that remind me of the sweet and innocent things in the world is exactly what I need. Until I catch sight of something strange in the spot where I've cleared the bubbles.

The overhead light reflects off the glittering surface, and a strange shadow blurs through the light. I sit up, dragging my hand across the surface of the water, spilling the bubbles onto the tile floor, and wait for the surface to smooth out again.

Two pure white eyes, sunken into cracking and burned flesh, gaze back at me. A perfect line of horns jets from the demon's forehead, pointing toward the ceiling. I automatically reach up, and pain erupts in my palm.

Blood drips into the tub water, tinting it red.

I scream.

INNER DEMON

FLAILING, I SINK underwater, my vision blurring in a red haze. I accidentally inhale, swallowing water. Hot hands grip my wrists, locking me in place. I can't move. I can't breathe. I can't do anything except watch the demon hover over me, now outside the tub as it threatens to kill me.

Death in a lavender-scented bubble bath wasn't how I imagined I'd go, but I guess it could be worse.

"Blood to blood, from red to black. Hell will take your body back. A demon you will surely be, I'll use your blood. I'll let you see."

The demon's face cuts through the water, hovering so close to mine that I can see the firelight burning in its white eyes. I freeze, fear paralyzing me. I wonder if Mary somehow figured out how to find me past Ezekiel's shield and if she managed to get a portal to Hell open strong enough to shift all power to her.

The demon cups my face. It presses its boney fingers to my eyes, forcing me to close my lids. The world changes, and I'm no longer in the bathtub in Vivian's house but standing in a room with gleaming onyx floors, blood red walls, and a window overlooking a gnarled forest of silently screaming trees.

My feet glide across the floor without making a sound, and the window transforms into a mirror, fire lighting it from within. A demon, the same demon who drowned me in the bathtub, stares at me from the mirror, its hand outstretched to me. My heart thuds in my chest, threatening to rip through the feather imprint still branding my skin.

Black blood drips from the demon's smiling mouth, its sharp teeth gnashing and threatening me as it bangs its fists against the glass separating us. Anger rolls through me, burning from my core to outstretch into my legs and head. Demonic power erupts in my palms, and I turn my gaze from the snarling demon, trapped in the mirror, to the ruby red liquid swirling in my hands.

I thrust my hands out, shooting my power, hitting the mirror with enough force to shake my world, knocking me off my feet.

Wind escapes my lungs in a deep gasp, and I launch myself

from the floor, now sopping wet. I slip and fall on the tiles, pain shooting up my back. A scream rips from my mouth, my stomach and lungs heaving, expelling the soapy water I swallowed.

"Faith!"

Arms hook around me, yanking me from the floor. I slam my fists into a muscular chest that leaves my hands aching. My eyes sting as I blink. Red fog blurs my vision. The world shifts from red to white, and I catch sight of familiar black wings.

"Faith, calm down. It's okay," Ezekiel says.

But it's not okay. A demon was in the house. It was trying to drown me—it *did* drown me. I saw its horns. They cut my hand, made me bleed out into the water. It dragged me into the sunlight prison world.

"It's not safe here." I cough and spit more, the force of my scream searing up my throat.

Ezekiel's hands slide around my back, his wings enclosing me in a place of light to clear the haze from my vision. His nose presses into my cheek, and he embraces me tighter like he can hug the visions right from my head.

Visions.

The demon I saw wasn't real...I think.

I release another shuddering breath, now ultra aware I'm naked, dripping soapy bathwater onto Ezekiel, and he's giving me an intense look full of concern and fear, my own panic shining from him and back to me.

I choke back a sob, catching my breath. "So, this is what it took to get you to snuggle with me naked." I don't know how else to suppress my panic than to snuff it out with what Dad would call inappropriate banter that definitely makes Ezekiel blush.

Instead of dropping me and making a run for it, he only moves his hands up my back and away from my waist while burying his face into my neck. Water slides off his wings, unable to cling to the soft feathers, but his shirt clings to him with my damp skin against it.

His breathless laugh, mixed with relief and something I can't pinpoint, tickles against my dripping hair. "I can't even leave you for a second, can I?"

"I don't want you to anyway," I say.

Ezekiel envelops me in his wings until my breathing evens. He reaches for a towel hanging on a hook on the wall and drapes it around my shoulders, half covering me up without separating me from him with the warm fabric.

He rubs his hand up my arm, drying off some of the water I flooded the bathroom with. To my surprise, it's as clear as it was when I got into the tub. The blood? The demon? All in my head.

"I think I'm going crazy," I whisper. "I saw something. It felt so real."

Ezekiel lifts me off my feet and carries me from the bathroom and wraps the towel completely around me to set me on the edge of the bed. Water drips from my face, and I realize I'm crying.

"Something in me is changing. I don't know how much

time I have." I wipe my face on the towel before Ezekiel can do it for me. "Maybe thinking I'd have a human lifetime was stupid. Mary's spell shifted something."

The bed shifts next to me, and Ezekiel hugs his arm around my shoulders. "Even if the spell did, you're still you, and I don't think we were stupid at all. I have hope for both of us, Faith, and I know you still have a long, long life to live."

I think he has his hope confused with his wishes. But how can I ruin his hope? How can I murder what makes him my beautiful angel? If I don't though, I'm afraid losing that hope could destroy him.

I sigh. "Even if that's the case, I want you to promise me something, Ezekiel."

He swivels to meet my gaze, rubbing his lips together, his jaw tightening.

I draw my stare to the floor, to the water dripping from my toes and onto the rug. "I saw a demon," I say.

"It's daylight."

I shake my head. "Listen to me. It was real. And—" I pause, summoning the courage to say the words out loud. "The demon, I think it was me. I was in the daylight prison realm. I cut myself on my own horn."

Ezekiel pulls my hand into his. "This is from Kristin," he says, inspecting the puckered, healing cut.

I hold out my other hand, my palm suddenly stinging. The blood from the tub might be gone, but it was so very real. It wasn't in my head after all. "This isn't."

He stiffens, his arm muscles flexing. Running his finger across my palm, he traces the thin scratch, red but not bleeding. "It could've happened when you fell. Maybe you tried to catch yourself on the edge of the sink."

Out of all people, Ezekiel was the last one I expected to try to explain away an injury. I know it was self inflicted by the demon threatening to cut through my skin to take over my existence. Knowing he's trying to force reason on me hurts me in a way that leaves disappointment washing through me. I need him to accept that I know what happened. He should trust me. Especially after everything.

"I didn't."

"Maybe you—"

I wiggle out of his arms and stand, wrapping the towel around me tighter. "Ezekiel," I say, cutting him off. "It's fine if you don't want to believe me, but I know what happened. And because I saw my personal demon with my own eyes, felt the fire of my power, I need you to promise me that you won't allow me to be a demon. Ever. If there is even a slight possibility, you must end my life. Destroy my body. I—I can't live an existence torn apart. It's bad enough you hold my..." I let my words trail off. It's unfair to remind him of something we can't change.

"I—" He stands up and unfurls his wings, knocking over the row of Cadence's pictures on her nightstand near the bed. "I won't fail you again."

I nod. "Thank you. You don't know what this means to

me. I know it's what my dad has wanted since he discovered it was possible, but not like this. Not without my soul."

He opens his arms, inviting me into them. "Anything for you, Faith."

Slowly lifting my chin, I meet his lips for a kiss. It's soft and sweet, gentle, not ignited by the fire burning within me nor the desire to push our limits. It's a kiss to seal a promise, to assure my eternity. The idea of a short life feels more real than ever. But it is what it is.

I smile, though my heart's not in it. Because I don't want to have to make these kinds of decisions. I don't want to put the angel I'm falling in love with—already *in* love with—in such a terrible position again. If our positions were reversed, I don't know if I could follow through. But I don't trust anyone else. Not Kristin. Not Dad. Definitely not the angelic army. I only trust my fate with the one person created for me. The person I'm certain I was created for, too.

A knock sounds on the door, drawing our attention away from each other. Without waiting for a response, Kristin swings it open, her hand covering her face to shield her eyes. "Are you decent? I could hear you guys from outside, and I have to say, your dad will freak—"

Ezekiel eases back but still keeps his fingers twined through mine. "Unfortunately, there wasn't any angel corrupting going on."

His words surprise me, and I release a laugh so loud I'm sure the whole sunlight prison realm heard it through the muted veil.

Kristin drops her hand from her eyes and gives us both a once over even though she knows an angel wouldn't lie. "So, what happened?"

I huff a breath. "My inner demon is what."

Her shapely brows rise on her forehead before knitting together, creating wrinkles over her smooth skin. "Are you okay?"

"Wait, you're not going to question my sanity?" I ask.

"Faith, you have the sight. I'll never doubt anything you see."

My stomach churns, and I clutch my knees, inhaling a deep breath. My insides, probably only filled with soapy bathwater, threaten to come up at any second. "Oh, God. It's really real."

"Relax, Faith. It's inside you. It's just a possibility. You're going to be fine. It was because you touched Hell."

I open my mouth to tell her she should try to relax with this sort of possibility hanging over her head, but Ezekiel squeezes my hand like he knows I'm about to snap—that I'm about to break, explode even.

I groan. "You can't shut it off?"

"I've done what I can."

I cover my eyes with my hands but drop them immediately, afraid to see my inner demon staring back at me. "I don't know how much longer I can take this."

Kristin moves closer and wraps her arms around me. "Just a little bit longer. Get dressed. After we eat some lunch, we'll go werewolf hunting. Should be fun."

"A total blast," I say, sarcasm dripping in my words.

"Better than dwelling on things here. It'll distract you for a little bit at least."

She's finally right about something.

I eye Ezekiel in my peripheral vision. "If only it were a good kind of distraction."

Hell's Palace is a joke.

A complete and utter joke.

I don't know if it's because I've spent years hanging around Dad's favorite nightclub, the Morningstar, but this place—a supposed haven for creatures not aligned with Heaven or the Hunter's Alliance but also not aligned with Hell—is neither as scary or cool as it sounds. Hidden underground in the middle of the desert, it's asking to be attacked by demons come nightfall.

But apparently Cadence loved it—or tolerated it—according to Vivian. Probably because it's the only thing to do in brown, dead, and dry Desertville, California.

"Okay, so what's the plan? Are you going to cast a spell to lure out the damned?" I ask, glancing from the metal elevator much too small to comfortably fit the three of us, especially since Ezekiel's wings remain in view, making him larger.

"No blood yet. We just want to lure one out. No need to start mass chaos and bring attention upon us. I'm about as safe as you are with the angelic army trying to intervene with Hell-bound witches," Kristin says.

"But my dad—"

"Sent me to you for a reason. Raphael is a master at deception and secrets. You think he even whispered my name to anyone?"

"Definitely not me."

Warmth washes over me, my heart aching while expanding at once because of how even after falling from Heaven, losing my mother, and being forced to do Hell's bidding, Dad still manages to do things demons don't do. They don't protect people or put themselves on the line. It reminds me that even though Heaven calls him a traitor, he still has something pure in his fiery heart.

"Raphael is different. You're the best example, Faith, despite what anyone thinks. He had every opportunity to ruin you and he didn't. He saw to it you made your own decisions. Why do you think he never told you about his past? About your mom?"

"To protect me?"

She shakes her head. "To protect them and allow you to have the ability to forgive. Your existence might benefit him, but he was so scared for you, bringing you into this life. He wanted to give you the best chance to pick the path your soul wants to follow."

"A lot of good that did," I mutter.

She squeezes my hand. "He might be a demon, but he still has faith. He has you."

Ezekiel clears his throat, interrupting a moment I wish lasted a little longer. I haven't had time over the past few weeks to process my family and what Dad and Mom went through to have me. What they gave up for each other. How could two people cling onto each other so fiercely even though it's not good for them? Love. Beautiful, dangerous love.

It's why I struggle with my feelings for Ezekiel—unbidden, untainted, and the best and worst thing for me.

"You're being watched, witch," Ezekiel says, stepping closer so his chest touches my shoulders.

Kristin peeks at us in her peripheral vision. "Actually, it's Faith. Just look at her. Raphael would burn this place down if he saw so many eyes on his daughter."

I glance down at the longest black dress Cadence had in her closet, which is still short on me considering I'm taller. Paired with fishnets and my boots, I didn't really think people would see me. But there was no way I was changing back into dirty clothes.

"Kristin, my shield. What have you done?" Ezekiel asks, locking his hands to my shoulders.

She huffs. "You're never going to trust me, are you?"

"Not after—"

"You've cast a spell?" I ask, interrupting the angel and witch before they start fighting while I'm still enclosed in an elevator with them with my only exit being a club full of people who are probably, maybe, a teensy bit after me.

"Of course I did. Think of Ezekiel's shield as being unbreakable glass, werewolf bait," she says. "And don't worry. It's tailored to lure a pure of soul who Mary might want."

Kristin pushes me forward and into the club without warning, getting in front of Ezekiel to block his way. As all eyes—okay, like half a dozen pairs—fall on me, I straighten my shoulders and keep my head up, channeling a fierce, badass hunter. It's a good thing I decided to wear the thigh holster with one of Cadence's blessed daggers. I wasn't actually planning to use it, but the outfit felt like it was missing something—probably because Cadence never goes unarmed.

At least Ezekiel was amused.

But now? If he could swear, he'd probably shout profanity toward Heaven.

I'm waiting for the day he does.

"They are harmless. You can melt their faces. No one messes with Raphael's daughter," I whisper to myself, through my forced smile. Dad engrained those exact words in my head since the first time he took me to one of his many demonic business meetings. But that was different. He was there to protect me.

And Ezekiel is now.

And Kristin.

I can damn well protect myself, too. Dad would lecture me for even humoring such doubt.

"There hasn't been a new hunter in town in years," a deep, throaty voice says from my right. I haven't even made it to the bar taking up the entire back wall.

And he thinks I'm a hunter? *Me?*

Funny.

I guess since I'm dressed like Cadence. I'm sure she left an impression on the whole community here. Hopefully a good one.

I force my mouth to smile even wider, my cheeks aching from the action. I might actually be baring my teeth if anything. "Does that mean I'm not welcome?"

"Thought the alliance changed their priorities is all." The young werewolf's presence begs for my attention, his close proximity invading my space, but not in the good way Ezekiel's does.

I swing my gaze up to his, and his smile falters as he blatantly stares at my eye. Ezekiel convinced me not to wear contacts, and now I wish I had protested more. My Demon Watcher might think I'm still beautiful, that I'm fine with my creepy looking glass to the realms, but clearly, his opinion is biased. "Not everyone agrees with the Hunter's Alliance."

There. I've neither confirmed nor denied I'm a real hunter.

"Now that's something I like to hear. You'd think it was our fault some packs got into agreements with a damn witch. Who even knew witches were still around? Did you?" he asks.

I shrug. "I had a feeling."

The guy glances from me to a table with two other werewolves, watching us. The woman narrows her eyes on me. And I recognize her. She was part of the Moonlight Shore's pack. Fear slices through me, gluing my feet to the floor.

"Why don't you let me buy you lunch? A drink maybe if

you're not hungry," the guy asks.

"I—"

A breeze picks up my hair from behind. "Decline," Ezekiel whispers in my ear. "I don't think this is a—"

"I'd love that. Thanks," I say, swallowing my fear.

The werewolf motions me toward the table of people. I peer over my shoulder, catching sight of Ezekiel frowning and Kristin smiling, though I'm pretty sure no one in the club can see them.

Pulling out a chair from the table, the werewolf offers me a seat next to him. He slouches in the chair, leaning his arms on the table. "New hunter's an ally," he says.

"She's also—" The woman on the other side of me leans close and sniffs my hair. "Faith, I don't understand. What the—"

"Hey," I say.

The guy leans over, brushing his arm against me. "You know each other?"

"All of the Moonlight Shores pack knows Faith," the other guy, another familiar werewolf, says. "She's a demi-demon."

There's no hiding the truth of my heritage from werewolves when they rely heavily on their sense of smell. And demons stand out. Aria used to say I smelled like a bakery. At least I don't smell gross like lower-level demons.

"You sure about that, Greg? She smells like—"

"A full-blooded demon?" I ask, wondering if they can sense what I sense about the demon within me lurking closer and closer to the surface.

The guy eases even closer and sniffs my shoulder. "No, definitely not. You smell like a nephilim."

Of course I smell heavenly. Ezekiel's scent lingers all over my skin. "My boyfriend is...angelic."

The man from across the table barks a laugh. "Leave Faith alone about her scent, Calvin. No one ever questions why you smell like you've been rolling in the dirt."

Calvin growls. "People like it."

I shift in my seat, ready to jump up.

"Knock it off, you two," the woman says. "Who cares about that stuff? What I want to know is why you're here, Faith? I thought Joshua got to you but obviously not."

I straighten my shoulders, hearing the Moonlight Shores pack leader's name exit her mouth. "I have the same question about you. Josh—"

"Isn't my leader. He only took me in after..." She sighs. "Damn it. I hate thinking about it. He ruined everything. Doesn't even know what he got himself into. I spent years as a half-broken hellhound. I'm not giving away my second chance again."

The guy across the table touches her hand. "Lola was one of the unlucky. We came here seeking refuge after the Hunter's Alliance basically disowned us all. But—"

Calvin releases a throaty groan. "Damn alliance."

"Can you blame them, Greg?" Lola asks. "Even distancing ourselves hasn't done much good. Josh is relentless."

"And as bad as a demon," Calvin quips. "Good thing Greg here can take a challenge. He's the only reason I managed to get out."

I'm going into information overload, and I can't help but wonder why they're telling me all this. Lola and Greg were nice enough, but they never really took much notice of me.

Turning my attention to the young wolf, Calvin, I take in his sandy hair, hazel eyes, and a boxy jawline. Something familiar captures my attention, digging into me. He's familiar, but I don't know him. He actually reminds me of Christopher, the traitor wolf from the Moonlight Shores pack and also Aria's cousin.

I drop my hands to my lap and link my fingers together to stop them from trembling. "I'm sorry to hear all this," I say.

All three of them nod, and then Calvin says, "So what brings you here? I didn't know there were any halfies around since the uprising. Someone must've been looking out for you."

I haven't heard the term *halfie* in years. I know it's what the human hunters in the alliance used to call the offspring of angels or demons, but the alliance has changed since then. There are few demi-demons still around. Most were lost in the war. As for nephilim, I'm not even sure. I've only ever met Dylan, and he ascended into Heaven's ranks after serving as a mortal. No one ever talks about angelic offspring. It's rumored the angels fall, but Ezekiel implied that it isn't always the case. Nothing is ever black or white. I'm living in a world of grays and unknowns. Of secrets. Even Ezekiel must keep things from me.

I realize I'm taking too long to answer and say, "I was one of the lucky ones until recently. Now, not so much. I'm..." I let my voice trail off.

"Tell him the truth," Kristin whispers from behind me. "They all know Joshua. They can help us."

"I'm here because I heard the hellhounds were rising, and I want to stop them. I experience enough Hell on Earth from being who I am. I don't exactly want to descend as a demon, and it's nearly certain that if Josh's witch has her way, I'll get my own broken pack of wolves. Possibly you, since you're the unwilling."

Ezekiel groans from behind me and the small pack gapes at me like what I said is the most ridiculous thing in existence. I may have even offended them a little. But it's true. Mary used a spell with my blood to force Christopher to change. She sacrificed the souls of his friends to try to rein in Hell.

The three wolves continue to stare at me for a moment, and then Greg smiles. "Well, if it makes you feel better, you don't look like you're heading to Hell anytime soon."

"Yeah, the goal is to avoid that," I say.

Greg chuckles. "Good to hear a demi-demon still has her good senses. I've had enough with the Hell-bound."

"Ask them if they'd be willing to help us," Kristin says. "I can only work with the willing."

I clear my throat. "I'm glad you said that because I could use your help finding Joshua."

Greg groans, rubbing his hands into his eyes. "I don't

know, Faith. If he found out that we were trying to set him up, he'd kill us. Right now, he thinks we're just being stubborn and will come around."

Lola and Calvin both growl, sending a wave of dread over me.

"I guess you don't need our help after all," Greg adds.

Slowly turning in my seat, I watch the elevator door slide open, and a huge, bulky man steps out and peers around. Joshua looks different than the last time I saw him. He's more muscular, rough. Any sort of gentleness gone with the goodness of his soul.

His eyes train on me, but he doesn't see me. He's looking at the others.

"Don't mention I'm here," I whisper through my teeth.

"What?" Greg asks.

"I'm being shielded," I respond.

He nods. "This isn't about you, anyway. But don't worry. I can handle Josh."

Good, I think to myself. Because I really, really don't want to be the one who has to.

PURE OF SOUL

EVERYONE TENSES, BUT no one moves from their spot at the table. I touch my fingers to the hilt of the dagger peeking through my hiked up dress from sitting. There's something about the weapon, about touching it, that gives me the courage to look at this dangerous werewolf, crossing the room way too fast, with everyone holding their breaths. I know, because the only one breathing is Ezekiel.

Joshua closes the distance and stops right in front of me, turning his gaze to Greg. Ezekiel stands close to the man, ready to pull him away. His black wings spread out on his back, and I expect everyone to drop to their knees to cry, the most common reaction from those never graced by a full-blooded angel, but he still remains hidden.

I catch sight of the werewolf's giant, shiny, gaudy belt buckle and frown. He even dresses differently now, considering the name etched into the metal isn't his own. It reads *Drake*, and I can't help but wonder what kind of power play he's making, taking over another pack's territory. I can see Greg's reflection in it but not mine. I'm eye level with Joshua's waist, just inches away, and it's like someone turned the light off on my side of the two way glass that encompasses the small wolf pack surrounding me. *Kristin did mention pure of soul.*

"Faith, don't let him touch you," Kristin says. "Not until I'm ready."

I ease back in my chair, keeping my lips locked tight, despite the anger rushing through me. It'd be so easy to ignite my power and blast Joshua in the chest. Nothing will ever make up for what he's done to me, but watching my power consume him feels like a good start. I shudder at the thought. Taking that kind of satisfaction isn't me. That's something a demon would enjoy.

"Well, isn't it the puppy pack of disappointment?" Joshua says.

It takes more in me than I expected not to rise to my feet to face him straight on. But killing him guarantees we won't find Mary. I barely even know the wolves who invited me to sit at their table, but a strange need for justice, to stop him from hurting anyone else flames my need to blast Joshua. The thought consumes me, and a small orb of power ignites in my palm.

"Faith, don't do it," Ezekiel says. "I know you. You will regret it."

I think I could live with that kind of regret.

"What do you want, Josh? We had an agreement," Greg says. He's calmer than I expect him to be. Werewolves tend to fight first and think later, but he's not reacting. His muscles bulge on his arms as he clenches his fists on the table, and all he does is hold the hellhound's glare.

Joshua turns his attention to the other two wolves. "Still time to return home. I'd hate to see you turn into prey."

Greg releases a low growl.

Calvin yanks me from my chair by the arm. We fall together on the floor in time to watch Greg launch from the table, knocking the whole thing sideways, spilling drinks everywhere. Fists fly as both Greg and Joshua throw punches, breaking all the furniture that gets in their paths.

"Get ready, Faith. I want you to blast the beast and run to the elevator. The pure of souls will give you enough time to get a head start. I need Joshua out in the open in the sunlight," Kristin says, standing over me.

I nod in response without using my voice.

Calvin helps me to my feet like I'm the one in need of protection from this vicious attack. Even Lola blocks me, too.

Kristin reaches out and grabs my hand, slicing a small cut

across my palm above the healing one. "Blood to blood from light to dark, gather the power, ignite the spark. A beast of night, consumed by Hell, peer through and see the veil."

Kristin motions to me, and I summon demonic power in my hands. Calvin and Lola startle at my sudden orb of Hell power, but instead of backing away or running, they step beside me to allow me to join their ranks.

Raising my hand up, I watch Greg push Joshua into a wall, but Joshua spins and kicks Greg's feet out from under him.

I take the clear shot and throw. Ezekiel flaps his wings, sending my power off course, and it explodes into the wall next to Joshua's head. He freezes, jerking his attention to me. Our gazes lock, and panic seizes my muscles.

"Go, Faith!" Kristin yells.

My blank mind remembers I'm supposed to run, and I dash forward toward the elevator. Greg yanks Joshua by the leg, knocking him off his feet, giving me the precious moment I need to make it to my destination. Ezekiel's already on the elevator, holding his hand out to me. Someone pushes me from behind. I yell out, stumbling into Ezekiel's arms.

I ignite power in my fingers, but Ezekiel blasts them with Heaven's light, stopping me from throwing it into the face of my attacker.

"Whoa, watch it!" a masculine voice yells. "I'm on your side."

Calvin slams his hand on the button to close the door, sending the elevator back to the surface from the club's underground location. Calvin tugs me from the elevator the second the door opens into the underground parking garage above the club. The only way out I can see is up the asphalt hill that'll spit us out through the wide doors of a maintenance shed.

"My truck's over there." Calvin drags me a few more feet before I jerk my arm away from him.

"Thanks, but I can't leave. Maybe you should. Take Greg and Lola and run. Get out of this town."

Calvin's brows furrow together. I leave him and charge toward the exit where blessed sunlight waits for us. Ezekiel sneaks up on me, hooking his hands to my waist, pushing us both forward with his wings. A howl echoes through the garage, piercing my ears. I should've had more time. It would have taken time for Joshua to call for an elevator.

But it's not Joshua.

More howls erupt through the stale, concrete garage. Silhouettes grow in the light of the exit, a couple wolves blocking the way out. The sound of nails scraping on asphalt echoes through the air. A few werewolves in their true wolf forms slink through the cars parked in rows.

Ezekiel doesn't stop.

He runs us forward together, his hands gripping around my stomach. The wolves in front of the exit don't move. They don't even react. His shield blocks the both of us, making it so the unpure of soul can't see us without Kristin. She focused on Joshua. Only Joshua would see me, not his entire pack, which means this isn't about me.

Calvin yells from behind me, snarls and barks cutting over the whisper of Ezekiel's wings. I jerk in Ezekiel's arms, craning my neck to look over his shoulder and past his expansive wings. I catch sight of a few wolves surrounding Calvin, still in his human form.

I've felt unlucky these last few weeks, and now, I know I am for sure. Because I've just found myself in the middle of a battle between a broken pack. The three wolves—Greg, Calvin, and Lola have turned their backs on the Moonlight Shores and Desertville packs, banding together, but I don't think the packs will easily let them go. These three werewolves don't have the backing of the alliance, of a witch like Kristin, to protect them like the traitor pack had.

And I'm afraid the new, powerful hellhounds will tear these wolves apart.

"Ezekiel, stop," I say. "We have to help."

He doesn't stop right away but closes the distance between us and the outside air. The wolves blocking the exit bolt forward, clearing the way for us, and it's like the universe begs me to stick to the plan. But my heart wants to stop and help. Kristin said it herself, Calvin and the others are pure of soul. How can I stand by and not do something?

"Ezekiel, please. It'll just take a second," I say.

Ezekiel drags his boots across the asphalt without arguing. It doesn't take any convincing to persuade an angel to do the right thing, even if Joshua could exit the elevator at any second. I have enough enemies in the world that I can't stand back and watch possible allies get eaten alive. I think Ezekiel knows this. He'd never persuade me to think about only myself. If it were a demon, Kristin even, they'd force me to go.

I summon power in my hands and chuck it at the wolves tearing at Calvin's clothing. Blood trickles from the bites on his arms, but he still manages to keep the attacking wolves back. My power bursts into the side of a black and gray wolf, smoldering its fur. It yelps, a high-pitched noise causing the other wolves to stop mid attack.

I throw another orb of power, hitting a dark brown wolf. It flips around and snarls. But it can't see us. It would have to touch me to break through the shield. The moment gives Calvin the opportunity to jet from the wall he's trapped against.

I hear the ding of the elevator, and Ezekiel tugs my hand, yanking me away before I have a chance to see who it is. A loud whistle resonates over the sound of the wolves, sinking into my eardrums.

"Block the exit. We're going on lockdown here," Joshua says, nearly panting.

The sunlight from outside cuts off. Someone closed the shed door from above, and there's no way to lure Joshua out of the garage. The towering wolf reaches down and grabs something off the floor of the elevator. He tosses Greg out, and the young wolf skids across the pavement, rolling into a car. Lola shuffles out next, stiff and on guard.

But where's Kristin?

Ezekiel nudges me toward a car. Joshua's focus remains on

the three wolves, and I realize something's gone wrong. He should be chasing me, looking for me. I thought he'd still be able to see me. But he can't. I'm sure if he could, he'd have his entire pack charging at me right now to drag me back to Mary where she'll force my existence to Hell.

"We need to find Kristin," Ezekiel says, not even bothering to whisper. "I don't think she accounted for the possibility of this pack being divided or that the universe dropped us amid the chaos for whatever reason."

I glance at him. "Can't you tell the universe to stop pushing fate on us? We're supposed to have freewill."

"You made your choice to stay," he says, puffing out his chest, turning into the angelic warrior I rarely see.

"Leaving wasn't a choice for me."

Ezekiel stares at the wolf pack ahead of us from over the top of the car. "So what do you want to do now? The sun will set soon. If it does, we'll lose our chance to get Mary out of hiding for another day."

"Well, we can't stand here and do nothing. The last thing we need is three more wolves joining Hell's ranks. People do things out of desperation. You know that," I say.

He nods. "I do. It's one of the few things I'm certain of...apart from you."

"So, divine intervention or summoning Hell?" I ask. Ezekiel and I argue over disagreements sometimes like with helping Kristin in the first place, but he ends up leaving the ultimate decision up to me. He's my watcher, and as much as he would like to do things his way, he can't mess with my supposed choices and freewill.

"Unless you're going to figure out how to break the entire pack by yourself, my power won't be as persuasive without them in Hell form. I can cause temporary blindness, though." This is what makes this pack, like the one of Moonlight Shores, so dangerous. They're making a power play in a world they're dividing all over again. And without being demon broken, they can continue to walk the Earth as what they were born and use the night to ignite their devotion to Hell through Mary.

Even if she never gets to access Hell to bring the wolves an eternity on Earth, these part-time Hell beasts can return the nights back to a Hell. Demons will start testing their ranks or keep souls for more power just to fight off the competition.

I never thought I'd ever in a million years be okay with breaking a werewolf, stripping them of their humanity to place them in the hands of the few demons who can control them, but they've made their decision. They've aligned with Hell and the uprising of power Mary's taken advantage of.

Both Heaven and Hell let their guards down with the truce. No one expected this.

And here I am, stuck right in the middle with the ability to do irrevocable damage.

I suck in a breath and cover my eyes with my hands. The brown haze of the daylight prison realm greets me, the underground parking structure morphing into a crater under the quick moving sun in the sky. In the realm, where time speeds by, the demons have only minutes until the veil drops.

Before me, I catch sight of the hellhound pack, flaming in what I imagine is the hot air under the demon sun. My heart picks up speed, watching their forms straddle the veil, revealing to me the Hell beasts that hide in their souls. They're not really in the daylight prison realm, but with the veil, I can see who they are.

I drop my hand from my good eye, merging the two worlds together. Seeing the hellhounds through my soulless eye helps mute my brain from saying that these monsters are still people—still flesh and blood. Still able to be saved even when I know they're not.

I summon my demonic power into my hand, and my arm morphs. My skin cracks and burns, stealing away the flesh of my humanity so much so that I can see the black blood flowing in my veins. And then I move—my demon moves. I stand frozen in place, my inner demon stepping out of me to turn to face me. It's like I'm torn in two, facing off with the monster I'm so deathly afraid of.

Two white eyes shine from the burned and blackened flesh of my face, and my inner demon smiles.

I scream and drop my hand from my eye.

My back hits a car, setting off the alarm, and the garage around me goes silent. I wish Ezekiel's shield turned me into a ghost because unlike him, I'm not used to avoiding everything at all costs.

He latches his fingers to my wrist and tugs me away from

the car, pushing me into the concrete wall a few feet away. He sandwiches me in place, shielding me even though I don't think anyone can see us.

"I can't do it," I whisper. "I can't summon my power. It's making things worse."

Ezekiel releases a soft breath in my ear. "You can't fight an entire pack of wolves without it."

"I—"

The elevator dings, causing Ezekiel to stiffen.

Kristin's swears cut through the air. A cacophonous melody of wolf growls pierces my ears, and Kristin curses a second time.

"Oh, no," Ezekiel whispers. "My shield. I lost focus on her. She needed me for her spell to continue to work."

"Ezekiel, you—"

"You were my priority," he says, cutting me off.

I summon power in my hands, pushing away the dread washing over me. "It's okay. Just put it back up."

"I can't."

"Why?"

"Joshua's touching her."

"Damn it." I tilt my head to the concrete roof. "Why is the universe so against me?" I'm not asking my watcher, just putting the words out there, though I know better than to send that kind of thought out there. The universe could laugh and make my life even worse.

"It's a test," Ezekiel says.

"A test? I don't need any damn tests. I need the universe to back off so I can go home and live out the rest of my short life."

Howls echo through the air, stirring fury in my heart.

Stepping forward, I summon a softball-size amount of power in my hands. I can't think like Ezekiel. I can't gather my courage and fight based on the universe testing me. Because if I do, I'm afraid I'll fail.

I'm afraid I am failing.

"Throw it now," Ezekiel says, not responding to my remark.

I do as he says.

"Again."

I don't even hesitate.

This time, I unleash my power on my own without his guidance.

Guttural screams erupt through the air like strangled wolf cries. Kristin yells, and for the first time ever, I let my inner demon control me.

These hellhounds never stood a chance.

Neither did I.

DEVIL'S WICKED SERVANT

THE SCENT OF burning skin drifts through the air, the wolves scattering to take cover behind and under cars. Except one wolf.

Joshua stands tall, holding Kristin in front of him. Her rainbow amulet creates her own shield to protect her from demon power, and now Joshua is using it against mine to save himself. I could try to sneak up behind him, but his back is nearly against the wall.

"I smell you, demon," Joshua says from over Kristin's shoulder. "Mary was right about you. You can't help yourself when it comes to werewolves. I knew you'd come to try to leash us like some sort of pet."

I respond with a blast of power, his words getting to me. Mary twisted Joshua's mind so much so that he can't even recognize that she's the one who chains him to Hell. He's not free. He's the devil's wicked servant, but without any sort of purpose.

Every time I shoot power, it pushes through Ezekiel's shield, allowing Joshua to use his sense of smell to pinpoint me even if he can't see me.

"Let me get a good look at you and that nasty soulless eye of yours, Faith," he says. "Come on, I don't want to hurt your witch. Mary seems fond of you both. I just want one look."

Ezekiel tenses. "No, Faith."

"But Kristin," I say.

Kristin must know that when it comes down to her or me, Ezekiel will pick me. She says, "It's my spell. She can't break it unless I do."

Joshua shakes her. "Then break it."

"I can't if you don't let go of me. I need her blood."

I stay frozen with Ezekiel. All I need is him to let her go for a second.

"You think I'm stupid?" he asks.

"Was hoping," Ezekiel says from beside me.

I laugh. I can't help it. I was hoping the same thing. Kristin probably, too. "This is serious."

Ezekiel stirs a breeze with his wings. "So am I."

"What do we do now?"

Kristin huffs, interrupting my need to pretend everything isn't falling into the pit of Hell Joshua created. "No, but you can't expect me to be able to undo my spell from your arms. What are you afraid of? We're obviously outnumbered. You've blocked the door." Kristin's logic is enough to get Joshua to hold her out.

"I'm not letting go of you, so you better figure it out," he says.

I step closer, flexing my fingers. All I need is for Kristin to duck, and I can get him. Kristin straightens her shoulders, looking through me. When Ezekiel lost focus on her, he basically pushed her out of our protective bubble. She's not pure of soul with a contract to my dad, and her own spell won't work to allow her to see me.

But Greg? He sees me. He silently watches my every step from his place on the ground, his nose bleeding, his eye already swelling shut. I wouldn't have put it past his pack to try to beat him into submission or kill him, whichever came first. And here I was, showing up at just the right moment to intervene. Divine intervention? No. Fate? Maybe. Bad luck for me? Definitely.

"The wolf is going to get himself killed," Ezekiel says.

"Not if I can help it."

"You can't. The odds aren't favorable. It's Kristin or him. We can't lose Kristin."

"I thought you hated her," I mumble.

"Faith," he says.

"Exactly. Get some."

Kristin clears her throat, drawing my attention from Ezekiel, who always chooses the wrong moments to argue with me.

"From light to dark and red to black. Give me blood or he'll break my back," Kristin says in a singsong voice.

Joshua frowns from behind her, and I laugh.

"A demon born and stubborn as Hell, open your eyes, look through the veil," she adds, continuing to chant a rhyme that obviously isn't an actual spell.

I raise my hand to my eye and peer at Joshua. Engulfed in flames, the Hell beast snarls, black foam dripping from his mouth to burn the dead brush under his giant paws. In this world, he doesn't hold Kristin. He can't. Only demons and creatures of Hell appear in the daylight prison realm. Occasionally an angel will cross, but it's unlikely. They hate it.

And like Joshua, I straddle the veil. My inner demon steps from me, almost like a second entity, but it doesn't move against my will. It closes the distance to the hellhound because I think it. Yet here I am, still feet away.

"Cut your palm and summon Hell. With those things, I'll say my spell." Kristin's singsong words trickle through to me.

I yank my dagger from my hip holster and swipe it across my palm.

"A little assistance from a rogue of three, could really help set us free," she continues.

Greg crawls forward, reaching out to grab Joshua's leg. A wolf flies at Greg, jumping on him before he can even touch Joshua, but it causes enough distraction for Kristin. She elbows

Joshua in the nose, and he throws her to the ground to cup his face. Another wolf launches toward her, growling and snarling.

Ezekiel blasts his heavenly light at the wolf, sending it crashing into the wall. I summon my demonic power, my blood boiling in my palm but not burning my skin, and I shoot it at Joshua already reaching for Kristin.

It hits him in the stomach, smoldering right through his shirt. Joshua yells, running his hands over my power, but it burns his fingers as he flicks off the molten liquid worse than fire. Howls erupt through the air, the wolves slinking closer, ready to attack Kristin. I catch sight of Greg unmoving under the paws of the werewolf who attacked him.

My vision turns red.

"A wolf of Hell, hear my spell. Use the blood, sheer the veil. Demon broken you will be, bow to Faith, let her see."

Joshua arches his back, hollering toward the concrete ceiling.

"We need to get him out!" Kristin yells.

I dash forward, locking my fingers to Joshua's wrist and pull him toward the exit. A wolf charges me from the side, and I throw an orb of power at it. But the second it falls to the ground, another wolf jumps at me. Ezekiel blinds it with his light. I push Joshua forward, the wolf brushing my back instead of colliding with me.

The wolf pack leader realizes what's happening, and he snarls, swinging his arm to hit me. His eyes shine with fire and Hell, black streaks marring his bare chest from where my power ate through his clothing, leaving his skin coated in burning oil.

Our gazes meet, and he screams, trying to flee back, but a wolf snaps at his calf. It's not one of his pack mates. It's one of the rogue wolves.

"Get outside before I cut your heart out and send you to Hell," I say. "Mary can always find a new pet so I doubt you'll be missed. But you can't seem to see that."

"Please, Faith. Let me make a deal," Joshua says.

My skin buzzes, a strange desire coursing through me. My vision darkens even more. His words called to my inner demon, pulling a need from me I had no idea I carried. My chest burns, and I peer down, almost afraid the smoldering lip print I can't push from my mind is burning me again. But it's not.

Ezekiel's feather tattoo glows over my chest, sparking a beautiful light not unlike the power that radiates from his hand. It's fighting against me.

I catch sight of a shadow crossing the floor, horns spiking from an oval head. *My* head. Panic snuffs out the fury simmering through my blood, setting my heart ablaze in a bout of what feels like an inescapable rage. Now my heart seizes, freezing with dread, making each beat painful. I hold my breath.

Ezekiel's brows scrunch on his forehead, and he peers from me to Joshua, flapping his wings once to send a gust of wind forward to push the wolf toward the door. It's strong enough to send a few other approaching wolves back.

"Out!" I yell, my voice sounding weird, raspy, like I have a sore throat, but I don't feel any pain.

The closer we get to the exit, the more fear rushes through me. I summon more power in my fingers, clutching it like a hot baby blanket, like it'll somehow make things better. But it makes things worse. I imagine steam sizzling from my burning skin in the brisk coming night.

Ezekiel touches my shoulder, and pain erupts under his fingers.

"Oh, God," I say, my voice rising in pitch. "Kristin, stop! You have to stop."

My angel rushes forward. The wind created from his wings causes my skin to sting like he blesses the air around him with his presence. Orange and red sunlight sets the garage aglow, and I cover my eyes for a moment, seeing an image of my inner demon running her hand across a fiery hellhound's back. But the demon is no longer separate from me. I can see my free hand touching Joshua as he and his Hell beast merge together.

The sun glows on the horizon, bringing night upon us. As the veil thins, I see the worlds collide, not like a filter, but they blur together as one. Joshua flickers between his human and hellhound form, and me? My inner demon threatens to escape the light prison realm to take over my life, to guarantee my body and soul will forever be torn apart.

"A beast of night and firelight, bound to Hell, hear my spell. Shift your bones, split your heart, hide your fur, rip apart. A demon's daughter you'll bow to, your soul will rip, we'll get part of you." Kristin's chant rings in my ears.

My hands fly up to my head, blocking out the noise without my mind's consent. "Stop! No! I don't want this. I changed my mind."

I thought Kristin wanted to lure the wolf out to better track the witch. She never mentioned breaking the pack leader, especially trying to break him for me.

"Hell power from angel's light, ignite the curse and burn the night. At sunrise with the break of day, wolf you'll be, wolf you'll stay. Leashed to one of Heaven and—"

The sun disappears into the horizon, the air misting over.

"Hell, hear me now, hear my spell," Kristin finishes.

But she's too late.

Dozens of wolves burst into flames around her, the Desertville pack unleashing Hell onto themselves with the night. The veil rises up, leaving Kristin on the other side. Ezekiel unfurls his wings behind me. Silence greets me, the cacophonous growls fading as the Veiled Realm captures me for another night, leaving my witch to fend for herself on the other side of it.

I raise my hand to my eye to peer through, my heart sinking into my stomach. "Ezekiel, she's going to get eaten alive. Do something."

He doesn't respond. He doesn't meet my wide eyes either.

For the first time ever, his glowing wings dim.

My angel, my beautiful, innocent, loving angel loses hope. Hope for my future, hope for Kristin's life. Hope for him.

With the rising veil, the unfinished spell, and the pack of hellhounds unbound to demons, there is nothing I can do to help Kristin.

Even Ezekiel can't provide divine intervention.

I watch the hellhounds circle Kristin as she backs up, her hands raised, her lips moving in a spell. But I can't hear anything.

Three shadowed forms launch from the darkening night, and my heart races as the rogue wolves try their best to save the witch who tried to help them.

Ezekiel tries to pull my hand from my eye. "You shouldn't watch."

"I have to!" I scream, my voice echoing through the air of the misty Veiled Realm.

"Faith," he whispers, like if he says my name any louder I'll explode and release my inner demon.

My inner demon.

Summoning power into my hand, I aim it at the nearest hellhound, yanking on Kristin's leg, tearing and burning her jeans. I chuck it at them, holding my breath, just waiting for it to fly through.

It hits the veil, sending a sparkle of red light flickering through the air.

"What are you doing?" Ezekiel asks. "You have to stop. You can't damage the veil."

I throw another burst of power at it. "I'll do what I have to."

Ezekiel steps in front of me, Heaven's light erupting in his hands. When I release my power, he blasts it with his own, sending a cloud of smoke and mist into the air. I glare, tears burning my eyes, and I summon more.

"Be reasonable," Ezekiel says.

I throw more power. "I'm not letting her die."

"I can't let you, Faith. I'm sorry."

I ignore him and grow an orb of Hell power the size of a basketball. My heart races, exhaustion from the constant exertion of power taking over me. But I can't stop. I can't let Kristin die. I can't accept that I'm fated for such a life torn between Heaven and Hell, being ripped at the seams. Heaven's most wanted and Hell's most coveted.

Ezekiel charges me, his arms out, his wings extended to their full length.

I stand in frozen shock. His heavenly light blinds me and sends stars dancing through my vision. "I thought you loved me," I say, my words making him stumble.

Pain sweeps across his face, his brows lowering and his jaw tightening. He skids to a stop in front of me. "Faith, I do. I love you more than anything, but I can't let you do this."

"She was my mom's best friend," I say.

"I know, but you can't damage the veil. Not again."

My hair blows around my face, caught on his heavenly breeze. "She'll end up in Hell."

"She knew the possibility."

"She did this for me."

The vein in his neck pulsates, his Adam's apple bobbing. "And I'm doing this for you."

I shake my head. "You're doing this for Heaven. You're standing with those who want me dead, who would destroy my life for just existing. You're standing with those who call my dad a traitor for loving my mom. You're not doing this for *me*."

"Faith, please," he whispers.

I turn my back, shrugging away from him when he touches me. "Don't."

"Faith," he repeats.

I gather more power in my hands and straighten my shoulders. Spinning around, I launch myself into the air too fast for Ezekiel to even react. My Hell power explodes against the veil, raining fire through the mist, turning the world smoky. Growls and screams rip through the air, and I elbow Ezekiel and run to the hole I made in the veil.

Reaching through, I pull Kristin in.

Light erupts in the air, blinding me, and I fall back with Kristin. My chest heaves, my skin still buzzing with the power of Hell. I bring my hand to my eye and peer through the mist. The veil is back in place, and the hellhounds scatter. Ezekiel mended the broken veil with his power, but the muted whispers of snarling wolves muffle through louder than before.

"Faith, what you did—"

I shake my head without looking at Ezekiel. "Saved Kristin's life."

Warm hands touch my shoulders, and Kristin hugs me from behind without making me stop looking into the Earth realm. "The rogue wolves got away," she says. "We're all okay."

I swallow the burning in my throat. "How are you so sure?"

"Because I have you, Faith," she says, "daughter of Grace Blackwell and Heaven's Traitor."

I drop my hand and turn to hug her, tears burning my eyes. I peek up through my wet eyelashes to find Ezekiel, but he's gone.

A single black feather floats in front of me, and I reach out and pluck it from the air.

"I'm not sure for how much longer. Ezekiel thinks I've betrayed him. He might decide to kill me now."

Kristin holds me out and looks into my eyes. "He won't. He loves you. You're his purpose."

I frown but don't respond.

For the first time since he's told me, I'm not so sure anymore.

I'm afraid his purpose has changed.

RIGHTEOUS

"CAN'T FACE ME in real life so you're going to destroy the short moment of peace I have in my sleep?" I ask, turning my gaze toward the dark, endless ocean stretching out before me. After so many nights in the Veiled Realm, it's become easier and easier for me to gain awareness in my sleep.

I wasn't expecting Ezekiel to show up, since he was still hidden from me and Kristin when I was awake, but now that he has, it stirs a mixture of emotions within me I had no idea I could feel toward him. Ones I don't like.

He stands next to me without responding—ever the king of silent treatments—staring in the direction I glare.

I puff a breath through my mouth, sucking my top lip between my teeth. Tears blur my eyes, and I sniffle, trying to control the hurt gripping me. I'm sure I'll startle myself awake at any second.

It's not even that I'm angry at Ezekiel. It's that I feel stupid for ever believing he was truly here for me. In this world where everyone wants something from me—my power, immortality with me, to change me, to kill me—I thought I found the one being who wanted nothing. Who was happy with my existence.

And now? Being blasted in the face with the realization and betrayed, basically told to lose the hope he was so quick to fill me with when I knew better—it expands the hole inside me where my soul used to be.

I swipe my hand across my cheeks. "You will not make me feel like crap for doing the right thing."

Ezekiel drops to the ground next to me and pulls his long legs up to his chest. He looks incredibly human and boyish, resting his chin on his knees, his wings hidden from my sight. My brain screams to put space between us but my heart pulls my body closer to him, like if I'm touching him, a simple act of grazing my arm to his, I'll feel whole. I'll feel like my soul isn't in someone else's hands.

He sinks against me, putting enough weight on me that I bury my hand in the sand to prop us up. His heartbeat thrums in a racing symphony, a collection of perfect notes to ease the pain in my chest coming with every breath. But it doesn't stop the sting cutting right through my middle as I'm torn by wanting to tackle him and kiss him and punch him in the face before I push him away.

"And I will not apologize for my actions. I'd do it aga—"

Ezekiel brings his hand up and touches his fingers to my lips to cut me off. "Never again, Faith."

I close my eyes, suppressing my rising anger. "Don't tell me what to—"

"Never. Again," he repeats. "It was unfair to put me in that position."

I hop to my feet. I thought I liked his closeness, but now I'm suffocated by his high and mighty righteousness that has quickly turned from endearing to infuriating. "Unfair to *you*? Well, I'm so sorry you've finally experienced something that wasn't fair. It sucks, doesn't it?"

I can't move a foot before he's standing and closing the space faster than I can get away. "I knew life was unfair. I knew the world was. I've dealt with it before, but this? It's more than I anticipated."

"Now imagine multiplying that times eternity. That's how I feel every second. And then when you stood against me in a moment the world finally felt fair because it gave me something I could use to save someone and I'm—I'm so—I don't even know. You hurt me, Ezekiel." I turn away from him and toward the dark ocean. I can't run in my dreams. He's everywhere and nowhere. He's part of my very essence.

"Forgive me, Faith. I acted on what I thought was right just like you did," he says.

"You lost hope," I say, ignoring his reasons.

"I—" He closes his mouth and takes a deep breath. He can't deny it. He doesn't lie. So, he's not going to answer at all. His silence says everything while he says nothing.

Touching my shoulder, he turns me so I have to face him again. His glassy eyes, shining my own sorrow and pain back to me, hold me in their dark intensity. Not only do I feel trapped in his gaze, I feel vulnerable, lost and found at the same time. Empty and complete. Loved and despised even.

"I couldn't let Kristin die, Ezekiel. I couldn't stand seeing your light vanish with the sun. You wanted me to have hope, but how could I if even you lost it? So, I fought for it. And *you* fought to stop me. I didn't want to do it. I'm sorry."

He leans forward and brushes his lips to mine. "Just never again."

I shake my head. "I won't make such a promise."

He sighs, cupping my cheeks in between his hands and kisses me again. "Please, just tell me you will."

I grimace, pulling away to get a clear view of his shining eyes. "Okay, I promise." We both know I'm lying, and it scares me that he asked me to do it for him without actually saying it out loud, but there is no denying his request.

He releases a ragged breath against my lips. "Thank you. I mean it. I'm forced to fail you in moments I want nothing more than to succeed, but I—"

I interrupt him with another kiss, brushing my lips to his, pressing my chest to his, until I know he won't finish his thought. "You don't have to explain. I forgive you, okay?" He's an angel after all. I can't pretend he isn't, not like I have been doing all this time.

"You know, I want nothing more than to keep you alone in here with me forever," he says, smiling for the first time since he appeared.

"If only."

"If only," he repeats.

"Blood to blood, red to black, a fall from Heaven will send you back. Hell's fury so hot and true, will cut your soul, releasing you. With your death, comes new life. A demon born, Hell's creature of night."

Mary's spell rings through my head, pushing the sound of ruffling feathers away. I squirm, sitting up, pushing one of Ezekiel's wings off me. I knew he was with me in my dream, but I didn't realize he had returned to my side while I was sleeping, encasing me in his wings like the softest sleeping bag in existence.

His eyes snap open, and he glances around. "What's wrong?" Ezekiel doesn't sleep, but he enters another level of awareness to be with me.

Peering around, I catch sight of Kristin pacing in a circle a few dozen feet away. From looking at the moon, we still have another few minutes in this realm. I hold my hand to my eye and take in the Earth realm. Vivian's house glows with soft light, and I catch sight of a figure in her window.

"You moved me," I say, dropping my hand to stare at the stretch of empty desert of the Veiled Realm. Not even the gnarled, silently screaming trees encroach on her blessed property.

Ezekiel helps me to my feet. "We couldn't cross back over at Hell's Palace."

Obviously. "You should've woken me up."

He chuckles. "Glad some things don't seem to change."

I bat his arm, and he pulls me into a hug. I rest my cheek to his chest, listening to his heartbeat, my heated emotions vanishing with the oncoming sun.

"Have I ever told you that you test me in ways I had no idea were possible?" he whispers.

I smile. "All the time."

"I love you, though. Even if you're wicked enough to try to use it against me."

I purse my lips. "I am sorry for that."

"I know."

Ezekiel kisses me once more, and I pull away to catch sight of Kristin waving her arms in our direction. Ezekiel doesn't give me a chance to prepare myself before scooping me up to fly me the short distance to the witch.

"Everything worked out between you two? I'm not going to have to create a new shield spell to hide you from your watcher, right?" Kristin asks.

My mouth opens. "You can do that?"

"It's quite an annoying talent," Ezekiel mutters.

"You're lucky it's a difficult, costly process," she says, grinning. "And I'm not talking about money."

I frown, despising they sometimes talk about things that go over my head. I think she's referring to souls, but I can't be sure. I bet she's done it for my dad. I've never met or heard of his watcher. And since Kristin didn't know about me, and Dad didn't tell her I didn't die with my mom, she never needed to make one for me. Dad also didn't expect Heaven to assign me a full-blooded angel as my watcher, either.

"I'll keep this new shield in mind," I say, nudging Ezekiel.

He returns my smile with an eye roll. He might be hanging out with me too much. "You're asking for me to hide you away on some mountain inaccessible to anyone without wings."

"Maybe I'm begging for it," I say, biting my lip, teasing him.

His cheeks redden with blush that makes me laugh. It's almost like last night didn't happen between us. Almost. Kristin standing with us in our usual private world makes it impossible.

Kristin pulls my hand up and slices her ivory blade across my palm without warning. "Don't even start. The sun's almost up and I have to be ready to face the mess we left."

"*We* left?" Ezekiel asks.

I'm pretty sure they'll never be able to have a conversation that doesn't end in an argument.

"You could've helped a little more, Zeke," Kristin says.

He sighs. "I have limitations."

"You're afraid to even test them."

I groan. "Stop! It's bad enough the universe is fighting over me, but I don't need you two doing it, too. I need us all to be on the same side."

"That's on your angel," she says. "I'm always on your side, Faith."

Ezekiel expands his wings.

I tense, clenching my hands into fists. Blood seeps from my palm and drips to the desert dirt. Flames burst from the ground, engulfing my legs, startling me. I scream out and try to pat away the flames.

Neither Ezekiel nor Kristin react to the sight of my flesh burning and flaking, leaving behind my inner demon in my place, begging to take over my body and existence. The world hazes brown, Ezekiel's and Kristin's voices suddenly muted though I see them talking. The veil to the sunlight prison realm thickens, and to my despair, it encloses me in, cutting me off from my watcher and witch. Sweat—no blood—drips from my forehead and into my eyes, and I hit my fists against the veil to shatter it again, but I can't touch it. I keep stumbling into nothing.

"Blood to blood from dark to light, steal the vision, blind the sight. A demon's blood will be the key, mirror the vision, let him see."

Cool hands lock onto my shoulders, and Ezekiel spins me around. His narrowed eyes widen for a second before they harden, and he composes himself. Red veils my vision, my tears now coated in the blood seeping from my head. I open and close my mouth, trying everything I can to push air from my lungs to make me speak. But the air is too hot, too thick, smothering me like the fire that smolders out, stealing away my humanity and everything Ezekiel fell in love with.

I shift, trying to turn away.

He doesn't let me go, his blessed stare takes in every little hellish bit of me I don't want him to see. Standing in front of him naked and Hell-bound would be better than showing him who I've become without my soul. My demon blood wants to show the world what a monster I am. How could Ezekiel ever love me now? How can he even bear to look at me?

"Faith, can you hear me?" Ezekiel asks.

I squeeze my eyes shut and nod. If I can't see him, it's not so bad. Because the way he's looking at me, wings outstretched, Heaven shining in his eyes, not letting me shift away—it sends alarms ringing in my heart.

His fingers dig into my hot, charred skin. "This isn't real. Drop your hands. Stop looking."

He moves his hands from my shoulders to my face, and confusion washes over me. I snap my eyes open again at the odd sensation crossing my skin. The pressure of his fingers shifts, but I don't feel him touching my cheeks. He's touching my hands that I'm now aware are covering my face. The two blackened arms pressing against his chest aren't mine. I don't feel them, though I see them as clear as everything else—the barren nothingness of the daylight prison realm now lit up in the brown sun, the shadow cast by me stretching out with a new row of horns, and even the ash from my burned skin floating through the air.

"Drop your hands," Ezekiel repeats. "Please, Faith. Please. Please."

Panic rises in his words as he chants and pleads for me to listen, piercing my heart to rip it open. His voice isn't filled with disgust, and he still doesn't turn away from me like I expect him to. His dark eyes remain unblinking, his muscles tense, and his jaw twitching, but he doesn't grimace at the sight of me in my true body horror. He leans even closer, his cherry blossom breath drifting over me in a calming cloud.

I gasp, the thick, hot air entering into my lungs as it thins and finally allows me to breathe. "Ezekiel, please stop looking at me. I can't stand it. I don't want you to see me like this."

"Like what?"

"A demon."

"Faith, look at me. You're not a demon. This isn't real. And even if you were a demon, I'd still look at you like this, because it wasn't your body I fell in love with. It was everything else."

I thrash my head back and forth, hitting my strangely oily yet charred hair against my face. "Which I've lost. I have nothing left for you but—"

"You haven't lost anything. Now, look at me." Ezekiel grips my wrists, prying my hands from my face. The sunlight prison realm disappears, leaving me standing with Ezekiel and Kristin outside the yellow Victorian house.

I slowly blink, my eyes adjusting to the shift in light. It's like someone opened the door after a hot shower, letting the steam dissipate.

I lick my dry lips and sag my shoulders. Turning my head to Kristin, I say, "Oh, God. I don't understand. I was a demon. I know I was."

Kristin twists her lips to the side and runs her fingers through her messy hair. "The transition isn't always easy on a mortal, Faith. The Veiled Realm takes a toll, especially after all the power you used last night."

I don't believe her. I feel I'm right about this deep in my bones. I might be mortal and able to walk in the Earth realm during the day, but I'm losing this battle faster than I thought. I had hoped for years, months even, but not weeks. "You're wrong, Kristin. It was real."

"It was a vision."

"Then I'm going crazy because I couldn't tell the vision apart from my reality. Something's not right. Mary is getting stronger or maybe my demon is."

Kristin steps closer and grabs my hand, pulling it up to press it to my own heart. "It's you. You're getting stronger, Faith. You haven't had the need to use so much power all these years triggered by dark emotions. It's different than summoning demonic energy to practice with."

I wring my hands together and flick my gaze to Ezekiel,

who doesn't take his eyes away from me. "Then I can't use it anymore."

She sighs. "You're not good with a weapon."

Dad never taught me how because demons don't have the need to ever use human weapons. I've gotten a few lessons over the years from Cadence, but nothing sufficient enough that I could protect myself in a situation that would require me to fight.

"You don't understand," I say. "You didn't see what I saw."

Ezekiel clears his throat.

Without him even saying the words, I know he saw me. Whatever spell Kristin performed allowed him to see what I was seeing, and now I'm even more mortified knowing I was right in my state of panic about him seeing me as a demon.

My cheeks flourish with unbidden warmth, and I yell through my teeth, the noise coming from me sounding more like a growl from a werewolf. I throw my hands up and spin, stomping away. "I can't believe you let him see me like that, Kristin."

Dirt crunches under her boots as she follows me. "I'm sorry, okay? We couldn't snap you out of it. I can't get into your mind's eye like he can."

"Faith, stop," Ezekiel says.

I don't.

"Just give us a minute, featherhead," Kristin says.

She races up next to me, keeping pace at my side. I head down the gravel road away from the house, though I don't know where I'm going. I just need to get away. Jogging faster, she turns to walk backward in front of me. I expect her to try to stop me, but she keeps perfect step without even looking over her shoulder, probably afraid I'll knock her over if she slows.

"I need to be alone," I say.

"And I need to apologize."

"It's whatever. It shouldn't bother me he saw me like that," I say.

"You're right. It shouldn't. He's an angel, Faith. I can't say exactly how angels think, but I'm pretty sure their desires run soul deep. That guy will love you regardless."

"That's beside the point. I was awful. Terrifying. I—he's so perfect, you know. I'm—"

"The beautiful, perfect halves of both your mom and dad put together. Don't you dare argue, either. I made sure you got the best of everything." She presses her lips together. "And I'm sorry. I really am. I didn't know of another way. I'm not some all powerful witch. I've been making things up as I go since you were born."

I roll my eyes. "You're just saying that to make me feel better. Dad wouldn't put his trust in someone who couldn't get a spell straight."

"You're right. I was barely an adult when I cast the spell to help Raphael gain some humanity. But your dad and I made a deal," she says. "Your mom was like my older sister, and the second I agreed to help her, I knew my life was over. My coven shunned me. I lost all my protection. My home."

"Then why did you do it?" I ask.

She stops, forcing me to halt in place. "I loved your mom, and I'd rather have taken her soul and used it to create something beautiful and pure and everything she had lost than lose her to your dad and Hell. Watching your mom fall in love and then go through all that—" A tear drips onto her cheek, and she swipes it away. "Faith, I swear I'm going to fix this. I regret asking for your help to begin with. I should've accepted my fate and the decision I made."

"You couldn't have known Dad was being set up. *I* was being set up. Mary would have come for me whether or not you'd asked me. And even if you hadn't, I didn't want the angelic army to send him to Hell." I tilt my head toward the sky. "I just don't understand how beings who are supposed to be all love and light and whatever could even think Dad to be a traitor. Why punish him for love?"

Her brows crinkle together. "Raphael isn't Heaven's Traitor because he fell in love, Faith. I told you this."

"Yeah, I know. His purpose. But he changed it because he was in love, right?" I ask. I had assumed. Dad hasn't had a chance to talk to me for more than a few minutes since the night I found out. Ezekiel told me it was something he didn't know for certain and that Dad would add any revelations he shared to the list of reasons he would break Ezekiel's wings. If I didn't know any better, I'd think Ezekiel worried about what my dad thought of him more than the threats my dad continues to throw at him.

Oh, Dad. I miss him so much right now. He's been the only person I ever really had since Grandma died. And I could really use a hug from him, even if he'd probably yell at me for being embarrassed in front of Ezekiel—for being mad at Kristin for helping.

"When Raphael was an angel, he was the Demon Watcher of a powerful demon. Your dad was the only one in Heaven's ranks who could keep the demon at bay. But then your dad slipped up. He lost sight of his purpose. Other angels tried to rise up to take over but in the end, the demon was too strong. Some said he was Lucifer incarnate, but even Satan would reject him." Kristin looks past me, and I glance over my shoulder to peek at Ezekiel, standing a few dozen feet away with his arms crossed over his chest.

I turn back to Kristin. "Are you saying Dad was the Demon Watcher of Malicevile Hellshire?"

"And Heaven's Traitor rose to be his right hand."

There's no denying it. I was there. I might have been young, but I know Dad had helped Cami's demonic father during the uprising and war. He did it for me, to protect me, especially after the Hunter's Alliance discovered my existence. But I had no idea he was Malicevile's Demon Watcher. How could I? I had no idea he fell until a few weeks ago. I thought he was always a demon, born from Hell, sent to Earth to usher souls. I had a feeling he was different, but I was so isolated. I had nothing to compare him to except the few less powerful demons he took me around.

But now discovering this? I don't know if it makes me feel better or worse. Because deep down, I know Heaven has every right to call him a traitor. So many lives were lost. My mom's life was lost. And he stood by and helped. He bowed.

I curl my fingers into the palms of my hands. "How could he?"

Kristin touches my hand. "Faith, please. You have to understand."

I shake my head. "I thought Dad was different. I thought Heaven was just out to get him because he chose to be with my mom."

Wind gusts through the air so powerfully it knocks me forward and into Kristin, cutting me off.

A howl echoes through the air. The sound cuts deep into my heart, threatening to spill it all over the desert. Kristin swears and pushes me off her to scramble to her feet. I automatically summon demonic power against my better judgment. My instincts kicked in before my mind, and I'm now too afraid to snuff it out.

But I don't have to.

Blinding light shines in my eyes, forcing my power away.

Strong arms lock to my waist. My stomach drops to my feet as the world disappears out from under me, and I'm thrown into the air. I scream, freefalling a few feet. Ezekiel catches me in his arms, cradling me against him. I turn my face away from the wind and to his taut chest, muffling my startled cries until my body catches up to my head.

"What the Hell!" I scream. "I thought you were the angelic army sent to kill me."

Ezekiel points down. "Wolves."

Another howl rips through the air.

"Oh, God. Not again," I whisper. "Ezekiel, we have to go back."

He shakes his head. "No, you made me a promise. If things got bad, we'd leave. I can't take any more chances. Not after last night or this morning."

"Ezekiel."

"I will not lose you, Faith. Not to them. Not to Heaven."

I cup his face and look into his dark eyes. "Please, I'm begging you."

He hugs me closer, flying higher. "Don't push me, Faith. If you do, I'm afraid I'll lose sight. I'm afraid I'll lose my purpose."

His words burn through me before ice overtakes my veins. I stare at him, my eyes watering from the wind, now freezing the tears splashing on my cheeks. "That's the last thing I ever want," I say, my voice nearly a whisper. "I'd rather die and be a demon than be responsible for pushing you to fall."

Demonic Affairs

A LOUD POP rings through the air, and I struggle to peer down at the commotion below. The howls of the wolves cease with the panic beats of my heart. Ezekiel dives down a few feet, sending my stomach into my throat.

"What was that?" I ask, squirming to get a good look.

Ezekiel does everything he possibly can to block me from seeing anything. "A gun."

"A gun? Who has a gun?" Guns aren't common in the demon world even with hunters—a blessed bullet might hurt a demon a whole lot, but they're not effective in killing mid or upper level demons. A hunter's more likely to turn a demon into a raging lunatic to merely injure it. It takes a dagger to the heart, and even then, you might have to cut the whole thing out if it's someone of high caliber.

"The Storyteller," Ezekiel says.

I huff a breath in relief. I thought the wolves might have armed themselves to attack. Demons aren't that susceptible to bullets, but I'm mortal. So is Kristin.

Another gunshot pops, making my ears ring.

"Vivian, stop!" Kristin yells, her words trickling to me on the wind. If my ears weren't buzzing from the sound of the gun and the whistle of the wind, I could hear her better. But now? I'm doing everything I can to mute the headache-inducing noise.

Ezekiel circles once, and I bounce in his arms as he skids to a stop on solid ground. Had Vivian not shot the gun, he might've already flown us out of here.

"What are you doing?" I ask. "I thought we were leaving."

"And I thought we were facing a threat," he answers.

Ezekiel sets me on my feet and spins me around. Kristin stands a few feet away, blocking three familiar wolves cowering in the brush away from Vivian, standing on her porch, a shotgun still aimed.

"No wolves," Vivian says, motioning her gun toward the gravel road that'll lead to the wrought iron gate to leave the property. "The Desertville pack isn't welcome at my house. They should know that."

Kristin glances between Vivian and the wolves. "They're rogue, Seer, and they helped us last night. You're right about the Desertville pack. It's worse than I thought."

Vivian lowers the gun, watching the wolves for a moment. "They have to change back if they want to come inside." She turns in our direction and nods. "I'm glad you returned with Faith. I have a message for you."

I frown. "A message?"

"From your dad."

"This is risky, Faith. I think we should wait until nightfall and have Kristin meet him," Ezekiel says, staring at the piece of paper with the name of a cemetery I've never heard of located halfway between here and the Hunter's Academy. It's a strange location for Dad to want to meet, considering demons don't ever focus on the dead. It's the living they want.

I snatch the paper from his hand. "If it was something for Kristin to pass along, he'd have waited or asked for her. I'm going. Dad wouldn't ask to meet me again if it weren't important."

"There's a lot of angelic activity around the academy. This is already too close for comfort," he argues.

"We'll drive."

"Dad? She knows her dad? I always thought demons were quick to take the souls of those who, uh, ya know..." Calvin's voice trails off as he ponders the possibility of my conception. I guess Lola and Greg haven't had the chance to catch him up to tell him Dad is the demon and not my mom like he's implying.

I turn my head to look at him, eyebrows raised. Ezekiel makes it too easy to forget there are others outside our little shield. Since Kristin still hasn't had a chance to break her spell allowing the pure of soul to see me, Greg, Calvin, and Lola have been listening to me have a one-sided conversation. I think all three werewolves are too nervous to ask who I'm talking to, and they haven't even mentioned how Kristin and I vanished into thin air last night.

"Raphael doesn't have a soul to lose, and it takes a lot more than intercourse to conceive a demonic spawn," Ezekiel mutters like the werewolves can hear him. He touches my cheek, and I turn back to him. "Do we have to talk about this in front of them? What happens if their pack comes back to break them and word of your survival gets out?"

"Faith's existence will disappear from their minds if Joshua manages to force them to return," Kristin says. "And if they even think of mentioning her now, they'll be demon broken come sunset."

Greg releases a low growl. "You have our vow to never speak of Faith. To have someone powerful enough to take on Joshua show up out of nowhere exactly when we needed her was a miracle. And you, witch? You were our prayers answered. We are here for anything you need."

"And we will die before we bow down to Joshua," Lola says.

"Demon broken?" Calvin asks, his Adam's apple bobbing

as he swallows.

"Faith's mom was the human," Kristin says, keeping her face straight. "Dear old demon dad is the one who has the power to follow through with my threat."

The smell of Vivian's hot breakfast disappears amid the sudden fragrance of nature—wet dirt, cut grass, strangely the scent of pine trees in this dry desert... I blink, jerking my attention from Ezekiel's dark eyes. Fear has never smelled so good.

I hop to my feet and cover my nose. I'd rather suffocate than breathe in Calvin's oncoming panic at the revelation that my demon dad and I have a relationship—something unheard of, especially with half demons nearly going extinct.

"No one is getting broken, so stop freaking out," I say.

Greg presses his lips together. "No one's freaking out."

My chest tightens, my lungs begging me to gasp, my racing heart agreeing, but not for the same reason. A series of quick thuds push the sound of my own heartbeat away, and I pull my dress up to cover my face.

"I can smell everyone's fear now. Your hearts are beating wildly," I say, my voice rising. I groan. "I gotta get out of here."

Without waiting, I run to the backdoor and out onto the patio where Kristin moved her SUV. I climb behind the wheel, snatch the keys from where she left them in the center console in case we needed a quick escape, and start the engine.

Ezekiel appears out of thin air and expands his wings. "What are you doing?"

"What do you think? Get in now or I will leave you behind."

A door slams, and Kristin steps out. "Get in back, Faith. You can't drive. We might need your power."

I frown. "I'm not using it ever again. You should stay here and fix your spell."

The rogue wolves come out of the house behind her, looking all sorts of fierce in the shadow created by the awning.

"For one, I'm not leaving you. And two, I need your blood," she says. "Featherhead can drive."

"I'm not driving," Ezekiel says.

"I can't drive and fix my spell."

"Then we'll wait."

I rev the engine. "I'm leaving now. Get in or don't."

Kristin sighs and steps forward. The three werewolves shadow her moves in a strangely protective way.

I wave my hand. "Nuh-uh. You guys stay."

Kristin's lips twists downward. "Actually, who's the best driver?"

Calvin slowly raises his hand.

Ezekiel huffs. "No way."

For the first time today, I agree with my guardian. "You remember what happened the last time we had a car full of werewolves?"

"What happened?" Greg asks.

Kristin glares at me. "Not much. It's just how Faith got that pretty white eye."

I automatically raise my hand to cover it but stop short. I

wish she hadn't pointed out my soulless eye, because I already knew they were looking at it, but now they'll stare at it even more. I had given up the colored contact I was wearing since no one except Ezekiel ever saw me. Now? I regret leaving them behind at our old apartment.

Greg must be aware of how awkward I'm feeling, because he says, "I think it's pretty badass."

Calvin steps closer to look at me behind the wheel. "And freaky."

Lola punches him hard enough to make him teeter.

I'm starting to like her now that I'm getting to know her.

Kristin opens the driver's side door to the SUV and drags me from the seat. Calvin switches places with me while Lola gets in the front seat. Greg gets behind Lola and Kristin gets in the middle.

Ezekiel rests his hands on my shoulders. "I guess the trip won't be so bad, Demon Spawn," he says.

I grin at him, my annoyance over the sudden shift in my plan to include the rogue pack now melting away. Ezekiel pats his lap for me to sit on. If only the last time I played lapsies with him didn't involve my new friends dying.

I glance toward the sky. "Grandma, if you can hear me, please don't let history repeat itself."

"You pray to your grandma?" Greg asks.

I smirk. "Yeah, I can't pray to Heaven. They think I've died and gone to Hell."

I had no idea how handy werewolves were until I stepped out of the SUV and into the shade of dozens of blossoming magnolia trees peppering the small cemetery nestled away from the freeway and any local church affiliated with the Hunter's Alliance.

Star bursts of sunlight litter the ground through the trees, and all three werewolves transform into their true bodies to slink quietly through the tall headstones. There might not be demons around, but they can pick up the scents of anything out of the ordinary.

"We're alone here," Ezekiel says.

I nod. "I know, but we can't be too careful. Plus, I don't exactly want an audience when I talk to my dad."

His brows knit together. "You mean..."

I pout my bottom lip. "I'm sorry, Ezekiel." I hadn't realized what his betrayal had done to me last night, and it's obvious in this moment. "Demonic affairs."

He reaches out and touches my cheek. "You don't trust me now." It's not a question.

We might have forgiven each other for the terrible positions we were in at sunset when I was pulled back into the Veiled Realm, but he's right. His actions put a rift in the trust I had for him. And I'm not sure how I feel about it.

I open my mouth to say something, but I can't find the words. Hurt sweeps across his face, his eyes glassing over in the bright sunshine. Ezekiel's wings sag for a moment before they disappear from sight.

"I—" Still, nothing comes from my mouth. I'm afraid if I

put the words out there—if I even whisper what I'm feeling—I'll ruin everything we have between us. It's so unfair that my heart and mind would go to war with each other over the angel who tried everything to make sure I was okay in the end, who keeps fighting for my life, even if I feel like there's no point sometimes. When death is inevitable for me and my perfect life as a demon's daughter is long gone, up in flames with everything else in my world.

Ezekiel leans closer, not letting me turn my gaze away. "I'm going to fix this. I'm going to prove to you that you're what matters to me."

But how can he? I'd never let him do anything to fall.

I respond with a nod and a quick kiss, pulling away before he can lure me to him with an offering of a hug I want to dive into and live the rest of my limited days in.

But then that rift inside me sparks pain in my already aching heart, and I force my legs to work. Ezekiel doesn't follow me deeper into the cemetery. He lets me close the distance to Kristin, standing by a weeping statue that once was an angel—but the wings have been long since broken off.

And then I see her name.

Grace Tabitha Blackwell

Dad wanted me to meet at Mom's grave. A grave I had no idea even existed. Grandma told me my mom was cremated and scattered out to sea because she loved the ocean. I didn't know it before, but I'm sure it's why Dad bought the house in Moonlight Shores.

"Something must be terribly wrong," Kristin says. "I never thought your dad would ever bring you here."

Without commenting, I raise my hand to my eye, my chest tightening at the possibility of seeing my inner demon come to life once again. But only a familiar smiling face greets me. Dad closes the distance between us, raising his hand to my face without touching my cheek, just framing my head in his hands like I'm all he wants to see.

"You brought me to Mom's grave," I say, trying my best not to break down and cry. Everything is so overwhelming, but I can't let Dad see me like this. He raised me to bottle up my emotions to strengthen me, not to turn into a sobbing mess every time something goes wrong in my life.

His smile hardens with his tightening jaw, and it's clear he sees past my fake smile. "What has Ezekiel done?" I'd give anything to hear his voice, hear how deep it gets when he's turning serious.

I release a small, breathless laugh. "Dad, I—"

"You will not try to make excuses for whatever that Demon Watcher did to make you look like you're about to cry at any second."

A tear slips on my cheek, and I cringe. "How do you even know it was him? A lot has happened Dad. Things are—"

"Bad," he finishes. "You broke the veil, Faith. I felt it. The whole angelic army felt it."

I suck in a breath. "It's fine. Ezekiel fixed it."

"So then why are you crying? I know what heartache looks

like, and I hate the sight of it on my beautiful daughter's face."

"It's fine, Dad," I repeat. "We're working through it."

He groans. "You're seventeen. There is nothing you should be working through with anyone, but especially that angel who I've entrusted your wellbeing to, including that pure, innocent, uncorrupted—which I've gone through a lot to guarantee— heart and soul of yours."

"We fought, okay? He tried to stop me before I could break the veil to save Kristin. We got into some trouble—"

"You broke the veil for Kristin?" Dad's voice rises loud enough that it cuts through the veil muting us. "Do you know what danger you put yourself into?"

"You're taking Ezekiel's side?" I ask. "Kristin was Mom's best friend."

"Kristin is why your mom is dead!" he snaps.

"She's why I'm alive!"

"I don't care." He runs his fingers through his hair.

"Of course not. They don't call you Heaven's Traitor for no reason. You don't care about anything, do you? Just your power and existing."

He winces. "I've made some—"

I curl my hands into fists, my gaze silencing him. I'm so angry right now. "The only reason you care about me is because I make those feelings possible."

"Faith?" Dad asks. "Faith, what are you doing?"

"Being honest unlike you."

"Faith?" he repeats.

Oh no. I didn't actually curl my fist. I watch as the strange hand jets out from me, summoning Hell power in a bright orange color different than the usual red of Dad's power. In one quick motion, the arm chucks it, expelling the power at Dad, sending sparks into the air.

Dad yells out, jumping back. His wide blue eyes lock onto mine, and he holds out his hands, palms up. The strange hands that look a part of me but move at their own freewill summon more demonic power and thrust it at Dad again.

"Kristin!" I yell.

But she's gone from my view. The whole cemetery is gone. All I see is Dad rubbing his smoking hands together. For the first time ever, he can't control the power in my veins. It's not the same as his. It's shifting, becoming my own as I lose my humanity.

"Faith, control yourself," Dad says. I hear his voice clearly like there isn't a veil at all.

I squeeze my eyes shut, nausea twisting my stomach. "I'm not doing anything. I don't know what's happening to me."

"This is impossible," Dad says. A pinch to my shoulder forces me to snap my eyes open. He stands only a foot away from me, one hand touching me and the other raised up to my cheek. His fingers brush over my skin. "I can hear you. I can feel you."

My lip quivers at the realization. "I can hear you, too."

Before Dad has a chance to say anything, I fling my arms around him and hug him, burying my face into his chest. This is the hug I've so desperately needed for weeks now. Tears well in my eyes, and I didn't know how much I took our time together for granted. He's been there for me every night for years like clockwork, and I've missed him so much now losing that. But here I am, hugging him like all the hugs we've shared when night allowed him to cross back to Earth. But it's me crossing through to him.

Dad stiffens in my hug and steps away. When I'm not quick enough to let go of him, he shoves me back, shocking me. I trip over a gnarled root twisting from the dirt, and hit the ground hard. The jolt makes my entire world quiver. Shadows edge my vision with dizziness.

"Get out of here now," Dad says. "You don't belong here."

"What?" I ask, now struggling to breathe in the too hot air. The hot world around me presses against me, making me feel sick. But I'll fight through it for Dad. "What do you mean?"

"Get out!" he hollers.

Strong fingers dig into my arms, yanking me from the ground. Dad's voice rips through the air as he shouts, cursing the whole universe.

"What have you done? You shouldn't have brought her here." Dad ignites power in his hands and launches it directly at me, but it goes over my head. Someone groans.

"Faith, drop your hands," Ezekiel says. "Do it now."

I stare in shock at Dad, who summons more power in his hands to toss at my Demon Watcher.

"What's going on? Dad, stop," I say, my knees weakening

and forcing me to the ground. "It's okay. It's just a vision." At least I think. I can't tell anymore. The air's too hot. But I see my blackened hands. My demon. But I'm not one yet.

Dad snarls at me, his horns cutting through his skin, leaving trails of black blood dripping down his forehead to splash on his cheeks. "You can't be here, Faith. I mean it. Leave now. I don't want you ever coming back. They'll know."

"Who?" I ask.

"Everyone!"

"But Dad," I say. "How will I ever see you again?"

He shakes his head. "This was a mistake. I should've left you out of it. I should've trusted that you'd live the rest of your life happily without me. But I was selfish."

"Dad." I groan, my stomach twisting. I cough and spit, black bile burning across the desert ground.

"Take her. This world wasn't meant for her."

Ezekiel flips me around, expanding his wings on his back, shading me from the hot sun glowing through the brown, hazy air. Bending his knees, Ezekiel launches us both into the air, leaving Dad to turn into a speck below.

Ezekiel squeezes me closer. "Lower your hand."

"It is lowered."

He releases a small groan. "Then close your eyes."

Raising his hand to my face, he covers my eyes with his palm.

The daylight prison realm melts away.

But so does the world.

PROMISE

I'M TRAPPED IN darkness.

I can't move or open my eyes. I can't speak.

But I can hear.

I've been listening to the soft sound of Ezekiel's breathing for what has felt like an eternity. The whisper of his wings whooshes every other breath, and the soft sounds of my angel are the only things keeping me from full blown panic.

My meeting with Dad spins over and over again in my mind. He's never acted like that toward me, and I'm hurt. My whole being tenses, my heart breaking resonating all over me.

It's all I am in this moment. Heartbreak incarnate. Broken. Shattered. Lost. Alone.

Dad rejected me. He was the one person I relied on. The one person who always managed to pull me off the floor and dust me off, to tell me I was strong enough to keep going. That I was his daughter, and because of that, I was powerful.

And now?

I don't know. He was afraid of that power.

I'm not even sure what happened. I was only watching him through the veil like the few times I've done before, but things changed. I could feel and hear him like I was there, and he could hear me, too.

For the first time ever, I think that if I had relented, if I had just accepted what Dad had wanted for me—to die and revive as a demon with my soul intact—I'd have been better off. I'd still have a life. I'd still have a home. A bunch of angry angels are far better than an army of avenging ones—demons, too. But I want so badly to prove I'm deserving of a mortal life. I don't want power beyond my wildest dreams or power to be feared. But life isn't fair, and obviously no one cares about my good intent, all because of the possibility.

Everything I was ever given has been ripped away like maybe I was undeserving in the first place. Not because I was a demon's daughter, but because I was too good. Too pure. It's like trying to do the right thing gets me nowhere. How am I ever to survive when being good and pure comes at a price more costly than if I turned my back and accepted my fate?

What's the point of fighting?

What's the point in finding Mary if even Dad fears me?

"I need guidance," Ezekiel whispers so softly that if I had any of my other senses, I wouldn't have heard his voice. "I need answers. I'm afraid."

I expect to hear someone respond, but only silence greets him. It's not the soft quiet that fills up the empty space, a reminder that someone is listening. It's the cold void of nothingness when no one is there. No one is listening. No one cares.

"I'm angry," Ezekiel continues. "She deserves a better life. She deserves so much more than this. Than me. I can't see the right thing anymore. I'm failing. I'm failing her. This isn't right. How can everything be wrong when I don't feel that it is?"

He releases another soft breath, the heat and pain in his words digging into me. I feel it in my soul that he holds in his hands, in his heart, in his entire being.

"I need to know why? Why send me to her to rip her away just as quickly? Why test my purpose? Why put me in a position that can ruin the world?"

I don't know what he's expecting or maybe he can hear something I can't, but whatever it is, he doesn't get the answer he needs or wants, because he grows silent, and I swear I hear a drop of water splash something—not water, tears. Each little teardrop blossoms warmth over me, igniting my sense of touch. I can now feel my face, feel his tears pooling on my closed eyelids to drip down my temples.

I lick my dry lips, tasting salt and something sweeter, and whisper, "Because you won't ruin the world."

Ezekiel inhales a shuddering breath. "Thank you," he says, his voice soft, shaky even.

Tilting my chin, I incline my head so his tears run down my face. He sits me up higher and smears his fingers across my cheeks. Staring into his dark eyes after listening to the struggle he fights over with himself, seeing the streaks of tears shining on his handsome face, and feeling his heart pounding on my shoulder, it's so clear to me how vulnerable he is under all the muscles and bones and beautiful black wings.

I hug him, putting my arms around his arms for once instead of the other way around. "You don't need to thank me, Ezekiel."

His pouty lips stretch into a smile, and he leans forward and kisses my cheek. "Of course I do. You answered my prayer."

I purse my lips. "Demonic intervention isn't a thing."

"But having my Faith is."

I laugh.

He smiles.

"My dad set me up for an eternity of angelic pickup lines."

I reach up and hold his face between my hands, kissing him like I've been starving for his lips against mine, to breathe in his breath, taste his sweet mouth. I have no idea what is going on or where everyone else is, but at least there's one thing I'm certain of—Ezekiel and I will be okay even if everything else isn't. The trust I thought I lost wasn't my trust for him. It was my trust for me. Because I can't trust myself anymore—or what I see.

Slowly pulling away, Ezekiel allows an inch of air between us, giving me just enough space to make me crave to close it. "What am I going to do with you?"

I know he's teasing me, but I can't help the uncertainty ignited within me by his words. "What *are* you going to do with me? What even happened? Where are we?"

His jaw flexes as he clenches his teeth. "We're in the SUV, heading back to Vivian's."

Confusion washes over me. "Wait, I'm sleeping?"

"Knocked out, actually."

I blink.

"I'm sorry. I had to. You somehow managed to cross the veil to your father, Faith," he says. "One second you were standing with Kristin, and the next you vanished. It's taken a toll on your body."

Goosebumps prickle up my arms. "I didn't mean to, I swear. I didn't even know I broke it. And Dad, he—" I can't bring myself to repeat what my dad said. Ezekiel was there. He knows.

He runs his fingers through my hair. "We have greater things to worry about right now. But I promise you, Faith, we'll figure out a way for you to see Raphael again. He was overreacting."

I sigh. "You think so? He's never pushed me away like that."

"He was afraid for you."

"He wanted to meet because the universe felt me break the veil open last night."

Ezekiel flicks his gaze away, and I follow his line of sight, realizing we're not in my normal dream world. This one is different. It's like I'm hovering in his arms in an absence of darkness. The light is so pure and bright and white, his black feathers shine in stark contrast but manage to radiate a different kind of glow.

"He agreed with you about Kristin, you know," I say.

I expect him to react, to tell me that he told me so, but all he says is, "You did what you felt was right."

"So did you," I say softly. "And I'm sorry for doubting you. But you have to understand—"

"I do understand. More than ever. I know I've failed you, and I'm trying to—"

I touch his cheek so he'll look at me. "Stop saying that. You haven't failed anything. This isn't some test. This is my life—*our* lives together."

A strange look crosses his face, a million thoughts flickering in his eyes.

I tilt my head. "What? You're looking at me weird. I'm not showing off my inner demon or something, right?"

He shakes his head. "I didn't realize I could love you more than I already do. Every time I ask for guidance, I have a moment of doubt when all I hear is silence, but then you always answer with exactly what I need."

"I didn't know you were talking to me earlier."

His lips pull up on one side. "I wasn't."

"Oh, well that's—"

"Blood to blood from dark to light, contain her power, tame the sight." Kristin's voice resonates within this pure world of radiance like an inky dark spot begging to steal all the light.

I hug Ezekiel tighter. "No."

He cradles me closer. "Don't be afraid."

"Please, no more magic. I—"

"Love's kiss will leave a mark, pull the light from the dark. An angel's devotion pure and true, will rise up and protect you."

A burning sensation crawls across my heart. "I can't do this anymore. Let's just run. Take me away somewhere no one can ever reach me."

"It's not want you want," Ezekiel says.

"It is now. I'm scared."

"Demon born and Heaven-bound, hear my spell, hear the sound. Whispered words, a begging plea. Awaken now, I summon thee."

One second I'm hiding in Ezekiel's arms and the next, I'm sitting up on a bed, gasping. I thrash, my mind trying to catch up to my body. I hate moving from one place to another when I'm not aware of my surroundings, even if Ezekiel told me where we were going.

I glance around the unfamiliar room. "Ezekiel?"

Something's wrong.

This isn't Vivian's house. The room is too sparse, too modern with sleek woods and chrome fixtures. I sling my legs off the side of the bed and rush to the window, pulling the black curtains askew to peer outside.

It's dark. But not night. A strange haze clouds the air, a fog strong enough to block out the sun. I flick the lock and try to pry the window up, but it doesn't budge. Shifting on my feet, I glance around the room, my gaze narrowing on a strange bronze statue on the nightstand. My instincts push me to pick it up and shatter the window. I don't even know whose house this is, but everything in me wants out.

"Ezekiel," I call out again in more of a hiss whisper.

A chill ices over my hot back, and I shiver, the creepy sensation that I'm being silently watched washing over me. Locking my fingers around the statue, I hoist up the heavy object and draw it back to swing at the window like a bat.

Soft music clicks on, coming from some hidden speaker. I hesitate, my hand shaking with the statue's weight. Someone hums, the low voice wafting through the crack under the door.

"My pretty little demon, the world can wait. Let me in and unlock the gate. Your fiery heart, burns so bright, the sun can't stop you, we'll rule the day and night." Mary sings the words like a lullaby, her voice swirling in my mind. "As the veil thins, you'll be free. There's no stopping it now, Heaven will see. An angel's shield will falter and break. All it takes is one mistake. An angel will fall from the sky, his grace will end and you'll both die. Hell will get you wait and see. A pretty little demon you will be."

"No!" I scream, swinging the bronze statue at the window. Glass cascades around me, exploding in a sharp sparkle of glittering pieces that fly in at me instead of out. Blood drips down my arms and into the dark wood floor, burning in small bursts of flames.

The door behind me whines open, and I spin and catch sight of a figure hovering in the hallway outside. Fog seeps in through the window, clouding the space between us, but two red eyes glow with the fire of Hell. I can't turn my gaze away from Mary's eyes. My chest burns with new fury, the witch's mark igniting to steal my breath away.

"Your Hell-bound witch will lose this fight. She can't survive Heaven's smite. As the veil shifts, you will see. My powerful demon, you belong with me. Heaven's Traitor has turned away, alone you will always stay. Now your blood turns from red to black, and Hell will take your body back."

Summoning power in my hands, I create an orb large enough to outshine the fog in brilliant orange light not unlike the power I saw in the sunlight prison realm with Dad. I launch it at Mary, setting the room aglow in flames, and she grins as they eat away at her until she's nothing more than smoke and bones, dropping to the floor.

Rushing from my spot, I head to the window and pick up the statue from the floor before using it to clear away the remaining pieces of glass. Something pricks my finger, and I stare at the statue more intently. An angel with folded wings holds up a curved dagger but doesn't aim it at anything. Black blood coats the small knife, and I hold out my finger and inspect my wound. Sure enough, a drop of black blood pools on my index finger.

I scream and chuck the statue out the window as far as I can into the fog. I don't hear it hit the ground.

An explosion rings out behind me, shaking the foundation of the space. I shift to watch the flames that consumed Mary lick and eat the walls. They warm my skin and send smoke into the air.

I inhale a breath and cough. I thought I was in a dream. I thought she managed to get into my head as Kristin was pulling at my consciousness, but this is so real. How did I get here? Where am I?

"Ezekiel!" My voice echoes through the foggy room.

The fire cracks louder than even my heartbeat.

"Faith." The whisper manages to slither through the destruction my life has turned into. Ezekiel's voice came from outside.

"Help me," I say, sticking my head out the window.

"Faith," he repeats.

A bright light cuts through the darkness, pushing away the looming fog. Fire burns behind me, crawling closer across the floor. If I stay much longer, I'll perish with the house. The light in the distance grows brighter and brighter, reminiscent of a rising sun.

"Ezekiel, hurry."

But he won't ever make it. Fire singes the back of my legs, and I'm left with no choice but to jump. Gathering my courage, I swing my legs out the window, sitting on the window ledge for a second before I jump. My stomach rises into my throat, the world blurring around me as cold wind whips my hair. I close my eyes, expecting to hit the hard ground below, but it never comes. I'm free falling in a dark world with only the sensation that I'm never escaping this foggy world. Light flashes, turning my closed eyelids red, and the world suddenly stops.

"Faith, please. Come back to me," Ezekiel says.

I groan, pain radiating through my whole body.

"Faith," he says again, my name on his lips sounding more like a whispered prayer. "Please. Please, I need you."

I flutter my eyes open, the light stinging my vision. "Mary," I whisper.

Ezekiel leans over me, coming into focus, greeting me with the most serious eyes I've seen on him. They're not the eyes of my pure and innocent guardian. They've been hardened by the world, by me, by everything that comes with my existence. The intense mocha eyes locking me in a gaze I can't escape are the eyes of a warrior. Of someone willing to rise and fight.

"This must end now," Ezekiel says.

I open and close my mouth, fear suddenly twisting my insides, making me writhe in Ezekiel's firm hold. I always knew Ezekiel would follow through with my last request to send me to Heaven when all is lost. But something burns within me to plead for my life. To ask for a little while longer. Death sounds easy when I know the alternative—but it's not so simple. "I—"

"I need time," Kristin says, cutting off my words.

"There's no time," Ezekiel says. "Faith is breaking. Look at her. A mortal body can only handle so much. Her mind— Kristin, we're losing her."

"The daughter of Heaven's Traitor is stronger than you think," Kristin says.

"I don't want to test her," he says.

Kristin takes my hand. "Then you have to fight, Ezekiel. If you want to extend a life with Faith, you can't just be here to pick her up when she falls. You need to see to it that she doesn't."

He doesn't respond to her words or take his eyes off mine. Ezekiel has his limitations. He can only do so much. And honestly, I'm not sure I want him to do more. I don't want to put him in a position where he'll have to make a choice between doing what's right or doing what's right for me.

"So, what now?" he asks. "We can't stay here much longer. They will come to investigate."

"They? Who's coming?" I ask, my throat hurting. I cough, and a tiny tendril of smoke escapes my lips.

"Everyone. Demons, angels, hunters. Word is spreading about the damage to the veil," Ezekiel says. "I knew it wouldn't be long. Power draws power, and with the arrival of unleashed hellhounds...I—I wish I could find things out for certain."

This is the first time Ezekiel has mentioned his desire to communicate with the angelic army. As far as they know, he's missing. Angels don't get a handbook, and they follow their instincts and what they know to be right. Someone of Ezekiel's rank doesn't answer to anyone but himself. For his purpose was set and when his purpose ends...I've never asked him. I'm not even sure he knows.

"But nothing is ever certain," I say, because I don't like seeing the sudden frustration in his eyes.

He nods. "Except time. We must act now. The werewolves will move once they realize what's happening."

Kristin sighs. "You sure about this featherhead? We can track them again."

"We can't risk them surprising us. Look what that witch has done to Faith. This link is killing her."

I frown. "What do you mean?"

He takes my hand and turns it over so I can see my palm. A black vein trails from a hole in my finger, snaking down my hand and to my wrist. I'm not imagining the black blood now. It's real. She's using my own body against me.

I jerk up and scramble away from Ezekiel and to my feet. We're outside of Vivian's house, and I startle at the sight of the shattered window above. A bronze statue—*the* bronze statue from my moment with Mary—stakes the ground a few feet away.

Power ignites in my palms without my consent, and I thrust my hands out like it burns my skin, though I just want it to get away from me. It zooms right toward the statue. Ezekiel flaps his wings, sending a gust of wind at me, throwing my demonic power off course and knocking me off my feet in the process.

My power splashes the dirt, sending a dust cloud in the air before fizzling out. Ezekiel's shadow falls over me, and he offers his hand out to help me to my feet. I dust off my hands on my dirty dress. Ezekiel strolls over to the bronze statue and hoists it from the ground to look at it.

"Drop it!" I yell, throwing power at his hands. It leaves him no choice but to drop the evil angel statue that pricked my finger. It's what caused these ugly black veins to spread over my hand like a knotted spider web. "That's Mary's."

Ezekiel's brows scrunch, wrinkles pinching his usually smooth forehead. "I don't think so, Faith. I saw it on Cadence's dresser. Mary wouldn't have a need for something blessed."

I hold up my hand to Ezekiel. "Blessed?" I shake my head. "That thing has Hell all over it. It's what did this."

Kristin steps closer from the spot she's been silently watching us. "Are you sure, Faith?"

"Yes. She was singing about—" I close my eyes, trying to remember the words I've suppressed. "She sang about Ezekiel, I think. She said his shield will break and he'll fall from the sky and..." I don't even want to think about the words she sang.

Kristin pulls her sleeve down over her hand and carefully takes the angel statue. "This is a totem. You must've manifested it somehow. The veil is too thin." She glances at Ezekiel. "Lock me out of your shield for a bit, featherhead. I need to cast a spell that'll leave a magical impression Mary will feel."

Strolling away, Kristin leaves me alone with Ezekiel in the dry front lawn of Vivian's house. I wonder where the rogue wolves and Seer are, but I don't want to look. I have a lot more on my mind. Ezekiel can see it, too. He stands there expectantly, waiting for me to bare my thoughts to him, the emotions I'm sure he feels in my soul.

"Can angels really die?" I finally ask.

Ezekiel's lips disappear into a fine line. He straightens his shoulders and outstretches his wings like he's steeling himself for the answer, like it's something he doesn't think about or refuses to even consider.

And then he turns away without answering me at all.

"Ezekiel," I say.

He sighs. "Yes, but not in the same sense as when a mortal loses their life."

"What's that supposed to mean?"

"It's not something to worry about, Faith."

"You don't return to Heaven, do you?"

His silence makes the answer obvious. Of course angels don't return to Heaven. If that were the case, they'd probably stand a better chance against demons. They'd have an infinite number of chances to take control of the night, unlike demons—Hell isn't so forgiving.

"The only real threat to an angel's existence on Earth is a demon," he says. "When demons leave this world, they return to Hell as failures. What happens beyond the gates, I have no idea."

"And demons wouldn't send angels back to Heaven," I say. It's not a question. "It's why Dad is Heaven's Traitor. He cost angels their lives."

"Their eternities, Faith," Ezekiel says. "Worth must be proven and fallen angels don't necessarily survive the fight to remain on Earth before falling into Hell. Demons are quick to send them. Your dad is an exception."

I curl my fingers into fists, digging my nails into my palms. "I won't let anything happen to you, Ezekiel. I mean it."

His shoulders relax, but he doesn't turn around to face me. He doesn't respond, either.

I close the distance and run my hands over the tops of his wings. They disappear under my touch, and I stand on my tip-toes and hug Ezekiel from behind, resting my chin in the crook of his shoulder. My heart pounds against his back, trying to escape my chest to get as close as possible to his. He shifts his head to lean against my cheek and slides his hands over mine to lace our fingers together.

"I wish I could make you the same promise, Faith, but it would be a lie. Look at everything you've been through on my watch." He lets out a small breath, just a whisper of sadness that shadows my own heart. "I don't deserve to have you in my life, you know."

I puff out my lips at his thoughts. "You're right. You don't. You deserve so much more than to have to suffer with me. You deserve a life with someone who isn't a losing battle. You shouldn't have to fight the whole universe for me."

He bends forward, flipping me over his shoulder to face him. My heart stalls, seizing at the look he gives me, peering through me and into the emptiness my soul left behind in me. "But I will."

"Loving me is hard, huh?"

He laughs. "You have no idea. But so worth it. You know, when we get a moment to breathe—"

"You'll let me corrupt you?" I ask, smirking, the weight crushing me drifting on the wind he creates, revealing his wings again.

I expect him to laugh, to blush, to return my teasing with something to make me giggle, but he doesn't do any of that. He pulls me closer, leaning in to kiss me so fervently, like kissing me is his new purpose in life. His chest presses into mine, and he picks me up off my feet letting me wrap my legs around his waist. His wings curl forward, covering us, encasing us in our own personal world filled with everything good, bad, and heart exploding between us. His cherry blossom scent mixes with the sweet scent of vanilla clinging to my hair.

He deepens our kiss before I have a chance, gliding his tongue over mine in a way that sends tingles through my whole body. His usual sweet kiss, the one that always teases me, leaving me wanting more, now fills me up, inviting me in, offering me more than a promise of exciting things to follow. Ezekiel's kiss promises me that he'll fight for me, for this, for us. For what we have together despite everything that threatens to ruin us.

Slowly, I break our kiss, gasping into his lips. "I love you."

"You said it out loud." He smiles and kisses me again.

I inhale a shuddering breath. "Still feels like the sky is going to come crashing down on us."

Laughing, he opens his wings. "But it won't. I promise you that."

I smile because he can't lie. "I love you," I say again.

"Have I ever told you that you always know exactly what to say to me? And I love you for that." He kisses me again. "And this."

I laugh and bat his shoulder. "You just wait."

A howl sounds through the air, cutting a moment I never want to end short. Ezekiel sighs but doesn't let any space fall between us. He spins to face the house to look at the porch, and I crane my neck to peer over my shoulder.

Sitting on his haunches, a muscular sandy brown wolf howls again on the porch of Vivian's yellow Victorian house. Kristin appears behind the wolf and pets the top of its head. It brings a blip of grief washing through me. It reminds me of the first time I met her, when the traitor wolves from Moonlight Shores brought her into their pack. Now she's an honorary member of the rogue pack of Desertville.

"Faith, it's time," Kristin says. "Word's out. The pack is moving. They'll lead us to Mary."

Ezekiel expands his shield to her, and she meets my mismatched eyes.

"And then what?" I ask.

She doesn't respond.

Ezekiel tenses.

I sigh. "I'm not going to like it, am I?"

She shakes her head. "I don't know of any other way with the time we have."

I rest my head on Ezekiel's shoulder. "Don't forget the promise you made me."

"The sky won't fall, Faith."

I bury my face in his shoulder. "Not that."

He flaps his wings once and squeezes me tighter. "You have my word."

PRETTY LITTLE DEMON

THE DESERT STRETCHES out for miles on both sides of the two-lane road. There's only one way in and out of town, so the Desertville pack will have to come this way. Ezekiel stands behind me, his fingers putting pressure on my shoulders, digging into my tense muscles to relax me.

"It's just one wolf," he says, mostly to himself.

"That now leads a pack of thirty," Greg says from next to us.

It didn't take much convincing to get Ezekiel to expand his shield to the three rogue wolves. After a moment of utter surprise and a few tears, Greg, Calvin, and Lola swore their allegiance and loyalty to Ezekiel like he was some sort of heavenly king. I laughed and Kristin rolled her eyes. Ezekiel wasn't amused, but he didn't argue. I suppose it's one way to guarantee the goodness of your soul.

"Thirty-one hellhounds come sundown..." Calvin's voice trails off.

"All for one witch who wants to gift the world with more Hell," Lola adds.

"Thank God it's only one," I say. "Imagine a coven. I'd be screwed."

Greg frowns. "The world would be screwed."

"It will be screwed if you guys don't shut up and focus," Kristin snaps. "Now everyone hold your hands out."

Ezekiel hangs his arm over my shoulder without arguing. I think this is the first time he's ever done what Kristin asked without needing to discuss it or have me beg him to be nice and go along with things.

"Before you freak out over the blood, I'm only doing a projection spell. It should be enough to break up the pack so we can separate Joshua from them," she says. Taking my hand for a moment in hers, she adds. "Not yet for you."

I heave a breath of relief. I'm pretty sick of spilling my blood, and I'm sure my palms will never stop aching.

Kristin gently holds Ezekiel's hand on hers. "I know we don't always see everything the same way, but I'm thankful that Faith has you. You have no idea how much she means to me. I want to do right by Grace Blackwell's daughter."

"I do know, Kristin," Ezekiel says. "I feel the imprint you and her mother have left on her soul."

I frown, wanting them to elaborate, but Kristin blinks the tears away from her eyes before they can fall and moves on to cut the palms of the rogue wolves. She motions for the wolves to drip blood into the dirt off the side of the road. Bending down, she scratches her blade through it, making three perfect circles. She slices her own palm and draws a fourth circle.

Kristin waves and motions Ezekiel to step forward. He swipes his hand through the air, his blood clinging to some invisible wall in front of him. What looks like a giant box forms around us when he's through. With his other hand, he summons angelic light, and Kristin runs her ivory blade through it, blessing it. She draws a rectangle along the walls Ezekiel created.

He then release more light, evaporating the blood until only Kristin's lopsided drawings remain on the ground.

"Come nightfall, if we're not out of here, this is where we will meet. The hellhounds won't get to us through the blessed barrier." She looks at me. "It's what I should've done last time, but I was overconfident in my plan. This time, I've already accepted the worst."

I think we all have.

"Have faith, witch," Ezekiel says.

"Maybe if you didn't hog her all the time."

Okay, now things are getting weird. I can hope for Hell to freeze over since my guardian and my self-appointed witch are joking about me.

Lola groans. "I'm sorry your parents named you that. I bet it gets old, fast."

I rub my lips together and say, "It hasn't until now."

Kristin closes the distance and runs her hand over my hair, pushing it from my face. "Cut me a break, Hell child. Ezekiel reminded me a lot of your mom. But now I'm back to annoying him, okay?"

I laugh. "It's my favorite thing."

Ezekiel raises an eyebrow. "And I thought your favorite thing was trying to corrupt me."

"Okay, annoying you is my second favorite."

All three werewolves gape at us, and I blush, my cheeks flaming, because it's not often anyone can hear my and Ezekiel's conversations. He ignores them completely, reaching up to touch my hot cheek before he runs the pad of his thumb across my bottom lip. I don't know if it's because he's finally made a decision he's happy with or if he's deflecting his nerves by focusing on things he's been trying to keep out of his head—either way, when he's teasing me and joking around, things don't seem so world-ending. When he's staring at my lips like he wants to kiss me more than anything, I can ignore the world turning to ash.

But then Kristin grabs my hand, pierces my finger, and swipes the blood over her closed eyelid. Ezekiel reaches into Kristin's bag and pulls out the angel statue.

"I know it doesn't feel like it, but you were lucky you managed to take the totem from Mary. I bet she didn't expect how powerful you really are," Kristin says, keeping her eyes closed. "Now, this might be hard because she's going to expect us now, but you must remember you can fight. Use her spell against her."

Ezekiel offers me the angel statue, and I grip it in my hands.

Kristin draws my branded hand up and places it over her eye. "Blood to blood, a demon's kin, give me sight, let me in. Thin the veil so I can see, if the witch is watching me."

The world around me morphs for a second, bending and stretching like I'm staring at everything in a funhouse mirror. My stomach rolls, nausea making my insides want to come up. Ezekiel holds onto me, and I wobble. Sweat breaks out on my forehead, dripping down to sting my eyes.

"I don't feel so good," I say, my breathing quickening.

"That's what happens when you reach out to me, my pretty little demon. It's so wonderful to see you now." Mary's voice drifts into my mind.

My stomach clenches, and I dry heave. "Kristin, stop."

I'm not sure I've even said the words out loud.

Mary's figure comes into view in my blurry vision. "Stop? But this is so fun. I see you've gathered your own pack of wolves to break. They're absolutely stunning. So fitting for Raphael Blackwell's daughter. And to think I almost wasted such a marvelous life for Hell beasts. I'd much prefer to make a demon bow."

I open my mouth to respond, but instead of words, I throw up black blood all over the dirt. My stomach convulses, sending me forward to grip my knees.

"See? It's not so bad. It'll get easier when you're reborn into the creature you were made to be. And now, I know where to find you. Your father could never resist such strong wolves. I knew you'd be the same. Your angel can shield you, but he can't hide you forever."

I groan, the pain coursing through me sending me to the ground. My hair drapes down, veiling the world around me. I swallow, forcing my mouth to work. "I'm not my dad," I say. "He's Heaven's Traitor. I will never be like him."

Something hot touches my shoulder, scorching my skin. "You'll be worse. You'll make all of Heaven fall."

"I won't."

"Graced by Heaven and born from Hell, hear my words, hear my spell. An angel's light will steal the dark. An angel's hope will fill your heart. From blood to blood, from dark to light, return the shield, block her sight."

Mary glides back, crossing her arms over her chest. I struggle to get to my feet and lose my balance as another wave of sickness washes over me. My cheek hits the sand, and I blow a puff of dirt into the air.

"Such lovely power," Mary muses. "If only she hadn't thrown away all her potential...then again, she gave me you."

"Daughter of dark, daughter of light, use the veil, control the night." Kristin's words pull at my very essence, stinging me in my core. It feels like I'm being ripped apart while Mary holds me in her gaze and Kristin struggles to pull me back.

"Faith!" Ezekiel yells. "Now!"

It takes everything in me to remember what I was supposed to do. The second Kristin started saying the spell, it was like my brain turned to mush with the rest of my insides that threaten to spill out again.

Taking a breath, I push to my knees and summon Hell power in my hands. The perfect orb swirls in my fingers, shining with the new orange light that has taken over the usual ruby-red color.

Mary smiles. "Beautiful."

And then the angel statue appears.

Mary leaps forward toward the totem, and I jerk my arm back and throw the ball of power at her, but instead of hitting her, I aim for the space next to her. The world shudders, her form blinking in and out of existence. Her eyes widen as she tries to pick up the angel statue. I summon more power and throw it directly at the statue. It sparkles and beams, and Hell power scatters around us.

A strange crack fissures the invisible wall. Darkness seeps through, dripping like black oil to burn on the ground around Mary. My eyes train on the oil, watching it crawl across the dirt, smoldering everything in its wake except for two oval shapes.

Footprints.

"A demon's kin, full of might, break the spell, break the sight. With Hell power, you'll burn through, the witch's words binding you. With blood so black but soul so white, come together and always fight. Destroy everything that you see, use all your power, and return to me."

I ignite power again, willing every last drop of it to fill my hands until I can't summon any more. I thrust it forward, shooting it at the footprints separating the oil. A scream rips through the air, piercing my ears, burning through my head. Mary's image splits in two as her projection protecting her falters. She explodes before me, showering me in the black oil.

Strong hands wrap around my waist, pulling me to my feet, and Ezekiel wipes the oil from my face with the hem of his shirt. I heave, my stomach still reeling. I throw up again, black, greasy blood splashing across the dirt.

Ezekiel rubs his hand across my back until I get my body under control. The others watch me silently, waiting for me to say something. I thought I was prepared to face Mary, but I don't think I ever will be. She was stronger than ever, stealing my sight, getting into my head.

"You did great, Faith," Kristin says. "Mary might be a powerful witch, but she doesn't have what I have."

I grimace. "If you even say me, I'm going to—"

"She doesn't have the devotion I do. She wants you for power, but me? I want you for you. You're family, and I'm not letting go of the one person I have left, not so soon after I've found you," Kristin says.

"So, did it work?" I ask. "Did I sever the link from her mark?"

Kristin tugs the front of my shirt just low enough to look at the skin over my heart. In the center of the feather tattoo is an empty space where the lip print should be. I touch my fingers to the spot, my skin feeling icy.

"You did it," she says. "She won't be able to get into your head when your guard's down now."

"But she knows where I am," I say.

Kristin pats my shoulder. "Don't worry. Ezekiel's shield protects us. We'll get her when her back is turned."

The sound of an engine hums in my ears, and I draw my attention toward the empty road. I can't believe I managed to cut Mary off from me by blasting the very essence she dug into me as she hid behind the same kind of projection we're about to use now. I haven't been able to fend Mary off, because she knew I'd attack her, so she basically used a decoy to fool me. And that stupid, evil angel statue helped me do it.

The three rogue wolves release low growls simultaneously, the deep rumble sending goosebumps over my skin. I spot the caravan of cars in the distance, heading in this direction and out of town like we predicted.

Because come dark, the demons will cross into the world. And they're gathering here. I can feel them. The same shiver I used to get at sunset clings to me now. Raising my hand to my eye, I peer around. Forms shift and move through the gnarled trees of the sunlight prison realm. There will be a second while crossing the veil where they'll feel me if I don't escape before, especially since Ezekiel can't take us to the sky.

Because when demons gather, the angels will soon follow.

All of them looking for the spot where I've weakened the veil. And if they find me, half will bow, half will rise. All of them waiting to tear me apart.

And then there's Mary.

If I can't get to her first, she'll be there to stitch me back together.

So, I'll die. I will never be her pretty little demon.

16

SEVER THE BOND

"A WITCH WITH her wolves of three, mirror our bodies and let them see. A creature of Hell tied to night, hear our voices, give them fool's sight. Draw them out, lure them in, make them bow, to a demon's kin. Break the hold of Hell's witch, hear my spell, make them switch."

"Oh, damn," Calvin says, releasing a whistle through his teeth. It's like he's looking in a mirror.

Greg reaches forward and waves his hand through the visual manifestation of himself standing next to Calvin's. "So how do they work?"

"They're your doppelgangers. They'll do what you do but are what the pack wolves will see. When we were forced into hiding by the demons and hunters, it was one of our defense mechanisms and something we're taught to do the moment we can talk. It's helped keep us alive. Very few people actually see a true witch. You're more likely to see their doppelgangers or familiars."

"Familiars?" I ask.

Sadness lines her eyes. "Wolves are mine. An unfortunate connection I share with Mary. Christopher found me first through your dad. The others followed." Her gaze flicks away. "I don't go searching or breaking people to use if that's what you're thinking. They were my family."

"I wasn't thinking it," I say.

She nods toward the others. "But they were."

I peer at Greg, Calvin, and Lola and back to Kristin. "Now them?" I whisper.

She smirks. "They don't even know it yet."

My heart swells at the thought that after everything we've been through, after everything we've lost, the universe still manages to give us something to keep us going. For Kristin, it was me and now her new wolf pack.

But even if fate brings us together, it's cruel enough to rip us apart.

Tires squeal, jerking my attention toward the two-lane road. The sun hovers low in the sky, counting down the short amount of time we have to separate Joshua from his pack and complete the botched spell Kristin performed. We need to finish it to get to Mary. She's coming for us, but all it takes is turning the pack leader against her to give us a fighting chance.

The pack is too large and will rise to fight against anyone who threatens the witch who offered them immortality. She knew exactly how to pick a werewolf for her cause, to shift power from Heaven again, to bring Hell onto mortals instead of the demons born from the pits of Hell. It was only a matter of time that someone would try to undo everything the angelic army had done to help mortals flourish—everyone thought it would be another demon to try. I don't even think werewolves were on anyone's radars. And witches? There are so few left.

"Get ready, Faith. I need your blood, power, and access to the veil," Kristin says. "And we must be quick. The moment it's done, Ezekiel will get you out of here and you'll wait for my summons."

I bob my head, fear snaking around me, tying itself to my chest and stomach, squeezing me so tightly it's hard to move or breathe. "And then we'll take care of Mary."

"Yes, and then we'll stop that witch from ever trying to turn you again. We'll show the angelic army you're not a threat."

At least one of us has hope. All I can wish for is to not end up as a demon. I can't stand to think of turning into the creature taking over my vision.

Kristin takes my hand. "I won't let you down."

I nod.

She turns to the rogue wolves. "Spread out. I need the pack to scatter."

I turn away as the werewolves transform with a resonating cracking and shifting of bones that makes me shiver. They leave their clothes near the safe spot Ezekiel helped Kristin make, and race away with Greg leading the way before they break off in different directions.

Car doors slam, and howls rip through the air. Standing with Kristin, we watch the wolves make their move. Greg, with his black fur, creeps closer to the cars, releasing a small whimper. He sits on his haunches, staring at the caravan. Cacophonous howls rip through the quiet desert out of sync, forcing me to concentrate on the soft panting coming from Greg so I push the rest of the noise away.

Joshua struts down the line of cars, several people following behind him. I expect him to glower, to send his pack after the rogue wolf, to do everything in his power to see that Greg pays for leaving his pack and taking others with him. But Joshua only grins.

He holds his arms open. "I knew you'd return to us, little cousin. You're making a good decision. Come nightfall, you won't have to worry about demons anymore. Mary is coming. She will perform your blood rites. And luckily for you, she has expressed great interest in you, Greg. Said you had great potential to rise from the ashes."

Greg stands, hackles shooting up on his back, and then he

launches himself at the pack leader. Joshua snarls as the wolf collides into him, and they both fall to the ground. Greg snaps at Joshua, but the pack leader locks his fingers into Greg's fur and thrusts him away. Greg skids across the dirt, sending a brown cloud into the air.

He snaps his frothy jowls, releasing another growl. Joshua whistles, the high-pitched noise ringing in my ears, and the familiar sound of breaking and shifting bones overtakes the sound of Greg's growls.

The rogue wolf launches at Joshua once more, but instead of smashing into the prepared pack leader, he lands on the hood of a car, denting the metal, before darting off in the other direction. A few figures streak through the cars, running so fast I could never dream of outrunning them if I had to, and they chase the black wolf into the desert.

Both Calvin and Lola sneak out from the brush, charging toward the pack leader. They don't get a chance to get within reach of him before more wolves race from the caravan. I count a dozen more wolves remaining, but twelve is better than thirty.

"Think we can handle them?" I ask.

"Not we. You," Kristin says. "Zeke, last chance to back out from the fight."

Ezekiel summons heavenly light into his hands. "This is for the greater good. This is for Faith."

"All right. Faith, you get Joshua. I'll be right behind you. Featherhead, separate the others but stay alert. We have thirty minutes until sundown. We have to be out of here in twenty unless you want to force me to spend the night here when Hell breaks free."

Ezekiel smirks.

I smack his arm before he can say anything. "We'll be out in fifteen."

Kristin inhales a long breath, opens her palm, and cuts herself. She motions for me to do the same, and I squeeze a few drops of my blood into her uncut palm to use when she's ready. Ezekiel leans over, kisses me softly, and expands his wings.

"I won't be far," he says. Bending his legs, he launches a few dozen feet into the air, but never leaves my view.

I press my hands together, staunching the small cut on my palm and pull Hell power from the depths of my being. A wave of dizziness sends me reeling. I teeter, taking a few steps to find my balance. Looking at my hands, I realize there's barely a quarter size orb of power. Confusion washes over me, and I concentrate on growing the demonic power, but nothing happens.

"Faith," Kristin says from next to me. "You're going to need more than that."

I twist my lips to the side. "You don't think I know that?"

I squeeze my eyes shut, my legs wobbling again. My shoulders droop, my arms suddenly feeling heavy. But it's not due to gathering more power. I'm tired. My adrenaline fades the longer I stand, and the few minutes with Mary wore me down.

Kristin pinches my wrist. "Your power doesn't just go away. With every heartbeat, that demon blood pumps through you, giving you more. You better find it."

I open my eyes. "I'm telling you, it's not there."

"It is."

"It's not."

Kristin yanks my hand up and forces my branded palm over my soulless eye. "Look for it. Now."

I startle at the shift in my vision, the sunlight prison realm overlaying the desert landscape in a new Hell appearance. A strange glow covers my hand, sending my black veins aglow. Though the firelight shines, it's like something dark slithers through me, threatening to consume me and take over.

I turn my attention to Joshua, to the caravan of cars and the eerie symphony of howling Hell beasts, burning in front of me. My vision flashes between wolf and hellhound, the inner evil of the wolf pack on full display for me to see. They're tethered to Earth by their humanity like I am, yet the absolute darkness eating away at us binds us to a world we're not made to enter.

"Faith, hurry!" Kristin's voice tugs at my consciousness, tearing me away from my vision to drop me into reality.

Bright orange molten power erupts in my hand, summoned directly from my inner demon only showing itself in my vision, and I drop my hand from my eye. The power remains moving and shifting, swirling with life like the very essence of Hell manifested into my hand to give me what I needed to push forward. To fight.

Narrowing my vision on Joshua, who waves his hand to instruct his wolf pack what to do as part of them chase the rogue wolves, I turn off the world around me until all my senses devote themselves to him.

I separate my power, pooling it in both of my hands, and charge closer. Wind blows my hair as Ezekiel flies forward, making the first move. Blinding light flashes through the air, drawing the wolves' attention up toward the sky. He blasts his power, sending the werewolves still remaining in human form to the ground. Those in their true bodies yip and bark, taking cover under the cars.

Joshua releases another whistle.

Pulling my hand back, I focus on the car next to him. I chuck my demonic power at it, and the door explodes right off the frame. The shockwave of the blast knocks Joshua forward, and he scrambles to his feet, spinning wildly, searching for a threat he can't see yet.

Throwing another orb of power, I hit the dirt next to his feet. A man in a flannel shirt and jeans grabs Joshua to pull him away. I thrust demonic power at them again and strike a truck. The front windshield explodes, sending pebble-like glass spraying through the air.

Joshua and the man run for another car to take cover. If they manage to get in and drive away, we'll lose our chance. Charging forward, I race for the two werewolves. Ezekiel blasts light beam after light beam, startling and scaring the panicking wolves out of my way so they don't disrupt the strength of the protection shield Ezekiel covers me with. I can't risk Joshua finding out where I'm coming from until it's too late for him to run.

I close the distance, stalking Joshua like a demon stalks its prey, terrorizing him because I can. I want him to know what his plans have done to me. What his allegiance to Mary stole from me. Breaking this man down, showing him the consequences of his actions, making him bow—none of that feels good to me. Revenge doesn't taste sweet in this moment. It's bitter, leaving a dark feeling sweeping through my being. Because taking him down doesn't change the past. It doesn't change that I touched Hell, that Ezekiel holds my soul, that I can open the veil—destroy it enough to make the universe quiver.

I wish with everything in me that something, even just a second of what's happening, felt right. Because then my heart would stop pumping in overdrive, my inner demon wouldn't fight so hard to relish in the destruction of this pack who might yearn for power but really acts out of desperation.

And how can I truly blame them for trying anything they can to not feel weak. Or broken. Useless. Pointless. Because we are alike. We're both victims of our heritage, of our circumstances. We're both tired.

But the difference between me and Joshua, the difference that pushes me to keep going, is that he's turning into the very thing that has hurt him. He'd rather be the tormenter—he's willing to take everyone he loves down with him to be what he has despised all along. And me? I want to learn to live with myself. I want to rise up to defend against the monsters who haunt me. I want to see to it that they stop leaving a path of bodies in their wake. Joshua, a man who fights evil with evil still isn't good. He'll leave a path of destruction, ashes as his only heir.

For me, the path I leave will bloom with hope and promise.

Joshua pulls the man with him, and they race into the brush, running from the fiery cars. I send one more blast of power, hitting the ground in front of them, and Joshua pushes his pack mate into it, stepping on the man's body as he screams.

Hands grab my sides, yanking me forward faster than I can run. I extend my arms and wrap them around Joshua from behind. Ezekiel releases me, and I force the pack leader into the ground. He roars, bucking under me. The world flashes, one second he's a man, the next, a hellhound. My two fire branded arms shove his face into the dirt with the strength of my inner demon.

I breathe long gasps through my teeth, my vision turning red. Joshua screams, his shirt smoldering under my touch.

"I'm sorry," I whisper, the realization of what's about to happen cooling the rage soaking my core. "I wish there was another way, but you made a choice while I've had mine taken away."

Joshua growls. "I'll tear your face off."

A shadow crosses over me and droplets of inky black liquid splash over Joshua's dirty cheek. He screams, his wails hurting my ears. I cringe, but I don't let go, watching as small tendrils of smoke waft from his skin.

Kristin kneels down and runs her fingers through the blood

on his face, smearing it. "A beast of night and firelight, bound to Hell, hear my spell. Shift your bones, split your heart, hide your fur, rip apart. Sever the bond, to the witch. You're mine now, make the switch. A demon's daughter will make you bow, your soul alight is hers now. Hell power from angel's light, ignite the curse and burn the night. At sunrise with the break of day, wolf you'll be, wolf you'll stay. Leashed to one of Heaven and Hell, hear me now, hear my spell."

Joshua's body contorts, his bones shifting and moving. His yells turn into a howl, and his wolf form collapses under me without a fight. An oily substance seeps from his fur, coming through the pores in his skin.

"Use your power now," Kristin whispers.

Tears swell in my eyes, and I do what she says. Through the veil, I watch the hellhound rise to his feet and bow forward in front of me. I reach out and rub my fingers across his head.

The sun dips toward the horizon so quickly in the light prison world that I lose sense of time. I drop my hand from my face, forcing myself to roll off the broken wolf. He's not cursed to an eternity at a demon's side, but his fate now lies in my hands.

I thought we were different until this very moment.

Because a monster stares back at me in the shine of his oily skin.

A soft thump sounds behind me and wind swirls my hair from my neck, cooling off the heat threatening to ignite my skin to reveal the true body of my demon self hiding in mortality under my flesh and bones.

Ezekiel kneels next to me, touching his cool hand to my shoulder. "We must go."

I turn to Kristin. "What now?"

She rolls Joshua over, his limp body unconscious, but his chest still rises and falls. "You wait for my summons."

I nod, a sinking feeling threatening to change my mind.

Because night will soon fall, trapping me in the Veiled Realm, which means I'll have to break the veil.

But this time it isn't to save Kristin.

I'm going to trap a witch.

17

BORN FROM LOVE

THE BRILLIANT MOON shines overhead, lighting a silver path down the onyx road leading into the mist. I sit on the ground, knees to my chest, and rest my chin on them. Ezekiel paces in front of me, hiding and revealing his wings over and over again. A black feather drifts through the air, and I reach out and cup it in my hands.

"You should sit down," I say.

Ezekiel freezes in his spot and turns to me. "This is taking too long."

I raise my hand to my eye for the millionth time. The dark

desert of Earth looms around us. We're far enough away from civilization that if Kristin doesn't succeed or if our plan fails, we'll be alone come sunrise. The poor inhabitants of Desertville will have had quite the surprise at Hell's Palace, and I'm sure the angelic army and the Hunter's Alliance would have arrived by now to keep the demons under control. It's what has Ezekiel on edge. Demons? We can handle. Everyone else? He won't fight them. I wouldn't ask him to.

I pat the spot next to me. "This might be our last chance to be together, you know. Do you really want to pace it away?"

He whips his gaze from the sky to me, a new darkness shadowing the light usually shining with intensity. I shrink back, digging my hands into the compacted dirt. He struts closer and towers over me, his expansive wings blocking the view. His hard jaw tightens even more, a vein bulging in his neck, and all I can do is gape. In a matter of seconds, the soft, sweet vulnerable side of my angel has been obliterated by my remark, leaving behind an angel deserving of Heaven's highest ranks—fierce, determined, unwavering, devoted. Everything about Ezekiel's goodness entices me as he embodies a true heavenly warrior so much so, that even my inner demon cowers. And I love that it does.

His nostrils flare as he inhales, and his wings disappear. "Faith, I..." Strolling forward, he kneels in front of me and takes my hands into his. He brings them up to his face and presses them into his cheek like the feeling of my skin against his can somehow make the world right.

I shift forward so my knees aren't separating us. I press my body to his, letting his wings brush my arms. Our foreheads touch, our hearts beat together, and his wings stir my hair from my shoulders.

"I know you want me to have hope, Ezekiel, but I can't hold onto something I know I might lose. It'll break me if I even think for a minute everything's going to work out for me," I say.

"It is," he says. "I'm not losing you."

My heart falters. He doesn't lie, but he can't possibly know it'll work out. And stating he's not losing me? That would mean... "You promised me, Ezekiel."

His eyes harden. "I'm not losing you."

"You don't have a choice in the matter!" My voice rises through the air, and I pull back. "Do you hear yourself? I will *not* be a demon. I will *not* be like my dad. Do you understand?"

He shakes his head. "Raphael has his flaws. We all do. People make it work. I love you, Faith. I don't think I will survive losing you. You are my purpose."

Tears burn my eyes. "Your purpose will change. You will go on."

His face falls, his steely façade shattering. He breaks, his wings sagging, his eyes glassing over. "But, Faith."

I clench my jaw. "I love you, Ezekiel, but I will not allow our love to destroy us like it did my parents. Look at where it left them."

"We're stronger."

I press my lips together, staring into his intense dark eyes. "You said you wouldn't fail me."

"What you ask would be me failing you."

"Ezekiel, please," I whisper. "If you do this, I won't forgive you. You'll ruin my eternity."

"Just like I've ruined mine."

Pain unlike anything I've ever experienced washes over me, tugging at my heart, ripping me from my core to tear me apart. How could Ezekiel have changed so suddenly? He knew what I wanted out of eternity, but it's like my wants don't matter anymore. And I'm afraid. His words claw at me, igniting alarms of panic through my being. I'm afraid of his undoing, and what that means for him.

I clutch his face, searching his dark eyes for answers. We were fine before sunset. We were fine when we caught Joshua. And now, something's shifted. I can feel it the longer I look at him, touch him, hear him breathing.

"Ezekiel, I don't understand. Have you fallen?" I have to get the words out there. He still radiates with light, with a pureness that sings to me, yet I can't get over the unbidden dread coursing through me.

"I don't know," he says, his jaw tensing. "I'm only certain that I can't lose you. I can't do as you've asked. It doesn't feel right."

"But it's what's right for me. It's my choice, and my choice alone to make."

"What about me?"

"This isn't about you." I frown as the words escape my lips. The words release a cloud of darkness through me. How selfish of me to even think that for a second. Because this is more than me.

He wraps his arms around me, burying his face into my shoulder. Dad always chided me for crying. He yelled at me so frequently that I started to despise crying myself. Crying makes me feel weak. It doesn't change the world around me. It does nothing but make things worse. But seeing an angel cry, feeling the injustice he feels, the anger and darkness snuffing out his light, it doesn't make him seem weak. It makes him feel human. And it does change the world around me. It might not give me the hope Ezekiel so desperately needs to cling on to, but it gives me the will to fight. And fight hard.

I will not back down. Turning into a demon or dying? I will not accept those fates. I'm the daughter of Raphael and Grace Blackwell. I wasn't born from evil. I wasn't born from their selfishness. I was born from love. From hope. From light.

"You're right," Ezekiel says.

I groan. "I didn't mean it like that. It's just—you say you can't live without me, but I can't exist without you. You've seen the monster inside me. You've seen what it could do. That demon? That's what I'll be. And it's not me. You carry my soul, Ezekiel. What do you think will happen to it? I can't live an existence split in two."

"You won't be," he says, his voice lowering.

"Of course Heaven will sever me and doom me. They'll

send my soul to Hell with my body."

He puffs out a small breath. "Faith, no one will let that happen—especially not Raphael and Kristin."

"But you have my soul. Heaven will make you—"

"I will not lose you," Ezekiel says. "I don't care about the consequences, Faith. I don't care what this means for my eternity. I won't lose you now. I won't. I can't."

"But being a demon? I'm still lost to you. I won't ruin you like that."

"We'll figure it out."

"No. There's nothing to figure out."

"Faith, ple—"

"From light to dark and dark to light, hear my spell through the night..." Kristin's words whisper through the air, and a tingling sensation washes over me.

A tear spills on my cheek. "Ezekiel, she's calling."

He stiffens. "I need you to stop thinking this is the end, okay? I know hope is hard for you to carry, but we will overcome this no matter what. I believe we will. I don't think my purpose is a lost cause. I think it was given to me, because I will fight for it. I will fight for you, Faith."

"Blood to blood from red to black, break the veil, I summon you back. With angel wings and love's pure light, use your vision, use your sight. A witch's call will leave a mark, use the light to see through the dark. A broken beast will lead the way, follow the fire, and do not stray. From blood to blood, a mix of Heaven and Hell, hear my words, hear my spell."

My whole body jerks forward out of my control, and I skid across the dirt unable to get to my feet. Wind gusts around me, and Ezekiel launches into the air. I scream, my voice echoing through the quiet of the Veiled Realm. Cool fingers grip my waist, pulling me from the dirt, scraping my skin.

Ezekiel yanks me back, but Kristin's spell pulls me forward, not giving either of us a choice but to follow her summons. Ezekiel flies, keeping me off the ground. We're caught on an imaginary tether, being dragged through the night and toward the gnarled, silently wailing trees that make up the forest.

"I'm scared," I whisper.

"I won't let anything happen to you."

"You told me you could never promise me that because it would be a lie."

Ezekiel dives us lower, sending my stomach to my throat. "I'm not lying."

Covering my face with my hands, I peer through the veil at the dark desert. Dozens of fireballs glow in the distance, the hellhounds of Mary's creation littering the night. Dread seeps through me, causing my body to tremble, and I drop my hands from my face.

"What if this doesn't work?" I ask.

"It will," Ezekiel says.

"Of blood and night, and love and sight, break the veil, summon Hell. Call upon the demon within, pull it out, let it win. The power of evil with Heaven's light, the power in you will give you fight. A witch's curse, you will break. A witch's life, you will take. A darkness shines from your eyes. The kin of Heaven's Traitor now will rise. To leash the Hell fury of night. Feel her power, feel her smite."

My entire being screams, fire erupting from my heart to consume my flesh in rivers of molten flames. The world blinks in and out, my vision blurring. The mist steams against my skin, though the coolness does nothing for the heat smoldering through me.

Ezekiel suddenly lets me go, and I free fall, dropping from the sky like a burning comet on a crash course to smash into Earth to unleash Hell's fury. I cover my eyes, blocking the freezing wind, and the desert of the Earth realm returns to view. More hellhounds gather like glowing beacons, creating a pathway directly where I'm supposed to head.

The ground rushes up on me, and I brace for an impact that doesn't come. Icy hands grip my fingers, slowing me down, and I hit the ground with a soft thud and somersault a few times until my body finally slows to a stop. Heaving a breath, I stare up at the bright moon above me and watch it crawl across the sky impossibly fast. But that's how the Veiled Realm is. Time rushes by until the veil thins to release me.

But even with the moon heading toward the horizon, I don't have time to wait. I need to open the veil and pull her in. I need to sever her power from Earth so I can end this and return the balance from creatures of Hell with no purpose but to destroy, to take, to break, to ruin the world without limitation and consequence.

Ezekiel towers over me, his glorious black wings glowing with ethereal light, pushing away the mist. He peers at me with a tight jaw and hard eyes, the grief and desperation now frozen over in a steely expression sharp enough to stab into me.

He extends his hand out. Blisters mar his skin, his hands red and burned. "I'm sorry. I tried to hold onto you."

I blink a few times and reach out to take his hand. My heart rams against my ribcage, my stomach twisting at the sight of my own arm now charred and smoking in the cool air. Orange liquid fire courses through my veins, trailing through my body, burning my power through me.

I suck in a quivering breath and cover my face with my hands instead of letting Ezekiel help me to my feet. Sharp horns prick my fingers, sending black blood dripping onto my shirt. "Don't look at me," I cry, my voice hoarse like I have a sore throat, though I feel no pain. "I don't want you to see me like this. What has she done? This wasn't part of the plan."

Ezekiel yanks my hands from my face and pulls me to my feet by my wrists. "It's just a spell reacting with this world. This isn't your true body, Faith."

"But it's what I'll become," I say. "How can you even stand to be beside me?"

He pulls me into his arms, hugging me. "I'll love you regardless. No matter what. No matter where."

He's not saying it to make me feel better. He's saying it because it's true. I feel it in my essence, in my soul radiating through his skin, glowing on the loose feathers drifting around us in the wind created by his wings.

"Ezekiel," I whisper.

"I'll walk through Hell for you."

"I won't let you," I whisper. "I'm not letting anything happen to you."

It's all I can say to stop the panic rising through me at his words. He's willing to fall from grace to see to it that I live, that I have an existence on Earth with him. But I'm not willing to let him give up everything he knows, turn his back on an existence with a greater purpose than what I've become.

He nods and smiles. The first one he's given me since...I can't remember. I was sure I'd die without seeing another one of his smiles again. Tilting his head, he brushes his lips to mine, kissing me softly even though I embody Hell.

My lips tingle, burning under his grace, but it's worth every ounce of pain to experience his kiss one more time—because this very well might be the last one we ever share.

I pull away at the same time I push the thought from my mind. Ezekiel brushes his fingers along my cheek once more and then takes a step back. My heart aches at the foot of space between us. I see the ache reflecting in Ezekiel's eyes, and he reaches for my free hand and laces our fingers together despite the spell making it painful for the both of us to touch.

Taking a deep breath, I draw my hand to my eye and peer around the dark night now set aglow with firelight from the Hell beasts.

I tense, a human figure standing in the night amid the

wolves. I'd recognize the red glow of Mary's eyes anywhere. Kristin was right about the witch coming here, coming for me. She promised Ezekiel would mess up and break the shield so I couldn't hide forever. She said—I refuse to even think of what else she predicted.

I step closer and notice someone kneeling at her feet. A wave of jealousy sneaks up on me, and I summon power in my hands. I startle at my reaction to seeing Joshua at Mary's feet in his human form. I knew he would be here with his pack, but what I didn't expect was for me to be jealous that the wolf Kristin bound to me was showing devotion, uncontrolled devotion to Mary.

I blow a puff of air through my lips. "I'm doomed," I whisper softly.

Ezekiel touches my shoulder. "It's the spell. Don't let it get into your head, Faith. You need to keep your sight clear."

He's right. If I forget for even a second about who I am under this demonic exterior, it's all over.

"From the depths of Hell, hear my spell. I summon thee to hear my pleas. I offer a vow and will bow. With this knife, I give you life. Heaven will falter and will fall, we will rise and rule them all. A demon holds the power of sight. She will break the binds of night. With blood and power and angel's smite, we will destroy all who fight. Blood to blood from red to black, I offer Hell a body back. A soul unbound will set free, a demon left behind, she will be."

Guttural howls sound through the night, and more figures

come through the darkness. I gasp at the sight of the three rogue wolves and Kristin being pushed forward through the brush to face Mary. The hellhounds close in, bringing more light to the scene unfolding in front of me.

I don't understand.

They weren't supposed to be here.

"No!" I yell.

Ezekiel grabs me before I run forward. "Faith, wait."

"I have to help them!"

"Calm down. Kristin knows what she's doing. This is part of the plan."

I turn to him with wide eyes. "No it wasn't, Ezekiel. We were supposed to do this alone. If I had known she was going to put herself in the line of fire, I'd—"

"Have never agreed."

Rage rushes through me, and I ignite more power in my hands. "How could you keep this from me?"

"I'm sorry. It was the only way," he says.

"What do you mean?"

"Because Kristin didn't think you'd break the veil otherwise."

I grimace. "She doubts my ability?"

He shakes his head.

"Then what?"

A howl screeches through the night, pulling my attention from Ezekiel. Mary circles the rogue pack and Kristin, her voice ringing through the night like there isn't a veil separating us, but I know it's still there. It buzzes against my skin.

Ezekiel unleashes heavenly light in his palms without answering my question.

"A witch with a pack of three, you will all bow to me. Accept the power of the night, Hell will let you withstand the fight. In the day you will thrive, and in the night you will survive. A contract to Hell, I will break, but I must have your soul to take. With a gift of blood to me. I now have the key. From blood to blood and light to dark, Heaven will fall apart."

My chest tightens at the words. "Ezekiel, then what?" I ask again.

But I don't have the chance to find out.

A hellhound zooms from the darkness, streaking across the desert. It launches at the rogue wolves, knocking them into each other and into the dirt. Mary grabs Kristin by the hair, exposing her neck.

Thrusting my hands out, I launch my Hell power at the veil. Orange sparks light the night, and a hole sucks away the misty air around me.

I charge forward through the Veiled Realm, my heart pumping demonic power through my glowing veins, my heart pounding so loudly, it's all I can focus on.

"Faster, Faith!" Ezekiel yells, pushing me forward.

Light explodes through the night, turning the dark desert aglow, but not with the fire of Hell. It's Heaven's light.

But Ezekiel's behind me.

And then I see the shadow of wings.

DAUGHTER OF A TRAITOR

I BLAST POWER at Mary, focusing my sight only on her. The onyx blade falls from her hand, and Kristin reaches down and picks it up. She swipes it across her palm, flicking her blood at Mary.

"Blood to blood from me to you, a curse will now ring so true. I lock your power in the night, you will fall to the light. Hell's fury from a demon's kin, will give you sight and let you in."

Power bursts in my hands, battling the bright ethereal light streaking and colliding in the sand around us. Mary swivels, searching the night, but she can't see anything beyond the glow

258

of her Hell beasts. All angelic shields remain up. It's the one thing I have on my side.

I thrust my power at Joshua unwavering at Mary's side, and he ignites in the flames of Hell, his bones shifting and moving, yanking away his humanity to serve by my side as a demon's daughter, now cursed to show my demon within for all the world—all the universe to see.

"A hound of night and firelight, you will now lose the sight. Bow down to a demon's kin, let Hell take you in. Skin and bones rip apart, ignite fire in your heart. Hear my voice, hear my vow, listen to your master, you will bow."

Mary spins again. Joshua launches at her, turning against the witch who promised him eternity on Earth by her side. He knocks her off her feet, snapping his teeth to her shoulder and dragging her in my direction.

The soft thuds of feet landing on the dirt draw my attention away from Joshua dragging Mary. Angelic light blasts through the air at the hole I tore in the veil as the angelic army seals it off, covering the very place I need to be.

Heaven's light erupts from the sky, hitting Joshua in the process, knocking him away from Mary. Summoning power, I throw it into the air without aiming. I need the angels to back off and let me finish this.

Ezekiel grabs my arm. "Faith, no!"

Bright light blinds me, sending shadows in my vision. I drop to my knees, screaming as pain blisters over my skin, burning me in the holiness clinging even to the air stirred by an angel's wings.

More light bursts out, this time from beside me. Ezekiel shoots his own power toward the sky, though it could never hurt an angel. It's pure and good, and hopefully they'll realize I'm not a threat.

"I'm trying to help!" I yell. "Stop!"

But nothing changes.

No one stops.

Pushing onto my hands, forcing myself up through the pain, I turn my head up and freeze. Mary's red eyes stare at me from a foot away as she crawls toward me. Ezekiel rushes to me, blasting light into Mary's face, but all she does is smile, her red eyes burning brighter than ever.

"Faith, the veil. Now!" Kristin yells.

I gather power in my palms, and another wave of light washes over me, making me scream once more.

"An angel's shield broken for me, revealing a demon I can see. With Heaven's power full of light, they will rip you from the night. Blood to blood from red to black, Hell will take your body back. An angel will rise to face them all, and then he will surely fall. You will bow down for me, my pretty demon you will be." Mary's voice sounds over the ringing noise from the angelic fight.

The world blurs around me, dust and dirt, light and night—everything blending together, making my head spin.

"Faith, again," Ezekiel says.

I summon power once more and just as quickly the angelic

army attacks me with light again, burning through me because of Kristin's spell.

"Ezekiel, you must hold them off. She has to open the veil," Kristin says, swiping her dagger toward one of the hellhounds closing in on her.

Ezekiel gives me a serious look, his eyes glassing over for a second before he blinks the sheen away. As his wings unfold and expand out, I freeze, holding his intense gaze that speaks volumes in this moment.

"Ezekiel, don't," I whisper. "Please. I'll surrender to them. I'm okay with my fate."

He offers me a sad smile, a look screaming this might be goodbye and that he loves me. His one look breaking my heart into a million pieces.

Because he's chosen to rise against Heaven. He's chosen to fight for me.

And he's about to truly and irrevocably fall from grace.

Bending his knees, he launches into the air, giving me a moment of darkness. The darkness I need to summon the fury within me to face Mary. This is her doing. She did this to me. But I will not let her take me. I will not bow. I will prove to Heaven that this is all for them and humanity. That my life is better off here.

Pushing to my feet, I yank her off the ground, gripping her wrist tight enough that she yells out.

"I will not be your demon," I say, siphoning the power of my rage and grief from the pits of Hell simmering in my heart, igniting because of the unjust world spinning around me. The world that stole everything from me because of who I am. Because of whom I love. Because of what I must do to survive.

The orange Hell power licks my skin, and I launch it into the night, exploding the veil that now filters over the Earth realm, inviting me back in. Angelic light flickers from above like bursts of fireworks sparkling in the air, but none of them gets to me.

I push Mary forward into the Veiled Realm, and the mist steams on both our skins.

She scrambles to her feet, scratching her sharp nail across her own palm and waves her blood through the air to set a spell into motion. She might have survived my power when I turned her to ash after she nearly succeeded sending Dad to Hell, but she has no idea of who she's dealing with now. No doppelganger or spell has a chance against my inner demon—against me.

I thrust a burst of power in her direction, but her image only wavers before me. The rainbow medallion lights up, sending beams of color through the mist. A low growl sounds through the air, and I straighten my shoulders as a hellhound slinks past me toward Mary.

"From the depths of Hell, hear my spell. A demon true, I summon you. Bound to day, destroy the night, you will let me use your sight."

Pressure erupts behind my eyes and the world shifts.

"From blood to blood—"

Pushing away the pain, I jerk my hands at Mary, sending

another orb of Hell power in her direction. Joshua snaps at the backs of her legs, keeping her in place. The whoosh of wings stirs my hair from my shoulders, but I don't stop.

Mary holds her hands up, shielding her eyes from the angelic light behind me. I expect pain to radiate down my back, to burn across my skin, but nothing happens. The light dims.

"Hurry, Faith," Ezekiel says, his voice pulling a huge weight off my shoulder.

"My pretty little demon, don't kill me. I'll stand with you, my help you'll need. With your watcher by your side, his shield won't ever let you hide. Heaven will come back for him, if you don't let my power in. With the sunrise you will see, the gates of Hell will open, and a demon you'll still be."

"Do it, Faith!" Ezekiel says. "Now!"

Summoning more demonic power from my blood, I force it onto Mary, breaking the protective amulet around her neck. She screams, trying to summon a spell, but I launch forward and land on top of her, cutting off her words.

I use her nail to cut my own palm, and I drip blood onto her eyes. Her skin sizzles and burns under me. Pressing my branded hand over her eyes and my other hand over her heart, I gather the same power she tried to use against me.

"Blood to blood from dark to light, you will bow to her might. Body from Hell chained to light, you will perish in the night. From red to black and black to red, she will get into your head. A demon's kin from loves pure grace, Hell is now what you face. Fury will burn, and love will bind, you will now lose your mind. I take the voice from your soul, you will never return whole. With the blade of your knife, she will now end your life. With blood and power from Heaven and Hell, you will fall by my spell."

A shadow casts over me and Kristin holds out the onyx blade Mary uses in her rituals. Squeezing my eyes shut, I gather power over her heart and ram the dagger right through my own hand to burn my power and blood straight to her heart.

Mary's body arches, fire blazing from her heart to crawl over her body, sending ash into the air. Howls echo through the night, the veil still ripped open because of me. Pain and fear battle with love and relief as Mary's body disintegrates beneath me, disappearing forever in the Veiled Realm.

With your watcher by your side, his shield won't ever let you hide. Heaven will come back for him, if you don't let my power in. Mary's last words swirl over and over again through my mind.

I pant, shaking, digging my hands into the smoldering ground beneath me. The burned skin of my arms flakes away, drifting through the night, leaving behind my smooth skin untouched by Hell. Ezekiel runs his hand on my back, rubbing away my sobs that make it hard for me to breathe.

"It's over, Faith," he whispers. "It's okay."

With the sunrise you will see, the gates of Hell will open, and a demon you'll still be. I shake my head, pushing up to my knees, Mary's words refusing to leave me alone.

I swallow, my throat burning. "Close the veil, Ezekiel. Hurry."

"But the angelic army needs to see," he says.

I ignite power in my hands, holding it in front of me. "Not now. Shut it. Please."

Ezekiel doesn't argue with me. Crossing the few feet between me and Kristin and the hole in the veil, he stands in front of the opening and presses his hands together.

My heart stalls.

"Oh, no," I whisper.

His heavenly light is gone. Mary was right.

Scrambling to my feet, I rush forward. Ezekiel stands frozen in front of the rip in the veil. On the other side, a small army of angels stand, Heaven's light glowing so brightly from them that it stings my eyes.

I grab the back of Ezekiel's shirt and yank him away, summoning power in my hands. "I don't want to hurt any of you. Please, just call my dad."

The angels don't move. They don't speak. All they do is continue to look at me like I'm Uncle Lucifer risen to Earth, but then, I'm sure they'll wish it was him if they try anything. I'm still running on fury and adrenaline, caught on a wave of fire because of Mary.

"I killed the witch who created the hellhounds," I say.

The woman angel with flowing golden hair, appearing eerily familiar, steps forward. I recognize her. She hasn't changed at all since I was young, but I don't remember her name. "You broke the veil. You pose a risk to everything we've done to keep humanity safe."

Ezekiel rests his hands on my shoulders. "Faith won't do it again. She knows of the consequences. Mary wouldn't have ever stopped, and you're all no match to the witch. Faith only did it to help."

"Help whom?" she asks. "The daughter of Heaven's Traitor helps no one but her father."

"You don't even know me," I snap. "I'm nothing like my dad."

She tilts her head to the side, peering at me for a long, quiet moment. "You're as soulless as he is. Look at what you've done to your watcher. Look at the position you put him in. You've stolen his eternity."

My chest heaves, the edges of vision shadowing. "I love him," I whisper.

"You destroyed him."

Ezekiel pulls me back farther like somehow a few feet of distance will do anything to save us in the faces of avenging angels too pure to see everything clearly. Too righteous to understand that sometimes you have to do the wrong thing for the right reason.

"Faith saved me," Ezekiel says. "She is my purpose. You cannot deny that. You cannot fault either of us for this. Now, please. Have mercy, sister."

"Traitors don't get mercy," she says.

I shake my head and pull away from Ezekiel. "No. He's not a traitor. He did not hurt anyone."

"He turned his back on his purpose."

"His purpose was me." My voice rises through the air, wind picking up as the angels flap their wings preparing for me to unleash my power. And I want nothing more than to show them what Heaven's Traitor's daughter is really capable of.

"And he failed."

"Liars!" Thrusting my hands out, I launch my power directly at the angels.

They scatter, sending blinding light in all directions, making it hard to see. My feet are knocked out from under me, and I hit my back hard on the ground. Heavenly light engulfs me, burning the remaining charred skin of my inner demon away, searing over me in a blessed glow that no longer burns.

I kick my legs up, thrusting myself to my feet, igniting more power, but the angels are gone. Mist wafts through the air, the veil now closed. I spin around, catching sight of a figure in the fog. But it's not Ezekiel. It's Kristin.

"Where is he?" I ask. "Ezekiel! Where are you?"

Kristin pulls me into a hug. "I'm so sorry. I thought they would listen. I thought they'd take a moment to reconsider."

My lips turn downward, and anger rushes over me. I bring my branded hand up to my eye, peering around the night desert of the Earth realm. The angels surround Ezekiel, shoving him to his knees with their heavenly light.

He doesn't resist.

He doesn't even fight.

Slamming my hands against the veil, I force my power against it, but nothing happens. It struggles to remain tangible in my palms. I do everything I can to fissure the magical wall, to force myself through, but my power is spent. I have nothing left.

I turn to Kristin. "Help me. Do something."

She brushes her fingers through her hair, pushing the stray strands from her face. "Okay, but your dad's not going to like this."

"I don't care."

"We're going to summon him."

"What if we don't have enough time? What if he can't do anything?" I ask.

She touches my shoulder. "Take a breath. I didn't go through all this tonight to lose you again."

My blood freezes at the realization. "Oh, no. Don't tell me..."

"Let's just hope your angel has some fight left in him."

It won't matter if he does or not.

I have enough fight left for the both of us.

FALL FROM GRACE

I PEER THROUGH the veil, watching the angels surrounding Ezekiel. "What are they waiting for?"

The fact that they haven't moved or done anything in minutes has me on edge. The moon soars across the sky, counting down until dawn will rise into a new day, the moon setting on possibly the last moment of my existence.

If I fail, I won't just fail myself. I'll fail Ezekiel. I'll fail my mom, who had given me her most costly possession to bring my dad humanity. So, if I fail, I'd be failing him, too. I'll be failing the world by bringing back Heaven's Traitor. It would serve the angelic army right, though he'd end up in Hell. And me? I can't think about it.

"I don't know but don't question it," she says. "Now, give me your hand. We have to summon him with your blood."

If only we could use phones in the Veiled Realm.

Kristin cuts my palm and motions for me to wave my hand in front of me. My blood sticks to the invisible wall that appears for me when I press against it. The whole world is a veil, and I can touch it no matter where I'm standing.

"Blood to blood from light to dark, I summon you through your heart. A vessel born from the depths of Hell, hear my words, hear my spell. An angel who has fallen from grace, appear before us in this place. I summon you to come to me, and when you do, you will see. A daughter lost and in doubt, needs more power to help her out."

My stomach ties into knots, threatening to rise into my throat at the pulling sensation crawling through me. I groan, heaving, but force my legs to stay strong to keep me standing. The blood hanging in the air sizzles, clearing the mist in front of us, allowing us to see through the veil without covering my hand over my eye.

I don't know what I was expecting. That my dad would materialize out of thin air or come blasting from the ground with Hell power. But what I didn't expect was for Dad to fall from the sky, landing on his feet before an angel lands behind him. White wings stretch toward the sky, so pure and ethereal, a stark contrast to Ezekiel's black wings. Stunning compared to the golden wings of those in the angelic army unassigned to a demon.

Dad freezes in place, his fingers clenching into fists at his sides. One look at Ezekiel sends him shooting power right at my angel. I scream out, smacking my hands on the veil, wishing with everything in me that the stupid veil would just drop.

"Dad, stop!" I scream. "Leave him alone."

Dad drops his hands, jerking his head in my direction. He heard me. I know he did. I might not have been able to break the veil, but I managed to project my voice loud enough for him to hear.

He waves his hands at the angels once and stomps in my direction, narrowing his eyes like he'd be able to see me through the veil. Kristin takes my hand in hers, linking our fingers together.

"A demon born from Heaven's smite, use your eyes, find the sight. A demon born from a fall from grace, look through the veil, see her face. A demon, the great servant of Hell, hear my words, hear my spell."

"Faith?" Dad asks.

"Dad, I'm here," I say.

He strolls closer and raises his hand to touch the veil, creating static against my skin. He's never been on the opposite side looking in at me. "Oh, my beautiful Faith. What happened? Are you okay?"

Tears burn my eyes. "I don't know. Am I?"

He sighs. "You broke the veil again after I told you not to.

What are you even doing here? That angel was supposed to keep you far, far away." He turns his gaze to Kristin. "And you. You had one job."

Kristin raises her chin, glaring at Dad. "Don't even try to put this on me, Heaven's Traitor. I've done nothing but fight to keep Faith safe. Fight to protect your own humanity. I've been doing nothing but giving to you. This far exceeds my contract. Faith broke Mary's link to this world, you know. And how does the angelic army thank us? Punishment. Do something. You know what will happen to Faith if they send Ezekiel to Hell."

Rage mars Dad's handsome face, and he summons power in his hands, turning toward the angelic army. His true body rips free from his skin, and he stomps back to the angels. I expect him to start fighting, to blast those pretty feathers right from their wings. To do something, anything.

But all he does is hold his power in front of him. "I demand Heaven to release my daughter's soul back to her. Do not punish her for her watcher's failure."

I blink, panic rises through me. "What?"

Kristin squeezes my fingers. "Faith, please. Let Raphael handle this."

"But he's not trying to help Ezekiel."

"This isn't about him. This is about you. He made his choice. You shouldn't have to suffer."

"He made that choice for me!" I scream. I bang my fists against the veil again, sending sparks of power in all different directions. "This isn't his fault!"

The angel who brought Dad expands his white wings, summoning light so white that Dad stumbles back, shading his eyes. He yells out but still holds strong, raising his hands with his own power.

They both release power at each other at the same time, creating a lightshow of red and white, Heaven and Hell, power so intense the ground shakes under my feet. But Dad's alone against the army of angels. He's powerful, but he has his limitations. He's always been cautious about picking battles he can win. It's how he's managed to stay on top, stay alive, keep me safe—until now.

The angelic army rises and beams their blessed light at Dad, causing his skin to smolder. He doesn't cower or move, just takes everything they have to throw at him until his legs give out, and he kneels on the ground next to Ezekiel.

Dad bows his head. "I will accept the consequences for both my daughter and her watcher. They were acting under my authority. All I ask is that you release my daughter's soul. You can save her."

The angel's stoic face softens for a split second.

"No," Ezekiel says, speaking up. Without warning, he rises to his feet, expanding his wings out. A new darkness shadows his usual light-filled eyes. He tenses, facing the angelic army without any sort of weapon or fighting chance. "I won't lose her, Raphael."

"Would you rather her soul suffers for your betrayal?" Dad snaps.

Ezekiel doesn't respond.

I clench my fingers, digging my nails into the palms of my hands. How dare everyone discuss my life and my existence without even giving me the chance to talk. How dare Dad agree to accept punishment for something he isn't responsible for. How dare the angelic army put us in this position. If they think I'm going to ruin the world, then I will ruin the world. I'll show them exactly what I'm capable of.

"You made your choice, watcher," Dad says. "I will not let you make one for my daughter." Dad ignites his power in his hands and launches it at Ezekiel. Ezekiel doesn't flinch as the ruby red orb collides into his stomach, burning the shirt away from him, leaving his skin glowing pink.

Ezekiel flaps his wings and black feathers scatter through the air, sending my heart racing. I can't stand here and watch without doing anything. I made a promise to him. I swore I wouldn't let anything happen to him.

"Faith," Kristin says. "Brace yourself."

I glance at her in my peripheral vision and open my mouth to ask her for what, but three angels launch themselves at Ezekiel. Two hold his wings and the other forces him back to his knees. Dad takes his moment of weakness to launch another burst of power at him.

"Stop!" I yell, hitting my hands against the veil.

"Was she worth it?" Dad asks.

Dad's words swirl through my chest, wrapping around my heart. I'm afraid to hear Ezekiel's response. Because I don't think I'm worth it. I never wanted this. I never wanted to see my beautiful, pure, innocent angel fall. I never wanted him to rise up to fight for me. I never wanted any of this.

Ezekiel stiffens, facing my dad directly, but he doesn't respond. His serious expression says nothing at all.

The angels circle my dad and Ezekiel, stiff and ready to act. The angels don't release Ezekiel's wings, and more feathers scatter through the air.

"If you accept this fate without a fight to stay, you'll damn my daughter's soul, watcher."

Ezekiel straightens his shoulders. "I will not allow it."

A wicked smile crosses Dad's face, and he launches more power. Instead of hitting Ezekiel, he hits the angel holding him in place. The angelic army reacts, blasting heavenly light again, but it doesn't shine as brightly. I turn my gaze to the horizon and peer at the coming dawn.

The angel with the pure white wings launches into the air, materializing a sword from nowhere, the light as intense as the sun. A strange sensation crawls across my skin, tendrils of smoke rising from me as I hold the angel in my gaze.

Dad throws power at him, but the angel's too fast. He zooms toward the space in front of Ezekiel, struggling to pull free of the angels still holding his wings. My stomach twists, my breath panting. Ezekiel told me what happens to the fallen who can't stand up and fight. Hell only chooses the worthy to walk the Earth.

A horrible, heart-stopping, soul-crushing feeling washes

through my very being. Flames crowd the edges of my vision, and I realize I'm seeing the gates of Hell open before me. The angelic army will push Ezekiel through and slam it shut, forcing my soul with him. Except something's different. I feel the heat of Hell. I feel it coursing through my blood. But then the world blinks out. Because nothing is tethering me to Earth. Once Ezekiel goes through the gate, my soul will travel with him, and I'll be completely soulless. I can't remain on Earth otherwise. Dad was right. Ezekiel's fall dooms my eternity since Heaven won't save me, the treacherous, enticing demon's daughter who can make angels break.

"Blood to blood from red to black, Hell will take your body back. I give you power, I give you the key, lock the gate, don't let them see," Kristin says from next to me. "Open the veil and use the night, I give you power to help you fight."

The thinning veil from the rise of the sun flickers against my burning hands. I slam my palms to the veil, thrusting power against it to break through. It shatters before me, causing the world around me to quiver. I will not fall. I will not allow anyone to force my soul. To destroy my life and existence.

I'm the daughter of Grace Blackwell, a soul so pure that she could see even the good buried deep in the darkness of a demon.

"A demon's kin born from light, give her strength, give her fight. Summon power from the depths of Hell, hear my words, hear my spell."

Orange liquid power erupts in my hands, sizzling through

my veins. I thrust it at the nearest angel, and golden feathers explode through the air as I hit its wing. My very being screams at the action, pain and anguish cutting through my heart like a sharp knife.

Tears burn my eyes. "I don't want to do this."

Dad freezes, his hands holding power, and something dark flashes through his eyes. Ezekiel's gaze locks with mine, the angel with the white wings standing before him, sword raised.

"Stop," I say. "I'm begging you. Please, don't do this."

The angel shifts, looking at me from over his shoulder, a strange intensity to his gaze, like the fire of Hell burns in his eyes, but I know it's not Hell. This fire burns brighter, it burns with his convictions, his own purpose.

And I can feel his despair, his grief, everything sad about the world coating his very essence.

"Forgive me," he says. "I have no choice."

The world slows, the light of day rising, sending the strange brown fog through the air. The terrifying angel turns away from me, raising his sword into the air. Silence falls upon me, like I've gone deaf to the noise of the world, all except the beat of Ezekiel's heart.

He closes his eyes, his face scrunching, his body tensing.

Power erupts in my palms, and I thrust it toward the angel. My very essence cries, pain and panic overtaking everything good in me. The female angel with golden wings flies in front of me, taking my power onto herself, stopping it from even touching the avenging angel.

His sword swipes through the air and cuts straight through Ezekiel's beautiful black wing, severing it from his back in a burst of flames so intense I can feel the heat radiating through the air.

I scream, the entire world shaking. Running forward, I summon more power in my hands, shooting it toward the angel as it raises the sword again. It hits his back, but he only wobbles for a second, my power burning the brilliant feathers of his white wings.

He thrusts his sword down upon Ezekiel's other wing, severing it before pushing my watcher back into the dirt. Black feathers smolder through the air, drifting on the heavenly breeze of the angels determined to send Ezekiel to Hell.

The avenging angel raises his sword once more, the whole world quivering with anticipation with the gates of Hell opening to take Ezekiel from me. I charge the angel, power flying, and I crash into him, knocking him away. We roll together through the desert, my fingers burning and blistering against his holiness pressing against my Hell power.

Heavenly light bursts through the air as the angelic army attacks me. The light no longer burns my skin. It merely steals my breath away, but I've learned to survive in a world that constantly suffocates me in everything that wants to see me gone.

I press my hand to the angel's chest, darkness washing over me. "I won't let you take him from me."

The angel doesn't fight under me, and the angelic army hovers around without doing anything either. He stares at me with shining eyes, his sword gone from sight, his wings now hidden. He looks merely mortal, but the intensity of his pure essence burns me in the void left in place of my soul.

"He's already gone. I'm sorry," the angel says. "Forgive me, daughter of Grace Blackwell. We have all failed you."

My chest heaves, my whole body screaming. I press my hands into the angel's chest, shaking him like if I somehow shake hard enough, I'll spill the answers I so desperately want without having to ask the questions I can't separate to form on my lips.

Tears drip from my eyes and splash onto the angel's cheeks. "I don't understand. I should be in—"

"He descended, Faith," Kristin says from behind me. "But he never crossed the threshold. You stopped him from entering Hell."

Pure, sweet relief rushes over me, filling me with the hope I have trouble summoning unlike the demonic power burning through my veins. If he's never entered Hell, my soul still remains on this plane. I'm still alive. I can still live. It's all making sense. Dad wasn't attacking Ezekiel to punish him. It was a test of worth.

"Forgive me," the angel repeats from beneath me.

I frown, turning my attention to him. "I..." I have no idea how to respond. "What are you asking me to forgive you for?"

He reaches out, pulling his hand free from me, and touches his fingers to my heart. "I couldn't save your mother, and I couldn't save you."

"But I'm fine. Everything's okay," I say.

He shakes his head. "Your soul is lost to Hell."

I straighten my shoulders. I don't know what I expected him to say, but I have a few words of my own for him now that he's finally listening. "It was only a matter of time. You damned me before I even had a chance. This is your doing."

A tear drips from the corner of his eye. "Forgive me."

My eyes widen at the sight of the angel's sword as it materializes in his hand.

He points it at me.

ENTICED

THE FLAMING SWORD blinds me, stealing away my sight for a split second. I shoot an orb of power directly at the avenging angel, hitting him in the chest. He drops his arm, giving me the opportunity to scramble away from him.

The angel flaps his wings, pushing me back, and I spill to the dirt. Kristin yells out and rushes for me. She throws her ivory dagger, sinking it into the angel's flesh, smoldering his skin.

The hope I gathered seconds ago flickers out as the angel unfurls his white wings, aiming his sword at me again. How stupid was I to let my guard down? The angelic army was never going to let me live. They can't see past their purpose to know that maybe others have their own purposes to live by, to fight for.

I was doomed to die, especially now that Ezekiel possesses my soul. Heaven would never allow another demi-demon to rise from Hell again, especially a soulless one like me.

I summon power into my hands, growing the orb larger and larger until I'm panting with exhaustion. This is the very last drop of power I can manage before my body gives out. This is my last chance to save myself.

If I don't, all of this was for nothing.

Ezekiel's fall. My mom's sacrifice. My dad's fight.

I can't face my death knowing what I'll leave behind in my wake.

Guttural growls rip through the air, catching on the wind, and I realize the wolves gathered for Mary now rise with the sun, shedding their Hell skin and returning to humanity. And they slink around the angelic army, surrounding them. Surrounding us.

An angel flies forward, colliding with Kristin, pulling her away from me. She yells out and punches the angel in the face, something I might have laughed at if he didn't launch her higher into the air. A black wolf jumps from the wild brush, sinking its teeth into the leg of the angel, pulling him back to Earth before he can adjust to the weight.

Kristin drops to the ground and lands on her feet only to

fall back. She hits the ground with a thud. Another wolf, a beautiful gray and white one, rushes in front of her. It skids to a stop, hackles raised, snarling and snapping at the angels.

They're defenseless against the wolves as Heaven's light can't hurt something pure and good.

Then I realize something. The angelic army's shield is down. If the wolves can see them, they've been weakened. I've weakened them.

The angelic army is scared.

I can smell it.

A dozen different scents waft through the air, swirling in a fragrance that touches my core, making my inner demon wild. Fire ignites through me, heating my skin, giving me more power than ever.

"This is your last chance," I say, holding my power out. "I don't want to do this, but I'm not letting you end my life."

The mighty angel points his sword at me. "You will destroy the world with Hell's hands. Is that what you want?"

"You don't know that. You don't know what I'll do. But don't push me. I'm begging you to give me a chance," I say.

His face remains expressionless. 'The risk is too great."

I shake my head. "I could've made a great ally."

"You will be all our undoing."

It takes everything in me to control my sarcasm. My fury. All the bad emotions this angel elicits from the pit of darkness growing with every passing second. His light fuels my fire, and I can't help the smile crossing my face.

"Last chance," I say. "I've already made one angel fall. Don't doubt that I won't take another."

The voice that comes from me, all low and raspy, dark, laced with threads of evil doesn't sound like my voice. The words, they didn't come from me. They came from the demon within, the monster infuriated by the circumstances Heaven forces upon me.

I've struggled for far too long to deal with my heritage, to fight the evil born in my veins, and now, without the light of Ezekiel, now that his good grace was cut away with his achingly beautiful wings, I have nothing to use against my demonic self.

I turn to Kristin, holding my hand out to her. The angels tense, but no one moves with the growls of the wolves sounding out around us.

I take a breath, willing to find some spark of goodness still clinging to my humanity, to find the will to care. To find the will to leave without tearing down Heaven, starting from this avenging angel. "I'm losing control. I don't want to hurt anyone, but I'm afraid I'm going to. They'll push me."

"It's Hell," she whispers. "You can still fight it. There's still hope."

I know better than to believe it, but my mind struggles with what I want to do. "You said you can make a shield from Demon Watchers. Can you do it now?"

"It's a steep price for your soul, Faith," she says.

"I don't have a soul," I say. "I don't have anything."

The avenging angel ignites power in his free hand, and the

other angels follow his lead. Wolves race around us, sending the angels scattering into the sky. White feathers drift around me, the angel jumping into the air, raising his blade.

"You have a broken wolf. He is still bound to you," she says. "His life and soul will do. But the consequences will be on you."

"I—" Could I? Is it worth it? What consequences? I don't have time to find out.

"He made his choice."

She's right. And now, I'm making mine. A choice that should feel so utterly wrong. But I'm desperate. "Okay. I accept the cost."

Just the thought of Joshua has the monstrous pack leader charging in my direction, hackles raised to the sky, jowls frothing, fire in his eyes though his coat is as dark as night. The mighty angel doesn't have a chance to move before the wolf collides into him from behind, knocking the angel from the air he hovers in.

"A broken beast and angel's smite, a gift to Hell to hide their sight. A life will end, a soul set free, bring the power, bestow it on me."

Joshua sinks his teeth into the angel's shoulder, spilling his blood. The angel raises his sword to Joshua, ramming it straight into the wolf's chest. A high-pitched, almost human scream rips through the air, and a strange light flows from both the angel and the wolf, expanding out.

Kristin grabs my arm, dragging her nail across my wrist

above the power she makes me split in two. My black blood drips into my palm, burning bright against my demonic power. "An angel's blood pure and true, burn with Hell, stopping you. A demon's kin, now Hell-bound, hear my words, hear the sound. A blood spell full of spite, will let you summon the dark in light. A shield will rise from a fall, hide her body, protect us all."

An explosion of light erupts behind the angel, black feathers scattering through the air. My heart punches my ribcage at the sight of Ezekiel's feathers mingling with the white ones of the avenging angel, burning and flickering as they hit against the blessed air circulating around.

Kristin motions for me to throw my power, and I jerk my arms forward, aiming it at the angel. He yells out, arching his back, my power burning away the blood spilling from the bite inflicted by Joshua. He thrusts the body of the wolf off him and gathers Heaven's light in his palms.

"As Heaven's light crashes with Hell, a shield will build with my spell. Angels will no longer see, the demon's daughter next to me."

The air ripples around us, the world blinking. I stare at the angels peering around, yelling, feathers flying, wolves still lunging, and then silently screaming trees materialize out of nowhere, the light prison realm revealing itself.

My head spins at the sudden shift in and out of both worlds, and I drop to my knees. Kristin's hands touch my shoulder, bringing my attention to her. I turn to look at her, a wave of nausea rolling through me, the after effect of her spell messing with my head as everything falls into place. I stare up at the sky, figures with huge wings taking flight, haloed in the glorious rays of sunlight.

They fade away as the gnarled tree branches come back into view, stealing my sight of the Earth realm. A tall figure looms over me, the brown air hazing him in dirty light, blurring my vision.

My chest heaves, and I roll on my side, pressing my face into the hard rock of the onyx road. I blink the darkness away, meeting the closed eyes of my beautiful angel...

My beautiful demon.

The angel I ruined.

The angel that fell from grace because I changed his purpose.

I reach out and run my fingers across his cheek, but I can't feel him. My fingers buzz against the veil separating us. "Ezekiel, what have I done?"

My words come out a whisper, a weeping breath so quiet, I'm not even sure I formed the words at all. Every part of me breaks open, cracking and fissuring, seeping with the darkness overtaking the light he had given me. The light I stole. When he fell, we fell together. But now? I feel us ripping apart.

His eyes flutter open, greeting me with their intensity, but he doesn't speak. He captures me in his dark eyes, unwavering, fiery yet icy, emotionless. Empty. Eyes no longer shining with everything I love, only eyes absent of light. Absent of love. Absent of me.

The avenging angel was right.

Ezekiel, my beautiful, powerful, loving angel is now the empty shell of a demon.

I've lost him.

And there's nothing I can do.

The light prison world fades away, and I curl my knees to my chest, wanting to fold up and disappear. The world around me falls silent like the universe holds its breath, anticipating my next move.

But I can't move.

I don't even want to feel.

A shadow cuts across the ground in front of me, and Kristin pulls me from the brush and onto her lap. She runs her fingers through my hair, pulling the sticky, dirty strands from my cheeks. She doesn't say anything, holding her arms around me, doing her best to keep me together, but it's too late for that.

Every broken piece of me scatters through the air, promising me I'll never be whole. Promising me that my world will rise with the smoke remaining from the destruction of my life, the descent of my angel, the loss of the best part of me.

"No one will hurt you ever again, Faith," Kristin says. "Mary's gone. Heaven can't find you. Hell will bow."

I should be relived. I should thank her. Instead, I say, "You should've cast the shield against angels to begin with."

She releases a deep sigh. "Faith, you know I couldn't have. Ezekiel's shield was all that was protecting you from Hell. You couldn't have had it both ways. Hell was the bigger threat."

I glare at the remaining feathers burning across the ground, scooping up a perfect black one untouched by my power. I cup it in my hands, running my index finger across the soft fluff. "And Hell still got to me."

"But you're alive. You're still you."

"I don't care about me. You should've just built the shield."

"Faith," she says.

I smack my hand into the ground, power exploding a hole in the dirt. "You should've done it! I'm not the one who needed protecting. Ezekiel did. From me."

She hugs me tighter. "He made his choice."

"He never had a real choice. He never stood a chance. My dad said it himself."

"But he gave *you* one."

Tears blur my eyes. "One I didn't deserve."

Kristin shifts back, staring at me with her dark eyes, her black hair blowing behind her. "Because you deserve more, Faith."

"Tell that to the universe."

She smiles weakly. "I'm sure it knows. Now, come on. We should move."

"I should be here when he returns," I say. "I—"

She shakes her head. "He'll be gone. Don't worry, Raphael will help him."

That's what I'm afraid of. Instead of speaking the words out loud, I bring my branded hand to my eye and peer around the sunlight prison realm once more.

My heart slides into my stomach at the sight of Dad helping Ezekiel to his feet. He rises before me, standing tall, eyes averted to the sky. I expect his wings to unfurl at any second for him to take flight, but he turns his back to me, peering around the new world that'll steal him away with every sunrise. Blackened and burned skin peeks through his charred T-shirt, a horrifying reminder of what I've done to him.

Like they feel the weight of my stare, Dad and Ezekiel turn their attention in my direction. My knees shake, my hands quivering. Everything hurts inside of me, threatening to obliterate me, because I can't stand to look at my watcher like this. I can't stand to see the emptiness in his eyes.

He takes a step forward, and my feet automatically step back.

Dad grabs Ezekiel's shoulder and shakes his head. I can't hear what he tells him. He only nods to my dad, brings his gaze back to mine, and smiles.

My heart races.

I hold my breath.

I drop my hand from my eye.

A wolf licks my fingers, and I run my hand over Greg's black fur. The rogue wolf pack surrounds me and Kristin. Beyond them, the rest of the Desertville pack. Dozens of wolves bow, some whimper, some howl.

I cover my ears. "Make them go away."

"You killed their pack leader. You killed their witch. Heaven is against them, Faith. Hell wants to break them."

"So?"

"Never hurts to have beasts of Hell on your side, ones who can withstand day and night," Kristin says.

I huff a breath. "No. They're the reason I'm in this mess. They're the reason I've lost everything." They remind me of those I've lost. Of Aria. Of Christopher and his traitor pack. No, I can't have that reminder. I don't want it. It stirs the darkness in me I'm trying to resist. The darkness enticing me, trying to seduce me to give in. To give up my humanity.

She frowns. "Everything? Faith, you haven't lost anything. You're alive. You're protected. You saved your watcher from an eternal fate in Hell."

"The angelic army will never stop looking for me."

She takes my hand, pulling me forward, walking me past the lingering wolves. "They won't find you."

"What about Ezekiel? He's Heaven's new traitor. They'll come after Dad. He took responsibility for this."

"You don't think Raphael is strong enough to take a stand against Heaven?"

Of course he is, but just because he is, doesn't mean I want him to. I remember the uprising. I remember the war. And this? This is all by *my* hands.

I tug away from her. "This isn't what I wanted! I don't want my friends being my enemies. I didn't want to have Hell breathing down my neck."

"It's in your blood. It gives you life."

"But a demon has my soul, and I'm mortal. I'll end up in the one place I never wanted to be. My eternity is still ruined."

She closes the distance and hugs me. "Demons deal in souls. Ezekiel will return it to you, Faith," she says. "This has made it all possible. You have to believe it'll work out in the end."

My hand flies to my chest, pressing into my heart, touching the black feather tattoo glowing with a new fiery light. It's the last reminder of who Ezekiel was. "Heaven will never take me back. I've started a war—one I never wanted. One I don't want to win. I care about the world. I don't want to ruin it. I don't want to prove them right."

"It's not a war. It's a small battle, and you will show them you're not a threat," she says.

But I am a threat. I can feel my inner demon begging to take control. To rise from the fire. It wants nothing more than to make me forget my humanity. It promises to take away the pain and heartache, the betrayal, the grief of everything I caused for the angel I fell in love with.

The angel I destroyed.

A flicker inside of me, a tiny spark struggling to outshine the fire of Hell coursing through me, begs me to remember who I am despite what everyone expects me to be. This was never supposed to be me against Heaven. It was me against Hell, me against time and the possibility of turning into a demon.

I want so much to hate the angelic army, to hate those who've wronged me, who've stood up to push me down, to tell me how I'm supposed to be, but a part of me knows they're trapped unchanging in an ever changing world. A world constantly threatened by power and darkness.

They can't help that they see me as a threat.

I'm the daughter of Heaven's Traitor. The daughter of Grace Blackwell, whose love for an angel nearly destroyed him and nearly destroyed the world. I'm a daughter born of Hell and night, of power strong enough to break the very veil that keeps the demons at bay.

And all of those things make up tiny parts of me.

But I'm more.

I'm born of love and hope.

Of faith.

It's all the good I have left. I won't let them take it from me.

COSTLY POSSESSION

I DIG MY feet into the sand of the stormy beach, watching lightning flicker across the sky in bright white flashes, lighting the dark world around me. An inky dread slithers from my chest and down to my stomach, tangling in knots inside me. A dark shadow appears behind me, and power erupts in my fingers, setting the dark beach aglow.

My lip quivers, my heart racing, and I squeeze my eyes shut. My once beautiful dreams storm with fear, with everything dark inside me, and I try to wake up. I try to summon the sun to cut through the clouds, but I can't.

"I didn't think you could still come here," I whisper, my voice shaking.

I wasn't ready for this. I'm still not ready to face Ezekiel. Not like this. Not in this world. Because here, I can feel the evil flowing from him. I drift on the darkness that stole the very light and good grace from him.

I count my breaths, trying to steel my aching heart. It takes everything in me to force my eyes open. I shouldn't feel like this. He is like this because of me. He might be a demon, but I still love him. It's the only thing I'm certain of.

I hear a small intake of breath, a whisper of my name.

And then nothing.

I shift to look behind me, but only an empty beach greets me. "Ezekiel, please. I'm sorry. Come back."

Tears blur my eyes, fear threatening to spiral me down a dark hole I'll never be able to pull myself from.

"Please," I whisper. "Come back."

A bright light peeks through the thundering clouds, lighting me aglow, and I tilt my head back to stare into the light. It expands across the sky, pushing the clouds away. Then everything is light.

I shoot upright, gasping. Raising my hand up to shield my vision, I block the setting sun from my eyes. Confusion drifts over me as I take in the unfamiliar room. I never even had a chance to say goodbye to Vivian, to thank her for the kindness, but I had to flee Desertville. And I still can't return to Moonlight Shores.

I groan. "It's almost sundown. You should've woken me up."

Kristin sits at a small table, drinking something from a coffee cup. "You needed to sleep."

"He was there," I whisper. "I felt him. But I messed things up."

She stands up, crossing the small motel room to sit on the edge of my bed. "It's going to take some adjustment, but you'll both manage. He wouldn't be the first demon you've ever loved."

"My dad doesn't count," I say.

She laughs, her voice filling me with something I thought I'd never feel again—a small bubble of happiness. "Don't tell him that."

I smirk. "I just—this is hard."

"You've faced harder."

But I don't think I have. I've been prepared for my end. I've always known I'd grow up and old, while everyone I loved remained the same around me. I knew the day for goodbye would come, but I knew it wasn't the end. I was prepared for an eternity at peace, an eternity to reunite with my grandma, to possibly spend it with a cute human I met when I finally managed to convince Dad to let me leave home and forge my own way in life.

But I couldn't have ever prepared for falling in love with an immortal, an angel. I couldn't have prepared that I'd be responsible for his fall. I could have never prepared for a fate destined for Hell, an unfair, heart-wrenching eternity where I'll always wonder about those who remain here, in this world I don't want to destroy. A world I don't want to leave.

Kristin touches my shoulder, pulling me away from my inner thoughts, the constant battle of dark and light inside me. "It's almost time."

I purse my lips, flicking my gaze at the sunset. "I don't think I want to go through with it."

She sighs. "Faith, you promised Ezekiel you'd fight for him. Just because he's a demon now doesn't mean you stop fighting. You haven't lost him yet. You will if you give up."

"I just need another night."

"Alone in the Veiled Realm? No. I'm breaking the spell. You'll already be separated by the sunlight prison realm. You don't want to hurt Ezekiel like that. He needs you."

"It won't hurt him. He's a demon," I snap. "It's hurting me."

"Faith, do you hear yourself?"

Louder than ever. Because agony fills my heart so much to hear me talk like this. I know Ezekiel doesn't deserve this sort of reaction, but I can't help it. "I'm so scared. You haven't seen him yet. His eyes—they're empty."

"So set them ablaze. Fill him up. Remind him of who he was," she says.

By doing so, I'm afraid I'll remind him of all he lost. All we lost. He's a demon after all. He'll use it against me.

"It's important he doesn't forget after he gives you your

soul back. He'll no longer touch your humanity when he does," she adds.

I don't have time to respond. The sun sinks into the horizon, and Kristin tugs me forward and out the door of the motel room. The parking lot is empty, the neighborhood we're nestled in rundown and lacking life. Demons destroy everything they touch, and I can feel the evil slithering through what I'm sure was once a beautiful neighborhood. A neighborhood where now only the brave or tainted reside.

The veil thins around me, the world shimmering with brown haze and cool mist. I keep my eyes trained on the asphalt. If I run now, Kristin won't be able to draw blood for her spell. I can hide another night, think in peace, accept my eternity isolated and alone where I can't cause further damage.

Pain cuts across my hand, Kristin slicing my palm for what I pray is the last time. Blood seeps between my fingers, dripping to the ground. I stare at the pooling blood, still so dark it looks almost black. I expect it to ignite in flames at any second to burn away the rest of my humanity.

"I need the feather you collected from Ezekiel's wings," Kristin says.

I gape at her. "It's all I have left."

"You don't need that sort of reminder, and unless you're going to get me some angel blood, it's what I need to break the link to the Veiled Realm," she says.

Tears burn my eyes, and I tug the small black feather, one not unlike the one warming my heart, from my pocket. I hand it to Kristin, and she dips it into the blood on my palm and holds it out.

"Blood to blood, from red to black, revive Faith and bring her back. Summon her body, hear my shouts, open the veil and let her out. Bound to a demon, bathed in his dark, holds her soul, and rips her apart."

Dizziness washes over me, the world flickering from Earth to the Veiled Realm, the barrier thinning for me, letting the worlds collide. My knees shake, and I fall forward, pressing my hands into the rough asphalt that shimmers to dirt and back.

Two boots step in front of me, but I don't look up. I lie down, trying not to throw up everywhere.

"As demon blood coats the ground, let Heaven and Hell hear the sound. A demon's daughter's very first breath, a heart now beats in her chest. An angel's light fades away, and in his place a demon will stay. The descent from Heaven felt by all, ignite the power from the fall. As darkness burns with a new light, a body will now rise in the night."

I groan, my head throbbing, my insides twisting and seizing, the link stealing me away from the Veiled Realm now severed. The cut burns through the empty spot where my soul should be, filling me with something new, something different. Something that feeds the demon clawing just under my skin.

I dry heave, my stomach turning against me in a moment I should be strong. I try to push to my feet, my body now weak from the weight of Kristin's spell lifting, throwing me off balance. I close my eyes, listening to the world around me while locking all my other senses out. Three heartbeats thud apart from my own, two even breaths slow against my own panting. And then a world of silence—all heartbeat and nothing else. No whisper of wings. No ruffle of feathers. But yet I still know the presence closest to me is Ezekiel.

A cool hand touches my cheek. "Give her a second. She needs to catch up with the rest of the world," Kristin says.

"I swear, witch, if you've done any more damage to my daughter I will—"

I clear my throat. "Dad..." It's all I can manage to say.

Shoes shuffle against the asphalt and two more, much warmer hands, grab onto my shoulders and pull me from the ground. "I'm here, Faith."

I still refuse to open my eyes. "If you're going to yell at Kristin, you need to leave. I can't deal with you right now."

"Faith, I—"

"No. I don't want to hear it," I say.

Dad drops me, and I hit my back hard on the ground, the wind knocking from my lungs. He releases a low groan, swearing to himself, and something explodes nearby, shaking the world around me. Another explosion rings through the air as Dad launches more power at some unsuspecting building.

But I do nothing to stop him or calm him down.

He has no right to be upset at Kristin. He has no right to be upset at all.

This is my eternity crashing and burning. Not his.

"Give Raphael a break, Faith," Kristin says. "This whole

situation has taken a toll on him. He was so sure he'd take care of everything for you. Imagine his surprise that his daughter is a force to be reckoned with and can survive on her own."

I don't respond.

She draws her hand back, the coolness of her fingers leaving a spot of ice on my skin that melts away with every beat of my burning heart. "Will you be okay if I make sure he doesn't burn the town down?"

Again, I don't respond.

I stay hidden behind the darkness of my closed eyes where it's safe. Where I won't risk seeing between the two worlds.

Heavy footsteps draw closer, and I tense, my whole body screaming with fear. Not because of who Ezekiel's become. I'm terrified of who I've become to him. Who we've become to each other. All that love and light, the hope he carried, is now gone, leaving someone I might not recognize. What if he doesn't recognize me either?

I listen to him shift next to me, and then he sits by my side. Hot hands lift me from the ground, and I automatically react, burying my face into his shirt. The usually light cherry blossom scent of his skin no longer lingers on him. He smells of something warmer, sweeter—dark chocolate, maybe. It summons a deep desire in me, something I've suppressed so long because I was afraid of taking things too far. But now...

Ezekiel brushes his warm lips to my forehead, breathing against my skin. "Faith, will you look at me?" he asks softly, his voice gentle compared to the hard edge of my sorrow.

I ease back from his chest, turning my gaze to him. When our eyes meet, a smile crosses his face, a smile that looks like the one he used to give just to me. He was always so brooding toward the world, but to me? God, I never knew how important that smile would be in this moment.

Then his eyes bore into mine, so dark, darker than usual.

And I break.

Tears spill onto my cheeks, my body trembling as I hold back a sob. Ezekiel's smile falters, and he reaches up and runs his thumb under my eyes, brushing away the tears faster than they fall. I try to turn away, to hide against his chest again, but he cups my face in his hands, stopping me from moving.

"Please, don't cry. Not for me. I'm fine, really," he says.

I can't tell if he's lying. The fact that he can? Oh, God.

"I'm so, so sorry. This is all my fault," I say, sliding my arms under his to hug him. He stiffens when my fingers graze over the holes in his shirt, touching the bumpy skin now healed over from his time in the daylight prison realm. It's almost like his wings were never there, but the phantom softness still tickles my fingers, my memory willing them to appear though they can't. They're gone forever.

"Faith," he says. "Don't."

"But your beautiful wings," I whisper.

He leans back, the corner of his lips curling up. "Don't tell me that was the only reason you loved me."

My mouth falls open. "I—"

"And you don't even like flying."

He has me there. I release a tiny, breathless laugh that disappears as I try not to start bawling my eyes out. "I still need to apologize."

He scrunches his nose. "For my choice? No."

"But—"

He releases a low groan and leans forward, closing the distance between us. Brushing his lips to mine, he cuts off anything else I can say with a kiss so full of fire it adds to the flames already smoldering in my heart. Moving his hands from my cheeks, he runs them into my hair, kissing me like he's never kissed me before.

I shift in his lap, his heat blending with mine, his lips sweet and delicious, tasting as good as he smells, and I link my fingers to his neck, losing myself to the new heat of his touch.

He nips my bottom lip, pulling it between his teeth, his desire washing over me in a hot wave that leaves me breathless. I want so badly to lose myself to his kiss, to devour every bit of affection he gives me, to throw all my guarded caution across the ground with the ashes from my burned blood and the remnants of the last feather of his wings.

I slowly ease back, and he leans in again, but I raise my finger to his lips. He smiles against my hand and tugs it from his mouth to lace our fingers together.

He traps me in his dark gaze, a gaze no longer empty and devoid. His gaze burns with fire, with Hell power. His gaze burns with my own reflection. "Have I ever told you that you test me in ways I had no idea were possible?" he asks, saying something so very Ezekiel. Words that remind me I might have loved his purity, his grace, but I'm in love with him and solely him regardless.

I smile without saying anything.

"That's better," he says. "That's the smile I remember loving."

My heart falters at his words, but I steel myself from reacting. He doesn't say it's the smile he *loves*, just that he remembers that he loved it. And in this very second, every little piece of him adds up to show me he might feel like my watcher, he might still make my heart race, make me feel better. He might act the same, but he's changed for good.

He doesn't love me but only remembers that he did.

I force my smile to remain and shift from his lap. He helps me to my feet, squeezing my hands between his. We stand together for a moment, staring at each other. A bright light flashes overhead, startling me, and I pull away, summoning power.

Blue liquid light erupts in Ezekiel's fingers at the same time, power not unlike mine, and he tenses. I gape at the demonic power in his hands, the perfect orb swirling and moving in his fingers. I wonder if my soul might be the reason for its likeness to mine.

The lights go out around us, leaving us in darkness.

Headlights beam across the parking lot, engulfing us in a glow, and a sleek Mercedes screeches to a stop in front of us. Dad rolls down the window and sticks his head out. He glances from me to Ezekiel and narrows his eyes.

"Time to go," he says.

Ezekiel snuffs his power out and holds his hand out for me.

I hesitate. "I—"

"Come on, Faith," he says.

"Maybe it'd be better for everyone if I just disappeared. I don't want anyone getting hurt because of me again," I say.

Dad swings his door open, hopping from the driver's seat, and grabs my arm. He motions for Ezekiel to open the back door. Dad picks me off my feet and sets me in back without giving me a choice in the matter. Ezekiel slides in next to me and helps me buckle my seatbelt because my hands shake so hard.

Getting back behind the wheel, Dad slams the door and swivels in his seat. "You really think I'm going to take my eyes off you again after everything? Never again, especially since your precious soul now belongs to *him*." Dad's look burns hot enough to make the gates of Hell look like candlelight in comparison.

Ezekiel laces his fingers with mine and brings my hand to his mouth to kiss. "I promise I'll take care of you, Faith. Forever. You don't have to worry."

I blink the confusion from my eyes. "Kristin said you can give me my soul back."

His expression hardens, his jaw tightening. "Now why would I do that? It helps me see. Feels just as good—better than before."

My heart smashes to my ribcage, threatening to run away

from me, from Ezekiel, from this entire situation. "Because it's *my* soul, Ezekiel."

He shakes his head. "It's not. It's mine. I won't give it up. You're my most costly possession."

Epilogue

FLY FROM THE ASHES

"**Y**OU KNOW, MY dad's going to power blast you if he finds out you're visiting my dreams," I say, turning toward the storming ocean of my dream world.

Ezekiel plops down in the sand next to me. "I like a challenge."

"Must be why you're so attracted to me, huh?" It's been thirty-three sunsets since Ezekiel lost his wings. Thirty-three nights of steeling myself to his charm. Thirty-three days alone in my new prison made of magic, concrete, and bulletproof glass. Two way locks with only Dad having the key.

I guess I deserve such a life. It's safer for everyone.

Ezekiel sucks in air through is teeth. "So much more, Faith."

"Obsessed," I say, smirking.

He chuckles, leaning in to kiss my cheek. "Very much so. You're just so...enticing. I love you."

I turn and kiss him, sinking against him. He says it in a way that I almost believe he actually feels the words he speaks with the muffled humanity he siphons from my soul he refuses to return. But he's only gotten better with his words, his act. I thought Dad was charming, but he has nothing on Ezekiel.

I shouldn't care so much. He deserves to keep my soul for everything, and I'm used to being a vessel of humanity to a demon anyway. But, it's just—I wish he'd give me the option. Because he fell with my soul, connecting the both of us, he's capable of feeling humanity through me. If he returns it, that connection will be lost forever. He'll change even more. If only he didn't block himself from truly feeling it in his fiery being. Everything he does comes from the hellish part of him and not his heart, now as black as his blood.

"I love you, too," I whisper into his lips. "You have no idea."

"Show me," he says.

I rub my lips together and climb into his lap. Wrapping my hands around his neck, I kiss him, sliding my tongue into his mouth, just flicking it across his tongue teasingly. I pull away and smile.

He tilts his head forward, resting it on my chest. "Show me more."

I bring my finger to his lips. "Stop trying to turn my dream into a fantasy."

He chuckles. "It was worth a try."

I laugh. "Now, it's your turn. Show me how much you love me."

Fire lights his eyes, and he flips me off him and sets me on my back in the sand, pressing his body against mine. I hold my hands to his chest, igniting a burst of power in my palms, singeing the fabric of his T-shirt.

"Not good enough?" he asks, putting his weight on his hands.

I shake my head. "No."

"Then tell me what you want."

I hold his gaze for a long moment, trying to lock him with my eyes for once. "My soul. Please, I'm empty without it."

"And so am I."

Ezekiel disappears from my dream world, leaving me alone to sit in a torrential downpour that startles me awake. The sunset burns through my bedroom window, lighting the hillside aglow in brilliant reds and golds.

I cover my eyes with my hands, sucking in a breath. Anger rushes through me. My eyes sting with the tears I try so hard to suppress. How can I love Ezekiel despite the fact that he refuses to give me the one thing that'll make me whole again? How can

I blame him? I stole his eternity.

The world shimmers with brown haze around me, and I catch sight of Ezekiel standing a foot away through the veil of the light prison realm. He laces his hands behind his head, staring at the final line of the setting sun.

I drop my hands and he materializes in front of me.

He meets my gaze with a raised eyebrow. "I was hoping to be the one to wake you. You're so beautiful when you sleep."

"Then why abandon me?" I ask.

He presses his lips into a thin line. "You know why."

Because in those short moments, when he's in my soul, engulfed in my being, he can feel something. And it scares him.

"And yet you still keep coming back," I say.

He smirks. "I'm a glutton. It's worse than you trying to corrupt me. But I can't resist you."

"You're going to lose this game you're playing," I say.

Laughing, he crosses the room and climbs into bed next to me, sliding his arm around my back, touching my skin under my shirt. His hot fingers stir everything dark within me in a good way. I crave to feel the desire, my deep-seated need. Because when I feel those things, I don't have to suffer the turmoil constantly trying to destroy me.

"This isn't a game, Faith," Ezekiel says. "There's no winning or losing. I wish you'd trust that I can take care of you. I know I've failed you as an ang—" He pauses, gathering his nerve to say his thoughts. "As an angel. But I'm stronger now. I'm finally worthy of you."

I pout. "You always have been."

He hugs me, reminding me of the angel who'd cry when I was feeling lost. Who called me his answered prayer. "We both know that's untrue."

I can't argue with him. There's no point. He's made up his mind. He can't see what I see or feel what I feel. He doesn't have the same desire I do. He's not trying to rise back into Heaven's good grace. And if he were to find out that's what I want to do...

Just thinking it makes me feel like I'm betraying him.

My beautiful fallen angel.

My charming demon.

I groan and rub my hands over my eyes. The Veiled Realm comes into view, cool mist drifting through the air around me. An ethereal light flashes through the mist, shining as bright as the giant moon overhead.

A figure emerges before me, startling me. The mighty angel with his flaming sword stands a few feet away, watching me watch him. He unfurls his white wings on his back, looking at me with the saddest eyes I've ever seen.

"Forgive me, Faith," he says, his voice lost on the pounding of my heart.

I nod my head, holding his gaze. "I forgive you."

Bending his knees, the angel launches into the air to disappear into the night. I drop my hand from my eye, and Ezekiel grimaces at me.

"You forgive me?" he asks. "I don't need your forgiveness. I only need you, okay?"

I nod. "Okay."

Ezekiel pulls me from the bed, tugging me across the room. "You should get dressed. Raphael's waiting. Want me to help you?"

I grin and shake my head. "Maybe if it were the opposite."

His Adam's apple bobs in his throat. "Your dad can wait. It'll be worth every bit of Hell power."

"Not yet," I say.

"I miss you trying to corrupt me," he says.

I laugh and nudge him toward the door. "Tell my dad I'll be there in ten."

Ezekiel kisses me once in the doorway, and I push him out before he convinces me to let him stay. Quietly closing the door, I rest my back on the wood and let out a breath. I bring my hand back to my eye to look around the Veiled Realm, but it remains misty and dark, only lit by the light of the moon.

I drop my hand and freeze.

A white feather drifts on an imaginary current in the middle of the room until it lands on the floor. Rushing to it, I scoop it in my fingers, cradling it in my hands. I ignite power in my palm, smoldering the feather. The action burns me to my core, because as much as I'm afraid of the angelic army, I can't deny what I want for my future.

Hell will not have me.

Heaven will not forsake me.

I'll make them see and prove Heaven wrong. I'll show the

universe I'm not a threat. I might not have wings, but I will rise. I will fly from the ashes of my life. I will soar.

TO BE CONTINUED...

Other Young Adult Series by Ginna Moran

PARANORMAL

Destined for Dreams Series
Demon Within Series
Finding Nate Series
Going Ghostly Series
Spark of Life Series
When Souls Collide Series
Demon Watcher Series
Call of the Ocean Series

CONTEMPORARY

Falling into Fame Series

STANDALONES

Life After Lila

Acknowledgements

AS ALWAYS, THANKS to my incredible team—Sarah, Katie, and Jan—for putting in tons of hard work and effort into the creations of my novels. Writing is the easy part for me, but without these talented women, the stories could never be what they are.

Without my mom, Faith's world would've never existed. I wrote my first demon hunting story as a Mother's Day present many years ago. From that short story, two series grew, and I'm so grateful that my mom supported me along the way. So, many heartfelt thanks to my mom.

Lastly, thank you to my readers for taking a chance on me. I'm incredibly humbled and inspired by the kind words and excitement you share toward my books. You are all amazing! XOXO!

About Ginna Moran

GINNA MORAN IS a writer from sunny Southern California. She started writing poetry as a teenager in a spiral notebook that she still has tucked away on her desk today. Her love of writing grew after she graduated high school, and she completed her first unpublished manuscript at age eighteen.

When she realized her love of writing was her life's passion, she studied literature at Mira Costa College in Northern San Diego. Besides writing novels, she was senior editor, content manager, and image coordinator for Crescent House Publishing Inc. for four years.

Aside from Ginna's professional life, she enjoys binge watching television shows, playing pretend with her daughter, and cuddling with her dogs. Some of her favorite things include chocolate, anything that glitters, cheesy jokes, and organizing her bookshelf.

Enticed

Ginna Moran loves to hear from her readers so visit her online at www.GinnaMoran.com. You can also find her on Facebook, Twitter, Instagram, and Snapchat. To stay up-to-date on new releases, sign up to her newsletter. You'll not only get exclusive access to the serialized retelling of *Diving Under* from Carter's perspective, but you'll be able to participate in monthly giveaways!

Ginna Moran is currently hard at work on her next novel.

9 781942 073277